TEACHING WITH THE ENEMY

JAQUELINE SNOWE

CITY OWL
PRESS

TEACHING WITH THE ENEMY
Shut Up and Kiss Me, Book 2

CITY OWL PRESS
www.cityowlpress.com

Cover Design by Mibl Art. All stock photos licensed appropriately.

Edited by Mary Cain.

For information on subsidiary rights, please contact the publisher at info@cityowlpress.com.

Print Edition ISBN: 978-1-64898-050-3

Digital Edition ISBN: 978-1-64898-049-7

Printed in the United States of America

To all the teachers in my family--CBMV, Vianne, CBMVI, Tina, Renee, Anastasia, Katie, CBMVII, Kacie, Mike, Jacob, and Ruth.

Praise for Jaqueline Snowe

"Brooding ex-athlete, check. Sassy yet thoughtful heroine, check. Jacqueline Snowe has written a lovely novel that ticks all the boxes for contemporary romance."
— *InD'tale*

"*Internship with the Devil* is an addictive, charming contemporary romance packed with snappy banter, tons of heart, and an immensely satisfying slow burn attraction that erupts into an inferno. The chemistry between Grace and Brock is absolutely scintillating."
— *Kat Turner, author of Hex, Love, and Rock and Roll*

"First rule for Grace's internship—don't fall for her grouchy boss, Brock. *Internship with the Devil* is a smart and sassy contemporary romance set in the world of athletic trainers for a college football team."
— *Miranda Darrow, award-winning romance author and #RevPit editor*

"Enemies to lovers, slow burn, AND sports? I am so in. If you're a fan of Mariana Zapata, then you'll love this novel. Grace is one of my favorite heroines--she's so down to earth and funny. Then there's Brock, wonderful, caring, sexy Brock. And the ending--I sighed and had the biggest smile on my face when I finished it. It's that good. Put it on your lists!"
— *Ashley R. King, author of Painting the Lines*

"This is a slow-burner that will keep you hanging on, just waiting for that first kiss!"
— *Melissa, the Archaeolibrarian*

Chapter One

EVERYONE HAD THAT ONE THING THAT SET THEIR HEART RACING. For some, it was sporting events. For others, it was bookstores or quirky coffee shops. My brother loved the nightlife, and my best friend craved to be on the football field.

For me, I never felt more myself than when I was prepping my classroom. It was my stage, my home, my *place* where not one of the twenty-four first graders cared that my grandparents had left me millions of dollars.

Winning Teacher of the Year for our district last year had filled me with a sense of pride that I carried around with me like an accessory, like I was doing the right thing at the right time. It was intoxicating, and I hummed as I unloaded the box of new supplies from my car and hauled it into my classroom. It smelled the same. Crayons and glue and markers. A very specific smell, and I breathed it in while eyeing the glass award on the corner of my desk.

I set the box down on my desk, anxious to open it. It was taped shut, and the words CARTER MOUNTAIN ELEMENTARY were written on the top with bold black letters. I treated myself every summer to buying materials for the year. Glitter, crafts, fun scissors, activity books. I'd splurged and got a Cricut to decorate the walls with all sorts of designs. The bounce balls and standing desks weren't arriving until next week, but I knew the students would be excited to try flexible seating.

It was better than Christmas morning when I opened new supplies. "Come to Mama," I said, using a letter opener to slice open the top part of the box. The smooth sound echoed in the room, and I couldn't stop the smile from spreading across my face when I pulled back the flaps.

I paused, my mouth stretching into a frown.

Blue folders, generic crayons, glue, and some sort of organizational file system stared back at me. I checked the box again, and it was my name, but this was not my stuff. I dug around until I found the receipt with the items ordered and frowned when I pulled it out.

Forty items ordered.

That was incorrect. I ordered triple that amount.

Annoyed that I couldn't prep my room as planned, I called the teacher shop and tried to explain it was the wrong box. It took ten minutes before anyone admitted there had been a mix-up.

"So how do I get my original order?" I said, plopping down in my computer chair and spinning around. "That's all I want."

"Uh, you might have to place it again. Someone picked yours up already, I'm so sorry," the woman said, her voice shaking a bit. "I'm seeing here two orders from Mountain Elementary were indicated, and—wait…hold on."

I tensed, the muscles in my neck tightening when she clicked her tongue. "What is it?"

"There were two orders with the name Carter and Mountain Elementary. Is there someone else with the last name Carter there?"

"Uh, no." I frowned and tried to picture our staff. Maybe one got married or changed their last name? We did have two new staff members joining our school, but the chances of them having the last name Carter seemed too coincidental. I would've heard about it before now. "I'll ask around, but in the meantime, could you repeat *my* order and let me know when I can get it?"

"Right, yes, of course." She cleared her throat. "I'm sorry about the mix-up, ma'am."

"It's fine," I said through clenched teeth. I'd spent hours over the summer coming up with a new seating chart system and a reward chart with color-coded stickers. I sighed and said good-bye as Larissa Lopes, my work-wife and best teaching friend, walked in with raised brows and a wicked smile. "My girl," I said, getting up and pulling her into a hug. "Mexico looks good on you."

"Gil, *Gilly*," she said, her voice all low and weird.

"What?" I pulled back from our embrace, and she raised her eyebrows up and down a few times. "What are you doing? I haven't seen you in a month, and this is how you welcome me?"

"Have you seen the newest first-grade teacher joining your team?"

"No, but unless he's famous or an exact carbon copy of my dream man, Chris Hemsworth, I don't see what the fuss is about."

"Uh." She paused, biting her lip and giggling. "He's a bit like him, yeah. He's *hot*. Like stupid hot."

My face warmed a bit, which was insane because I hadn't met the man. "Are you sure he's *my* new buddy teacher?"

"Oh shit. You're doing buddies this year?" She tossed her head back and laughed, clapping her hands and making her million bangle bracelets cling together. "Gil, you are going to struggle with a capital S. Wait until you see him."

We were not in high school, and it was just fine having an attractive man be on the team. Sure, it was rare to have men teach in an elementary school, let alone look anything like Chris Hemsworth, but it could happen. "Well, might as well put on lipstick when I go next door, huh?"

She eyed the box and looked inside while I found my favorite red matte lipstick from the top of my drawer. My mom never wore a lot of makeup but instilled the power held by a bold color. It made people pay attention to her mouth, and in the process, what she said. She was five feet tall and a powerhouse.

The additional color on my lips gave me a little of the confidence I needed. I'd been experiencing a dry spell. Nothing since the hookup I'd *thought* went well, only to find out he'd ghosted me.

I was either a one-night stand *or* a way for a someone to get money. The bitter memory of my brother's ex clouded my mood, and

I cleared my throat. I spent enough time letting *her* piss me off, and I forced my attention back on Larissa.

"Why'd you order boring stuff? This isn't you," Larissa said, pulling out a pack of pale-yellow Post-it notes. "You have a personality change when I was gone or what?"

"Orders got mixed up, somehow." I checked to make sure I didn't have anything in my teeth and popped my lips. *Perfect.* "Okay, guess I should go meet my buddy teacher, huh?"

"Assistant Principal Dave does encourage us to be leaders and reach out to newcomers. We are a *Mountain* Family," she said, mocking our boss by putting her hands on his hips. APD, as we called him, had a no-nonsense attitude more reminiscent of a military general than an elementary school assistant principal.

But he was the best advocate for his teachers.

"Wish me luck," I said, dabbing a tiny bit of lotion on my hands and rubbing it in.

"Come to my room when you're done. Helen wants us to have an in-depth *planning* meeting on the first day back. Kill me. I need ten margaritas already." She brushed by me and strode into the hallway. Her smile caused me to sweat just a little as she studied the room next to me.

I sighed and gave her a small wave, wiping my palms on my dress. Wearing bright and crazy patterns was something I'd starting as a teenager in an effort to stand. The vibrant colors hid glue, boogers, and leftover craft materials well, and like the lipstick, they made me feel bold. Plus, I wanted kids to see me as someone positive. They all came from home lives that were so different from mine, that being a consistently upbeat adult in their life could make all the difference. It was one of my professional goals—as was having more of a presence at the school.

APD wanted me to step up and be more of a leader on campus this year, and that would start by welcoming my buddy to our team. The buddy system provided a stepping stone into leadership and had helped new teachers at our school feel welcomed and part of the family. With a strong knock on his classroom door, I waited. After a few beats he got up from his desk and strode to the entrance, opening the creaky wooden door and showing me his face.

Oh my God.

Him.

I narrowed my eyes as a bolt of recognition lit me up. Sweaty palms, racing heartbeat. There was no way. *He* couldn't be a teacher. Here. At my school. He belonged at a firehouse or posing for photos or...places where he could be shirtless for everyone to enjoy. Christopher stood at his full height, one eyebrow raised and no evidence of a smile.

I sucked in a breath and willed my pulse to settle.

Be cool. Be cool, Gilly.

He looked better than I remembered. His navy polo fit his arms and chest in a mouthwatering way, and his curly brown hair was styled just right, like I'd run my fingers through it over and over. And his legs. My mouth felt like I'd swallowed a spoonful of baby powder it was so dry. Legs were a weakness. Strong and meaty with muscles.

Damn. This isn't being cool.

I cleared my throat and regretted not bringing extra tea because my mouth was dry as a desert. It wasn't every day an incredible, body-altering one-night stand showed up at my work and was assigned to teach next door to me. His gaze moved from my red flats, up my legs and to my face, without showing an ounce of recognition. Wait. What?

Does he...not...remember me?

He'd had quite a few drinks that night, but I hadn't thought he was drunk enough to forget me entirely. The overwhelming attraction turned to humiliation and anger quick. Like a snap of the fingers.

"Can I help you?" His voice was as deep and seductive as it had been during our night together. His lips twisted into a scowl, like he was annoyed with me, which made no sense. At all.

I held out my hand, because manners were preached to me growing up, and forced a sweet smile that hid the plethora of insecurities rushing through me. "Hey, uh, I'm your neighbor and buddy teacher for the year. Gilly Carter."

"Interesting name," he said in a calm, even tone that solidified he did not remember me whatsoever. I always used a fake name when I went out, and while Genie wasn't that far off from Gilly, it felt like a slap to the face. A total KO to any self-confidence.

"Yup." I nodded to him, regret and shame flooding my thoughts. We'd had a great time. A couple drinks, one night in bed, and an easy good-bye. Did it matter if he remembered me? I played with the ring on my middle finger, swirling it around over and over.

Yes. It did.

He stared, the slight tic of his left eye making me feel like I was bothering him somehow, which made zero sense.

I rubbed my lips together and shoved all the negative emotions down. Here I was, a leader, a mentor, a good teacher. It didn't matter that my face was so unforgettable.

"I wanted to see how you were settling into Mountain Elementary. Is there anything I can help with or any questions you have?" My ability to sound normal was exemplary. He had no idea my hands were balled into fists in my pockets.

His gaze moved over my shoulder for a beat before clicked his tongue. "Nope. I'm good. Not a first-year teacher, so don't really need all the *buddy-buddy* stuff."

"Ha, yeah, I get it." *I did not.* "Well, I'm next door if you need anything."

He didn't say a word before he went back to his desk, dismissing me with nothing more than complete silence. It was foolish to say my feelings were hurt, but they were. I tapped his doorframe twice before leaving and heading down the hall to the second-grade wing, wondering if he had a twin brother because the guy I'd had a great night with was fun and wonderful...not grumpy or an asshole.

I stopped by Larissa's room to analyze what the hell just happened, but she wasn't back from Helen's, so I went back to my room. As soon as I got into the first-grade hallway, I found Christopher leaving my room. He carried the box of supplies I had to return. "Uh, *what* are you doing?"

"This is mine. Why the hell you have it, I have no idea." His jaw tightened, like he was chewing gum, and he shook his head with so much disappointment and anger, my stomach twisted into knots.

"It's *clearly* a mistake," I said, moving closer, the energy between us cracking with tension. It wasn't often I could feel someone's dislike for me, but this time, I tasted it with each hard look he tossed my way. "Why would your supplies say Carter on them?"

"Because my name is Carter Christopher, I go by Christopher." He rolled his eyes, like I should've known that little anecdote.

"Again, how the hell is this my fault that the teacher store mixed up orders? Do you have my box then?"

"Hell no. They handed me a receipt for three hundred dollars. I wasn't gonna pay that for a bunch of unnecessary junk. Teaching should be about learning, not all the extra nonsense I'm *sure* you have." He eyed my outfit, stopping at my shoes before he shook his head and went into his room, not offering another word or explanation as to why he was acting like a total jerk.

My vision blurred with anger as I stormed into his room, pointing my finger at him from my position near the door.

"I need that back so I can return it and get the stuff I ordered," I said calmly, quite impressed I was keeping it together.

"No. That's a waste of time. They'll end up here anyway," he said, unloading the folders and setting them in a bin on his desk. "You're getting worked up over this."

Oh my God.

I clenched my teeth together and fought the urge to chuck the stapler resting a foot away from my hand at his face. "Christopher," I said, my voice low and laced with poison, "give me my stuff back, so I can get a refund."

He stilled, ran a hand over his jaw, and narrowed his eyes. Disbelief crossed his face before he went back to unloading the box. "I'm sure you'll be just fine. Figure it out. Now, excuse me. I'd like to get my class ready for students."

"With that?" I jutted my jaw toward the box, and his face hardened.

"Yes. I don't have to *buy* my students into liking me." He tilted his head, his meaning crystal clear.

I bolted from his room, not because he dismissed me, *again*, but because the temper and anger that took over my body was so foreign, it startled me. He was playful, sweet, and patient when we were together. Nothing like this irritation.

I didn't get angry here. My classroom was where I escaped the pressures of my life, not lived them. The shift was unsettling, and I sat in my chair, rubbed my temples, and took a few sips of tea. It was cold now, but the calming herbs helped me settle down and rationalize what the hell happened.

Christopher hated me, that was clear, and I had no idea why.

Chapter Two

IN THE MORNING, APD TEXTED ME ASKING FOR A FAVOR—HE'D
ordered a large box of bagels from a place a block away from my
apartment." He'd already paid for everything—he just needed me to
pick them up because his kid had gotten sick. It was no big deal, and I
added an extra box of donuts for our team. Meeting with the other
first-grade teachers was my favorite time of year because we could
share ideas and align our plans, and I refused to let thoughts of *him*
intervene in my happy place.

The first trip from my car was to the teacher's lounge, where I set
the box of bagels on the staff table and placed the napkins next to it.
It came with an assortment of cream cheese, and I set them all out.

Once it was in order, I picked up the box of donuts and hummed
as I left the teacher's workroom and stopped mid-step when Christopher stood on the other side of the door. He laughed at something
Kennedy, a fifth-grade teacher, said, and seeing a smile stretch across
his face sent a wave of lust through me. He was so dang good-looking
and that smile…whoa.

He mumbled something that sounded like "see you later" to her
when his gaze landed on me, and every ounce of joy evaporated. His

lips went into a flat line, and his face hardened as it dropped to the box in my hands. "Figures."

"What?" I snapped back, blinking a few times to see if I imagined the look of loathing coming from him. "What *figures*?"

He shook his head and scoffed, brushing by me and into the workroom without another glance. The interaction bothered me, again, and it was difficult to mask emotions when I continued to my classroom. His accusation made zero sense. He figured what? I liked donuts? Who the hell didn't?

His attitude wasn't my problem, and life was too short to worry about other people's actions. I couldn't control them, no matter how much I wished I could.

I put my hair up into a messy bun and opened my boxes of supplies and started decorating before our grade-level meeting. I chose purple and turquoise for the year as our classroom colors and spent way too much time cutting out stars and shapes to hang around the room. The behavior chart was up and straight, the carpet squares organized by color, and each student had a cubby hole in alternating colors. Content with my design, I played some Taylor Swift and lost myself in the process until Maggie poked her head in my room with a toothy grin.

"Gilly, oh, your room looks great!"

"Thanks, Mags." I beamed at her. She reminded me of my mom, who I missed since she and Dad decided to travel the world, and I eyed my watch. "Shoot, our meeting starts now, huh?"

"Sure do. In here is okay, right?"

"Yes. I printed an agenda, let me go get it real quick. Sit down. Have a snack." I pointed to the box of donuts.

While my teammates never questioned why I always brought them food, they certainly never complained. She clapped her hands and waltzed over to the snack area while I sped out of my room toward the teacher's lounge. It was a quick trip, and I grabbed the copies, stapled them, and smiled as I filed them in bright-turquoise folders. I loved getting packets ready for the team. Pride filled my chest as I put a laminated cheat sheet in the front. It had all the important numbers and emails for them, and with a smile on my face, I made my way back to my room.

My heart pounded against my ribs when I approached my doorway and found Christopher laughing with Maggie, Marisa, and Maria—the other three members of our grade-level team. He had that huge smile and had them in giggles, and I dug my nails into my palm. Did they not realize he was a jerk?

The second his gaze landed on me, the smile disappeared, and he sat straighter.

"Oh, Gilly, have you met our newest teammate? Christopher is just wonderful. He taught at Canyon for five years up in the city." Maggie reached over and patted his forearm, like she did with me.

"Yes, welcome to our team," I said, keeping my voice polite even though I wanted to take scissors and cut off just one eyebrow.

Christopher didn't answer. He crossed his legs so one ankle rested on the other, and he spoke to Marisa. "Who usually runs our meetings? Do we always have them in here?"

"Gilly. She's the best. She writes all these grants and gets all these donations to get snacks for the staff and supplies for the students. It is wonderful, and we're so thankful for her. Have you gotten something from her snack table? She always brings us stuff."

"I bet she does," he said, the insinuation making my spine straighten.

I bet she does? What the heck does that mean?

"Anyway, yes, I run the meetings, and since I like to bring food, we meet in here." I grabbed my chair and rolled it to join their circle, and his left eye ticked again when I pushed a student desk along the floor, making a loud sound. "To start, we need to go over goals and expectations." I passed out the folders to the group, and three of them started writing. Christopher did not.

"Is the whole *color folder and sticker* thing necessary? Can't we just write our goals on a sheet of paper and call it a day? Kids should learn. End of goal."

"I agree with you, Christopher," Maggie said, nodding and clicking her tongue. "The paper work and hoop-jumping always grinds my gears. We're here for children, why do all the song and dance?"

"Exactly." His jaw clenched, and his stare penetrated me. "Is this a you thing or a school thing?"

"Well, I always thought it'd be great for us to track our goals each month and hold each other accountable. It'll help us be honest with each other."

His lip curled up before he blinked away the hate and looked at Marisa. He lowered his voice and spoke so softly and kindly, it almost gave me whiplash. "What if we just verbalize our goal and talk about it so we can avoid busy work?"

I gripped the pencil harder, and a part of the plastic broke off, landing on the floor by his foot. His lip curved up just a little when his gaze landed on the piece, and he dragged his attention back to my face. "Unless that's not okay, *Gilly*. I wouldn't want to *steal* anything from you."

His nostrils flared, and for the third time that day, a weird sensation took root in my gut, churning and growing the longer he stared at me. My stomach bottomed out, like the elevator lurched and gravity had me thinking I'd crash. *What don't I know?*

The question played on repeat in my mind.

He raised one dark eyebrow and tilted his head. "Well?"

"Sure, yeah. Let's try it," I said, my voice shaky and uncertain for the first time since I'd grown to love this team. This was my zone, my place, my people, and Christopher made me feel like an outsider. The other three nodded and shut the folders I'd spent hours making and shoved them to the side.

"I'd love to go first, if that's okay. Be kind on the new guy, all right?" He smiled sheepishly at my teammates, and they ate it up.

How the heck did this happen?

Maggie and Marisa stated their goal to have ninety percent of their students to meet each standard, Maria opted for all students to score well on their literacy skills, and Christopher wanted every student to read at grade level. Maggie loved his goal and offered to help him get set up, and the two of them got up to leave our meeting as he joked around with her about the Chicago Cubs.

It grated my nerves seeing him joke around with everyone *but* me.

"I just love your room, Gil. It's straight out of Pinterest! I wish I had the eye, and wallet, for this," Marisa said, her loud voice carrying into the hall.

Christopher stilled and looked back at me, his gaze moving toward my wall with cutouts I had spent all night creating with my Cricut, and he shook his head.

"Thanks, Marisa," I said, swallowing down the unease. "I researched all summer."

"The kiddos are going to love it!" She beamed at me and studied the behavior chart wall. "I'd love to try this. Care if I take a picture and make one myself?"

"No, of course, go ahead!" I gushed, somehow needing to defend myself and make sure my team still liked me. "Do you need any help getting set up, Marisa?"

"Oh, now that you mention it," she said, her voice going low, "I could really use an extra set of hands cleaning out my library. My sister got a huge donation using a GoFundMe, so I'm going to donate these books to the library and replace them with a bunch of new ones."

"How wonderful!" I smiled and followed her out of my door and across the hall to her room. She was in between Maggie and Maria, leaving Christopher and me on the opposite side.

Marisa winced when she bent down on her knees, and I joined her.

"Here, I can unload into the box. You figure out how you want to sort the new books."

"You're a doll, thank you. I spent too much time gardening this summer, and my back does not agree with me."

"It's no worry." I spent ten minutes placing books in a box, mastering it like a game of Tetris, and stood to set it on the desk. I kept my favorite book on top, debating if I wanted to take it for my class library. *Chicka Chicka Boom Boom* would always be one of my favorites. "I'll run these to the library real quick."

"Oh, perfect. If you want anything before you take them, go ahead."

It wasn't too heavy, but it did strain my muscles as I headed down the first-grade hallway and toward the school library center. The maker-space section had Legos and all sorts of crafts. I would've *loved* having something like that when I was in school. I'd always loved crafts, but my time was always limited with all the traveling. Always an event, or a mission, that my parents dragged us to. Being a positive, consistent adult in these kids' lives that fostered creativity was a reflection of the time I had in school. It fueled me to be the best I could for them.

"Hey, Miranda," I said to the librarian. "These are from Marisa."

"She did mention that, yes." She pointed to a red-and-white table in the back corner. "Go ahead and set them there. I'll get to them in a minute."

I did as she asked, and when I set the box down, the flap opened, and I said to heck with it. I took my favorite book. The cover was still intact, but the pages were yellowed. I picked it up and ran my fingers over it. Marisa did offer I could have one of the books, and I smiled, already knowing where I'd put it on my shelf.

With the book tucked under my arm, I waved to Miranda just as the hairs on the back of my neck tingled. Christopher glared at me as he stood at the counter, mid-conversation with Miranda. He narrowed his ice-blue eyes at the book under my arm, and my stomach dropped with dread. It took a lot of effort to smile, but I managed. "Have a great day, Miranda!"

"You too, Gilly! Oh! Drop off all the materials you need laminated. I'll have time later this afternoon to get the machine fired up."

"Will do."

My neck hurt from how tight my muscles got whenever Christopher was in the same room, and I ducked my head and beelined for my classroom. The brief joy at finding *Chicka Chicka Boom Boom* disappeared from his accusing glare. I hated how flustered I was. Why in the hell was he so nice to everyone but me? Was I that unlikeable? Did I do something to him for him to hate me? I couldn't recall a single thing from that night together.

My fingers shook a little as I set the book on my shelf near my award and took a few seconds to settle myself. I didn't need him to like me. I had my friends and my students. It just sucked because it bothered me. I stretched my arms over my head and took a calming breath, pushing him out of my mind. The only thing I needed to complete my room was the flexible seating, and I got my phone to track the shipment and squealed when it said delivered.

That meant they were in the front office.

All thoughts of Christopher disappeared, and I practically skipped down the hallway and into the double doors. Sally, the office manager, wiggled her brows the second she saw me. "Oh, your order just got here, and I'm dying to see what else you got! Your room is just the absolute cutest, Gilly."

"Thanks," I said, blushing at her compliment. My room was a source of pride. There was nothing too expensive or time-consuming that I wouldn't do for my kids, and providing a creative, colorful, and engaging classroom was my passion. The large boxes contained four bouncy balls and four standing desks.

Sally got up from her chair and pushed a dolly my way. "Need any help?"

"Oh, I got it. I'm itching to get started with these new seating arrangements," I practically sang with glee as I loaded the boxes onto the dolly and pushed it out of the office. "Thank you so much."

"Let me know when you're set up, so I can peek in there. My baby girl is going to be a first grader next year, and I've already been telling her all about your fun room. Fingers crossed she gets you!"

That comment lit me up inside with pride and joy that I never got anywhere else. I smiled and let that high carry over as I unpacked the boxes in my classroom and made a game plan on how to set them up. I tapped my finger on my chin as a large, overbearing presence stood at my door and the happiness disappeared. "Christopher," I said, not hiding my dislike. "What do you want?"

He put his hands on his hips and studied the packages on the floor. His gaze swept over the bouncy balls, the half-created desks, and the adjustable table that could go up and down by two feet. He curled his lip up before tossing a package on my desk. "Miranda said you'd like these."

It was a pack of sticky glue, and I smiled. "Yes, I would."

He scoffed and a reluctant smile crossed his face. "You go all out like this every year?"

"Yes," I said, my hackles raising. "I do."

"Interesting."

Dang it. Before I could stop myself, I asked, "Why is this interesting?"

"You could've spent all summer planning lessons, figuring out how to teach students standards and how to spell and say words. But instead, you did who knows what to get all this stuff. Hundreds of dollars of junk that doesn't make a lick of a difference when it comes to doing your job." He eyed the award again and laughed. "Let me guess, you buy new toys and prizes for them all the time. You think students like *you*, but really, you use all this stuff to buy their affection."

"That's…that's not true," I said, my voice weak and pathetic as he hit me right in the center of my insecurity. "It enhances learning to have options and provides students different ways to absorb the material."

"False," he said, his tone stronger. "It overwhelms them. They need a teacher who cares and a teacher who meets them at their level so they can learn. They don't need all this crap." He waved his hand in the air and twisted his mouth into a scowl.

"I'd rather have all this *crap* than be boring. Your walls are bare, and you have nothing that says fun in your room. How can you possibly inspire anything?" My legs shook. I reached over to steady myself on my shelf. My normally calm and goofy demeanor was shot to hell around him. I hated confrontation.

But he wasn't done. His eyes flashed with warning before he took a step closer to me and lowered his voice to just above a whisper. "You think all these gadgets and knickknacks make you a better teacher? They don't." His gaze landed on the glass plaque on my desk. "I couldn't sleep at night if I didn't think I'd earned my accolades on my own merits. But by all means, you do you."

And with that, he stormed out of my room and into the hallway, all before my brain could catch up to even form a comeback.

Chapter Three

GIL—HERE ARE THE QUESTIONS ALL BUDDY TEACHERS NEED TO WORK ON together. I need them by Friday afternoon. Let me know if you need anything —APD

I READ THE EMAIL TWICE THE NEXT AFTERNOON AND GROANED INTO my hand. Spending time with *my buddy* Christopher seemed as appetizing as eating an entire pack of glitter glue, safety warnings be damned. Regret washed over me, making my face burn. His accusations replayed in my head like neon signs. *You can't bribe your way into getting awards.*

I didn't trick them. Yes, I spent hundreds of my own dollars on my classroom, but didn't all teachers do that? Sure, I had more money than most, but spending it on students never seemed like a trick or a ploy. Their faces lit up in my classroom when they got to play with clay or try something different. I rubbed my temples and hated that I thought doing the buddy teachers would help me prove myself to the school.

Instead of growing professionally and maybe making a friend along the way, I was partnered up with the jerk whose uptight expression—which seemed to be reserved just for me—made my jaw clench. That was the other part of the puzzle that made me lose sleep. He was nice to everyone else. He'd had Miranda cackling like a hyena when I dropped off calendars to be laminated. He flashed an easy smile to my team, the administration, the kids, but the scowl, the almost tangible hatred, was reserved for me and me alone.

Really made a girl feel special.

I switched from tea to water two hours ago, and it was almost time to switch to a cold margarita…which would be my reward once I survived going over these buddy questions with Christopher. APD wouldn't take any excuses, and telling him my *buddy* teacher hated me would make him laugh. Who would believe it when Christopher had everyone eating out of the palm of his hand?

I took a moment and built up my courage despite the hurt from his words the day before. I loved my kids, and they learned from me. Parents always thanked me at the end of the year, and my coworkers never said a word about my *crap.* They encouraged the exploration of new ideas. My Teacher of the Year award wasn't bought. I had earned it…right?

He was so darn wrong, yet my eyes still prickled at the wave of worry causing a small dark cloud over my confidence. Self-doubt was a dangerous thing, and I had it in waves when it came to my dating life, but it rarely crept in professionally. When I found out the woman my brother was going to propose to was actually a con artist and using us, our family money, for her own gain, it really put a damn damper on my outlook on life and love. But that didn't matter when I had my job to fulfill me. However, Christopher's words poked holes in that argument, hitting me where it hurt the most. My stomach ached with uncertainty, and I studied my classroom, unable to smile at all the decorations. They mocked me now.

Damn it. I sighed and shook my head, forcing my thoughts into better territory. I was good at my job and a professional, so I would get through these questions with Christopher and call it a day.

I grabbed my rainbow notebook and pulled the questions up on my phone before walking to his room. My flats were almost noiseless in the hall, and with a growing sense of dread, I knocked. The small window gave me a glance into his room, and I hated how plain and boring it was. He didn't have the quirky personality of Maria or the motherly-fatherly vibe that Maggie had, and he certainly didn't have my bubbly personality, so the fact his classroom was bare bones bothered me. Kids liked colors and visuals and things to stare at. The white walls with the black-and-white pledge of allegiance poster didn't exactly spark joy or creativity. The only thing it sparked was depression.

Kids need to learn, not have crap everywhere.

His lean and tall body appeared in the window, and the curious expression shifted to annoyance the second his gaze met mine. He didn't hide his disdain when he opened the door and leaned against the frame—not letting me in. "Hello, Ms. Carter."

"Mr. Callahan, I need ten minutes of your time."

"Mm," he responded, running his gaze up and down my body with a slight flexing of his jaw. "Surprised you can spare ten minutes. Just think of all the crafts you could make or wasteful trinkets you could buy."

I gritted my teeth to prevent myself from saying something I'd regret and walked right under his arm and into his room. I plopped down on a small chair and wasted no time. "Christopher, what has been your biggest challenge here, and how can I help?"

He took his time waltzing to his desk. His black slacks fit him well —too well—and his deep-blue sweater matched his eyes to a T. Dark lashes framed those eyes, and…

Dang it. Stop ogling him.

"Challenge?" He repeated the word and gave me a wide smile that sent my nerve endings haywire. Nothing good would come from that sinister smile. "Colleagues."

"Could you expand more?" I wrote down his answer as my face burned with anger. We both knew he was referring to me. "What exactly makes your *colleagues* a challenge?"

"Different opinions on what it means to be a teacher." He leaned back into his chair and smirked at me. "What would you suggest if a teacher had concerns about a fellow member of their team?"

"Say what you want." My heart pounded, and my face burned hot, but my tone was ice. "You sure said what you wanted yesterday."

"I did. That is true." He picked a piece of lint off his shirt and sighed before snapping his gaze to my face. "Next question. I'd like to get this over with as I have lessons to plan that don't require expensive toys and flashy objects."

"Fine," I said, ignoring the now pounding headache at the base of my skull. He'd baited me, but I refused to take it. "What is your goal outside our first-grade professional learning community team?"

"Winning Teacher of the Year." His gaze met mine, and he smirked. *Jerk.*

It took everything in my body to not throw something at him. "Hefty goal," I said between clenched teeth, clutching the pen so hard ink bled through the page.

He looked at me like he was bored out of his mind. Blank face, no smile, narrowed eyes. It was intimidating and made me stutter on my next question. "How, uh, do you go about achieving that goal? Is there anything I can do to support you?"

He ran a hand over his jaw and leaned forward onto the desk. To anyone else, it would appear he was interested in me or what I was saying, but I knew better. This was a challenge. "Yes, there is something you can specifically do to support me."

I blinked, unable to stop myself from asking the question. "What is it?"

He tapped his fingers on the desk for a beat, his lips curving into a menacing grin as his eyes flashed with mirth. "SPIRITS is coming up, right?"

"Our staff spirit week? What does that have to do with any of this?" I frowned, trying to anticipate his next move. Our SPIRIT week was an intense, five-day competition where teachers were given prompts and we dressed up as best we could to fit it. There was one winner for each grade level and a school-wide champion each time.

"I'm going to kick your ass at it without spending a single dime," he boasted and puffed out his chest.

"Uh, okay," I said, laughing. "You won't win, but it's cute you think you can."

"You misunderstood, *Martha Stewart*," he said, the nickname hitting me right in the chest. "You won't be spending a dime either."

"What makes you think I'll agree to this?"

"Because if you win, we both know it'll be because you bought your way into first place. Just like that award you got last year. It's easy to win Teacher of the Year when you spent money that's not yours to fund it."

I froze. "What are you insinuating?"

"Don't play dumb. It's not a good look on you. You know exactly what I mean. You waltz around like you're good at what you do, but it's all for show. Win without all the extra crap." He smirked and looked down at me as he made a fist on top of his desk. "Unless you know you don't have a shot."

My blood roared with competition, and before I could rationalize why this idea was absurd, I smacked my hand on the desk. "You're on. Not a dime."

He gave me a pathetic smile, one I'd used on mean girls in high school, and he patted my hand and spoke in a condescending tone. "Look at you, thinking you can manage. The woman responsible for keeping Hobby Lobby in business thinks she can win. I admire your confidence."

My eyes stung, and my stomach bottomed out as APD walked into the room with his typical whistle.

The features on Christopher's face shifted in half a second, and he grinned at our boss. "Dave, what brings you in here?"

"Oh, perfect. I was going to check in with both of you but can hit two birds with one stone." He adjusted his tie and sat down on a small blue chair, shifting the clipboard in his lap before smiling. "How are my two star teachers doing? I love that you two are paired up."

I sat up straighter and plastered on my best professional smile, the one I used when parents went on a soapbox about how they could do my job at parent-teacher conferences. "We're going over the questions you sent me."

"Perfect." He yawned and wiped a hand over his face. "Gil is great, ask her anything. Don't forget you have the new teacher program tonight. You're scheduled to do some observations of your team next week, but you'll want to check in with the head of the program."

"Right," Christopher said, his tone easygoing and his lips curving up on the sides. "Will it be done in time to catch the end of the Cubs game though?"

"I hope so. Man, they really have a shot this year." Dave was a huge Cubs fan and everyone knew it, but the fact Christopher knew and was oh-so-casually talking to him about it pissed me off.

"Tell me about it. I was at Wrigley last fall when they made a play-off run, and it was one of the best experiences. The food, the people, the crowds. Man." Christopher paused and got a hazy look in his eyes. "Can't wait to go back soon."

"I have tickets when the Cardinals come to town, and I'm counting down the days." Dave hit his knee, and his gaze shifted to me. "Gil, I have you down to collect the funds for the *Give Thanks* fundraiser. I want to get started early with it so we can raise more than last year. I have a bet going on with the AP at West View, and I want to raise more to rub it in his face. Also, to help those in need. Can't forget that."

"Of course," I said, nodding. "I've already started making flyers we can hang up and also post online. The NHS scholarship wraps up at the end of the month, so the timing works well."

"What is the *Give Thanks* fundraiser?" Christopher asked, his tone holding an icy edge. His gaze sliced into me when Dave scrolled through his phone. "I can help out with it too. I managed a lot of accounts at my last school."

"Oh, no need for that. I love this charity. We purchase food to donate Thanksgiving meals for families in the area. We raised about two thousand dollars last year, and it was awesome." I shared a smile with Dave, but Christopher's face remained hard and angry. "There's other fundraisers you can lead."

"You collect money from students?" he asked, his face paling. "Is there an account set up in the office where people deposit it, or do you hold on to the cash?"

I frowned at his insane round of questioning and looked at Dave. "Both, not that it matters. I keep a detailed account of who donates what," I said, brushing him off and releasing a long breath. "Is that what you needed to talk to me about, Dave?"

"Yup, for now." He tapped his clipboard twice and stood, totally unaware that I was fighting the urge to smack Christopher in the head. "I need to check in with the other new teacher, but seriously, Gilly is great. Be thankful she's your buddy." Dave left without another word, leaving Christopher and me in his room alone with his scowl etched onto his handsome face.

"What the heck is your problem? Seriously?" I seethed at him.

"You might think you have everyone fooled, but your act doesn't work with me." He stood and narrowed his blue eyes, his chest moving faster than before.

I reached my limit. I needed to get the hell out of there and pushed off the chair, hoping he didn't see my shaking limbs. Right before I got to the door, he said my name.

"What?" I spun around, giving me the meanest glare I could.

"Not a dime."

I should've told him to go to hell or flipped him off, but instead, I nodded. "Game on, Callahan."

Chapter Four

My anger hadn't dissipated at all in the four days since our showdown. It was Sunday afternoon, and my best friend, Grace, and my brother sat in my living room, laughing their asses off after I told them all about Christopher.

"What is so damn funny about this?" I spat out, pushing off the couch and placing my hands on my hips. "I can beat him at this stupid *not-a-dime* competition. I will."

"Uh, okay, sis," Fritz said, hitting his knees as his shoulders shook with laughter. He shared a look with Grace and rolled his eyes. "You spend thousands of dollars on your classroom and nails and hair. There's no way you won't cheat."

My face heated, and I pointed my finger at his chest, showing my teeth as I tried to come up with something to prove him wrong. "I can do it. I'm not *that* entitled."

"I dunno, Gil." Grace winced and wiped the smile off her face when I glared at her. "You need something, you buy it online in an instant. Should we check your Amazon account? I saw four packages on the counter when I walked in."

"Or her subscription addiction? Did you know she gets perfume, clothes, and shoes delivered to her every month?"

"I like those things! Sue me!" I yelled, super annoyed by the truth to their words. "Fine, I spend money a lot. I like it. It doesn't mean I can't work hard though."

"We're not saying that at all, Gilbert," Fritz said, using my childhood nickname and softening his tone. "You've always worked hard, *but*—now don't kill me—he has a point."

My left eye twitched. I sighed and ran a hand over my face. "So what the hell do I do?"

"You don't spend money on this competition. Prove him wrong, duh." Grace wiggled her eyebrows and picked up the pad of paper where I'd scribbled ideas down. "Dang, Fritz, wanna take a bet on if she can do it or not?"

"Oof, no, because I know she can't."

"I can do a damn week on a budget. I'm not *that* bad." A dull ache started behind my left eye, and I wanted to slam a pillow into my best friend's face. "Why are you looking at me like that?"

"I love you, Gil, but you can't do it."

"Yes, I can. I can even do it longer than a week. Two." I puffed out my chest as my pulse raced. My nerves danced at the doubt in their eye. "Swear."

"Make it a month," Fritz said, his voice getting serious. "One month, just your teacher paycheck."

"What do I get if I do this?"

"Bragging rights, respect, knowing we were wrong about you," he fired back, raising his brows. We weren't athletic like Grace or her husband, but competitiveness lived in our blood. We thrived on being the best.

"Fine." I swallowed. "I'll do it."

Fritz grinned and relaxed into his seat as Grace cleared her throat and scanned the pad of paper.

"Okay, let's brainstorm then," Grace said in her teacher voice. "Day one is opposite day. What does that even mean? Opposite?" She shared a smile with my brother. They doubted me, that was obvious. While I liked excess things, I still had my pride, and I would prove to them I could do it.

Tight budget for one month. No funsies or extras or pedicures.

I gritted my teeth and plopped down on the couch, determined to win against Christopher, but also to prove to myself my money didn't define me. "I found the coolest ideas online, but they all cost money. I've never needed to win something more than I do this SPIRIT week. If he wins, I might have to quit my job. Working with him all cocky and gloating…" I trailed off, and my entire body shook with dread. "Yeah, it can't happen."

Fritz laughed and picked up his phone. "Let's go through ideas?"

"Please."

Grace offered different ways to style my hair or wear two different shoes, which was a great start, but not enough. Christopher didn't have to know I spent money if I made things look like they were older. My stomach soured at the thought of essentially cheating, and I got my laptop from the counter. It hadn't even been five minutes since I made the bet with Fritz, and I was thinking about sneaking around.

I knew what I had to do.

"Looking up ideas?" Fritz asked, writing down something ineligible on the idea pad of paper. "I think if you wore different shoes, wore half your hair one way, and the other half different, that's a good start."

"I'm emailing Fred." Fred had been Fritz's and my fiduciary since our inheritance was released from the trust. Every transaction involving my money went through him.

"Um, thought we agreed for you to not spend money." Fritz frowned at me and tilted his head to the side. "Gil, come on. You *just* agreed, and you're flaking out?"

"No, I'm emailing him to make sure I don't have access to any money for the month, except for my paycheck. I'm updating my spreadsheet of exactly how much I need for food, gas, utilities for the next four weeks, and that I cannot touch anything else. Not a dime. Then, I'm giving you my credit cards."

"Whoa," Grace said, her eyes going wide, and her tone impressed. "You're taking this seriously."

"While you two were brainstorming, I was daydreaming about sneaking off to the store and not telling you." I looked at my best friend and brother and refused to feel guilty that maybe I was a bit high maintenance with money. "I want to get rid of any temptation so this guy can't say a single thing and"—I paused to swallow my pride —"I need to prove it to myself that I'm more than money."

"Well done, Gil," Fritz said, grinning at me as he clicked his tongue. "Once you get that figured out, let's come up with your outfits all week."

"Sounds like a plan."

DANG, I WISH I COULD SPEND MONEY. KNOWING I COULDN'T intensified the urge. I could always call my advisor to have him unlock my account, but that defeated the whole purpose. My normal confidence shattered into pieces when I got to school and saw teachers decked out in all sorts of opposite gear.

One third-grade teacher had an outfit that had one side white, the other side black. It was incredible. I nodded at them as I walked into the building with my teacher bag and hot tea, but it faded when my gaze landed on Christopher—who was walking backward as he talked to Kennedy.

"Oh, you're so clever!" she said, putting a hand on his arm, and he grinned down at her with amusement in his eyes. "I love it."

"Thank you," he said, nudging her shoulder with his. "I might look like a doofus, but it's fun. Your idea is great too. Big fan of the crazy hair."

I wanted to vomit. He was flirting with her even though her opposite day outfit was lackluster. His, though…

I gritted my teeth as my anger flared. He'd dressed like a student all the way from the light-up shoes, the blue shorts, a school T-shirt, the backpack, the name tag, and *what the heck?*

Jonathan Simpson, one of the students both Christopher and I had, walked out of his Christopher's classroom wearing a blue sweater with elbow pads, gray pants, and a name tag that said *Mr. Callahan.*

Damnit! His idea was *awesome.* My inside-out clothes and opposite shoes seemed silly in comparison to his student-teacher opposite idea, but I stood taller as I approached our classroom doors. He stopped walking and grinned at Kennedy before she kept heading down the hallway to the fifth-grade wing.

"Well, best of luck, Ken. I'll see you at lunch." He held out a fist to Jonathon. "See you in twenty minutes, yeah?"

The kid nodded, but my brain was stuck on how everyone seemed to like Christopher besides me. He'd called her Ken. He had a nickname for another teacher after just one week, and he looked at me like he wanted me to burn alive? Yeah, this was so not fair. My plan was to speak in opposites all day and do a handstand for my class as often as I could. Now those ideas seemed to evaporate when his icy-blue gaze landed on me.

He pressed his lips into a flat line as he scanned me up and down, his nostrils flaring. "Not a dime, huh? I doubt that."

"I didn't spend anything," I seethed, my face burning hot. "I already owned every item of clothing I have on. Trust me."

He made a face that said he did not believe me, but he arched one eyebrow and smirked like he knew he'd won the competition. He stepped closer to me, and his subtle cologne tickled my nose. "Wearing your clothes inside out is a little too cliché, don't you think?"

"It's fun and clever and cheap."

"It's interesting," he said, dragging out each syllable as his tone dropped. "You're just proving my point over and over."

"What point?"

"You *think* you're so creative and fun," he said, his gaze dropping to my mouth for one split second. "But you're not. The first time you're challenged to not steal or bribe or buy your way into first place, you're average." He barked out a humorless laugh and straightened his posture as he gloated. "Man, it feels so good knowing I'm right."

He spun around and moved to his classroom before I had a chance to react. My eyes stung, and my stomach hollowed out at the underlying doubt I carried around. I did think I was creative, and my students loved all the fun stuff in my room. They fought to take turns with whatever new gadgets I had, but now...I hated that they made me feel gross.

Like I did buy my way into being their favorite teacher.

I grabbed a tissue to make sure my momentary tears didn't ruin my mascara, and my hands shook a little as his words played over and over in my mind. The seed of doubt was growing into an entire tree in my soul.

I didn't have to wait long. The familiar sounds of the rumbles and engines of the buses carried through the windows and excited little voices echoed in the hall. Students were here.

They'd attended school for half days the Thursday and Friday before. Today was the first full day of class, and my belly danced with butterflies. My crazy pink-and-purple dress was worn inside out, my shoes were different, each knee-high sock was a plethora of colors, and I used body glitter to cover my arms and face. I positioned myself outside my classroom door and didn't have to pretend to smile as the first group of kiddos came walking my way.

"Good night! Good night!" I said to all of them as they either smiled or looked at the ground nervously. "Didn't you hear? It's opposite day!"

One young girl beamed up at me. "I hope you have a bad day!"

"That's the spirit!" I said back, my blood buzzing with the high of knowing this was what I was supposed to do. Teaching was my passion, my call to the world, and it didn't matter that someone thought I bought my way into their hearts and minds. I loved what I did.

"You have the funnest class," a young boy said, stopping just outside my door. I made sure to shake all their hands before they entered, and I nodded.

"We have lots of fun while we learn."

He went inside with the rest, where I had large nameplates cut out from my Cricut letting them know where their cubbies were and their desks. I might've gone a bit overboard by giving them each a packet of stickers and supplies, but seeing them use the cool pencil and show it off to their friends brought me joy.

"Yeah, we'll see whose class they enjoy more," a low voice said, making me whip my head to my left. Christopher leaned toward me, a smile still on his face as his students walked into his class.

"Is this another challenge, Mr. Callahan?" I asked between clenched teeth. I didn't want to scare my students on the first day with a scowl, so I kept my smile wide. "My former students have siblings, and they know how my class is."

"Yeah, I know how it will be too. All flash and flair from material-istic items you got from *grants.*"

He bent down to help a student tie their shoe, and my heart lodged in my throat at how gentle and patient he was. This was the glimpse of the man I connected with all those months ago, not the jerk who almost made me cry, twice. My muscles tightened with how unfair it was that I didn't get to see this nice side anymore.

Before I could say anything else, a new bus arrived and another wave of students flooded the hall with little voices. My cheeks hurt from smiling so much, and Maggie caught my eye across the hall and waved.

Ready or not, the school year had started.

Hours later, my throat was drier than a desert, and my feet ached. I moved around constantly when I taught, and after three months of being lazy, I lost all my stamina. I heated up another cup of tea in the teacher's lounge, and while I waited for it to warm, I plopped in a chair and rubbed the bottom of my foot. If I had access to money, I'd splurge on a pedicure, but between Christopher's words and the fact my best friend and brother laughed at me, it sobered me up.

I didn't need a pedicure. I could put my feet up when I got home and take a bath. That would work *and* wouldn't cost a dime.

That damn phrase. It was starting to rule my life.

After putting my shoes back on, I got my cup of tea and made my way back to the room to pick up for the night. My class was messy, and I always felt guilty leaving crap all over the floor for someone else to sweep up, so I spent ten minutes doing it before I left. I was halfway done when a high-pitched laugh made me stand up straighter.

There was no way that laugh belonged to *her.* Plenty of people laughed with a high tone and were a bit nasally.

I blew out a breath and focused on the last half of the room, ignoring the way my blood pressure spiked and blood rushed to my ears. All thoughts of her were shoved into a box in the back of my mind that I never allowed myself to think about or open. She was out of our lives, and that was it.

But that laugh…I chewed on my lip for a second and set my broom down. I just had to make sure I was imaging it. I took a few steps outside my door, and voices carried over from Christopher's classroom. Walking in there would be too weird, too sketchy. I needed a reason to go in there.

Buddy teacher. That's right. I could ask him about today, how attendance went, that sort of thing. The laughter rang out again, and with a fake smile that stretched across my face, I walked into his room like I belonged and stopped dead at the woman sitting on the edge of his desk.

My blood turned to ice, and my vision blurred.

It was *her*.

The woman I paid ten thousand dollars to leave my brother.

Chapter Five

MY BODY SEEMED TO STOP WORKING. MY LUNGS WOULDN'T SUCK in air, and my feet were glued to the white tile on the floor. Samantha Sullivan should *not* be here, in my school, talking to Christopher.

She should be anywhere else, conning men into giving her money and breaking their damn hearts. Time seemed to slow down when her gaze moved from Christopher's smile to mine. She was always heart-stoppingly beautiful, but the malice and thrill in her eyes gave her away. She was ecstatic at my panicked expression.

"Is there a reason you're staring at me in my doorway?" Christopher asked, his tone laced with irritation.

I willed my mouth to move, to say something, *anything*, but all physical abilities left, and the longer the silence stretched on, the worse it got. Samantha ran her tongue over her bottom lip as her eyes lit up with amusement, and she seemed to wiggle with joy. Never had the sight of someone sent a rage so deep. I could almost taste how much I loathed this woman. "I-I came for a question."

"Then ask it or leave," he fired back, his shoulders stiff and broad, and *why the hell is Samantha in his classroom?*

I had to warn him, somehow.

"Uh, did you have trouble today with attendance?" Wow, I sounded like a total idiot, and my face flushed.

Samantha ate it up and crossed one leg over the other as she watched me, like she was the predator and I was the prey.

"No. I know how to click buttons and hit submit. Is that all?"

"What are you doing here?" I asked her, but Christopher didn't understand. He tilted his head and scowled.

He cleared his throat and put his attention back on the woman in front of him, his gaze softening and his tone getting playful. "Ignore her."

Samantha didn't look his way once. She slid off the desk, curved her bright-pink lips into a smile, and held out her hand. "You must be Gilly Carter. I'm thrilled to see you. I'm a volunteer at the school and have heard *such* interesting things about you."

My teeth hurt as my stress doubled in size, making my lungs work overtime for each breath. It felt like drinking molasses, and I leaned into the doorway as she got closer. I was not supposed to see her again, ever. The fact she was in the same zip code as Fritz made me think about dark things. Like punching her in the face over and over. For a normally relaxed person, I had felt more anger and fury in the past week than in my entire life. Damn Christopher and Samantha.

"Let's chat about how I can help your class, hm?" she asked.

Christopher frowned in our direction and arched one dark eyebrow as Samantha looped her arm in mine and guided us out of his room. Shame at my lack of response was enough to make me choke on my words, and it wasn't until she shut my classroom door that words seemed to form.

"Why are you here?"

"Why do you think, Gil?" she asked, smiling and eyeing my desk. She ran a finger over the edge and picked up one of my staplers. "You seem to be doing well. Got the award, the classroom that looks like Pinterest fucked Hobby Lobby." She tapped her nails on the top of the desk before crossing her arms and leaning against it. "I need money, and I know you have it."

"It was a onetime thing," I said, noting how she looked more tired than she did six months ago when I handed her cash. She had gotten into her beat-up car without a backward glance and kept her word. Fritz said she never responded to any of his calls, and even though my heart broke into two seeing him like that, what she was doing was unacceptable. Me making her go away was the better option. She got what she wanted—money—and he never learned that the relationship was an entire con.

"Oh, honey, no, it wasn't. You know I can waltz back into Fritz's life and make him fall for me? You don't think I knew about the engagement ring?" She laughed and moved to run her hands over the sticker chart on the wall. "If you don't get me cash, I will return, and we can be family. Yay."

No, that couldn't happen. "I don't have access to it."

"Stop bullshitting me. You were always a shit liar, hon." She spun around, and the amusement left her face. Instead, a desperate anger made her features contort into pure ugliness. Red splotches on her cheeks, her eyes narrowed into slits. "I need five thousand dollars now."

God, my whole chest tightened with worry. She couldn't return to Fritz. I refused to let her hurt him even more, and I coughed to buy myself another second. "I'm not bullshitting you, Samantha. I froze my funds. I don't have access until the end of the month. I can show you the damn email if you don't believe me."

"Why would you freeze your funds?" Her brows pulled together, like I'd told her I hated puppies or something.

"It doesn't matter why," I said, hating that I put myself into this position in the first place. I had *encouraged* Fritz to date her, see her, try a real relationship with her. The woman I'd thought she was charmed me and made me feel like we were friends too. It wasn't just Fritz she betrayed, but I, at least, had myself to blame.

She studied me for a second, teeth on her bottom lip, before she nodded. "Fine. Let's see if little Miss Carter follows through at the end of the month. Good thing I'm here every day helping you and Christopher out. God, that man is *fine*. What's his story? He rich too?"

I swallowed down bile. "No, he's not. Not even a little bit." My voice came out louder than I intended, and of course, she caught it.

Her pupils grew as her gaze moved from me to the wall I shared with Christopher. "So, you and him, huh?"

She's searching for a weak point.

"Um, no. Hell no." I shook my head for emphasis, but it only made her laugh more. "You might be the devil, but you're not an idiot."

Her eyes flashed, and she crossed her arms. "Interesting," she said, drawing out the word. "Seemed like there was some leftover tension in the room."

"Not leftover, just regular tension. We don't get along. It can happen."

"Right," she said, taking a deep breath as she chewed on the side of her mouth. "Does Christopher know your past, heiress? Does anyone at this dingy school know you're a walking bank account with money that's not yours?"

I blinked. "Yes," I lied, my heart beating so hard there was no way she didn't hear it. It thudded so fast it made my throat shake. "They know."

"You and your brother share the same inability to lie." Her eyes lit up, and she clapped. "Oh, this is delicious. No one knows about your wealth."

"They do, and they don't care."

"Gilly, you naïve heiress, *of course* they care." She tilted her head to the side and gave me the biggest, fake smile I had ever seen on her. "You and Fritz are entitled, spoiled adults who waltz around without a care in the world. You didn't even earn your money—it was *given to you.* You are nothing more than a means to an end, and if you think differently, you truly are pathetic. You might judge me, but at least I know what I want in relationships—money and security. You and Fritz? You think y'all can find love? You can't. You're a bank account."

"Get out of my classroom, now."

I'd had enough. My fists balled into my sides, and my vision blurred at the anger building in my chest like a tidal wave. "Get the hell out."

She pursed her lips. "Or what? Precious Gilly won't hit me. She doesn't have the guts. You need to find me money, or I'll ruin everything you've worked to hide."

"I don't have it," I said through clenched teeth.

"But you know where you can get it," she said, the fury making her eyes go dark.

I took a step toward her as Christopher walked into my room, and it sickened me to see Samantha morph into her charming, bullshit personality. This was the woman who tricked Fritz into loving her, the woman who befriended me and who I thought would potentially be my sister-in-law.

"Hey, Mr. Callahan, are you here to walk me to my car like you promised?" She batted her eyelashes and walked by me as she strutted to him. He remained stiff and expressionless as he looked from her to me, but whatever concern he had in his eyes died when she placed a hand on his arm. "Come on, handsome. Ms. Carter needs to send some emails to people."

"Right," he said, looking at me a beat or two longer, but I shielded my face.

Tears threatened to spill over, and I refused to show either of them more of a weakness. I forced a smile, and Christopher frowned at me. He opened his mouth to say something, but I wasn't in the mood for him, for Samantha, for *anything*.

I held up my hand. "I don't care. Get out. Both of you."

He slammed his lips together and retreated into the hallway, leaving me in my room alone with the only sound coming from my rapid heartbeat.

Samantha was back, and she wanted more money.

I had to get the hell out of this place. My one home, where no one knew about my wealth, was tainted by her, and the dread in my stomach grew as the truth settled on me. She would expose me and return to Fritz if I didn't get her money. If people found out my *grants* were a cover and knew what I had in investments and bonds, they would treat me differently, but I could probably handle it.

Fritz, though…if he found out what I'd done, he wouldn't talk to me ever again. He was my best friend in the world, and the thought of hurting him sent another wave of hysteria through me. My sob escaped quickly and aggressively, and I covered my mouth with my hand as I shoved my stuff into my bag.

I refused to break down in school, but it seemed to be too late. I plopped into my chair and held my hands over my stomach, taking deep breaths to settle down, and after five minutes of it, I succeeded. My eye makeup was a mess, and I wasn't sure I could eat anything for a week, but I was calm enough to walk to my car.

With one more sniff and a quick use of a tissue, I got up with my keys in my hand and walked out my door. The last person I expected to see was Christopher in the hallway, alone.

He was stopped right in the middle, bending his head to look at his phone in his hands, but when my shoe squeaked on the tile, he snapped his gaze to me. "Gilly," he said, his brows scrunching together as he blinked a few times. "Were you *crying?*"

"Stay away from her." I walked faster than normal and looked at the ground. Only twenty steps until I would be at the double doors. Nineteen, eighteen…

His footsteps got closer to me. "Hey, wait."

"What?" I snapped. I was done. Emotionally and physically. "What do you want, Christopher? Do you actually care why I'm crying because let's not pretend you do, okay? You should be *thrilled* I'm upset.

His face paled, and he looked like I'd slapped him. I didn't care what his response was. I had bigger things to worry about than my teaching buddy who didn't remember me from a one-night stand and who hated me. I continued my path to my car and got in, wishing more than anything I could erase the last hour.

The first full week of school was my favorite time of year, and now, Samantha had ruined that for me.

Chapter Six

My competitive drive didn't seem to dull despite the fact my personal and professional life were a hot mess. The SPIRIT day was *favorite character,* and it was so hard to not buy a Ms. Frizzle outfit. I would've rocked an orange wig and crazy colored dress, but instead, I pushed myself to be more creative. *Take that, Christopher Callahan.*

I totally pulled off a green striped rugby shirt—courtesy of my dad—and khakis Fritz lent me, but little notebooks were my weakness, and a student had given me a *Blue's Clues'* dog to set on my shelf last year. My favorite character outfit was pretty good. I felt confident in my Steve impression. I had my handy-dandy notebook ready to go as I stood outside my classroom door to welcome the kiddos on day two. Across the hall, Maggie dressed like Minnie Mouse and looked adorable. I waved and flashed her my biggest smile.

Christopher intercepted the grin and raised his brows at me, so I turned that grin upside down, fast. Heat flooded my veins knowing he saw my tearstained, red-rimmed eyes yesterday, but I was better today —okay, better-ish. I scanned his outfit and had to choke back a laugh. The man was dressed in head-to-toe cowboy gear. Boots, jeans, the star things that spun on the boots, yellow plaid shirt with a vest, a bolo, and a hat. There was a huge yellow star cut out and written on it was WOODY.

"Not a dime, huh?" I said, my voice almost on the edge of flirting. *Where did that come from?*

"I owned this." He stopped walking and lifted up his boot to show the ANDY written on the bottom. "It was important to show you that detail."

"Why would you own an adult-sized Woody costume?"

"For…reasons," he said, smirking at me.

Why is he smirking? Why? Make it stop.

I cleared my throat and shrugged. "It looks all right."

"Mr. Callahan, cool!" a kid said, walking by us and smiling up at him. "I love Woody!"

"Me too." He bent down to talk to the little guy. "Why do you like him?"

"He's brave and the favorite, and I like his toy." The kid nodded a few times and high-fived Christopher. "Is he your favorite?"

"Jesse is actually my favorite. Do you know who she is?"

"Yes, the lady cowboy with red hair! My sister loves her. Why is the girl your favorite?"

"Because she's strong and fierce and is a good friend. Woody is great too, but Jesse is my girl."

"Nice." The kid beamed at him before Christopher stood up and jutted his chin toward his classroom.

"Want to help get the carpet squares out for reading circle for me?"

"Yes, sir!" The kid took off, and Christopher slid his gaze to mine. He looked guilty with his eyes swirling with something, but before either one of us could talk, Samantha walked into the hall.

"Good morning!" she yelled, making me jump back. "How is everyone today? Oh, Christopher, you look darling. I have a thing for cowboys. A real thing."

She got closer to him, and I used that as an excuse to drop my stuff off in my room. I needed to run into the teacher's lounge, but I trusted Samantha as much as I would Hitler, so I got my classroom keys and locked the door before heading to the lounge. I could feel

Christopher's stare on my back as I made my way away from them, her voice getting louder the whole time.

I knew her goal. She wanted to fluster me, but I refused to let it show.

"Did you ever hear about that lawsuit last year? About two siblings who destroyed some family members to protect their inheritance?" she asked.

My entire body locked up. Everything took place in Indiana. There was no reason for anyone in the city or our town to hear a whisper of it unless she heard about it there.

"No, I don't recall."

I exhaled and was almost drunk on relief. Samantha might be messing with me now, but she wouldn't spill the news yet. It was one of her two options. If she told my secret, then why the hell would I give her any money?

I can do this.

I made copies of the goal-setting activity I was going to do with my kiddos and smiled as other staff members came into the work-room. There was no malice on their faces or hidden agendas to ruin my life. These were my coworkers who I enjoyed talking to and working with. Christopher and Samantha couldn't take that away from me. With a new resolve to ignore them, I went back into my room and got ready for the day. An idea struck though, right before the bell. I went to my computer and sent a quick email to APD.

Dave—heard we need help unloading boxes in the basement. Can we send volunteers there today? You know I love help, but I don't want to confuse the students with another adult when we're forming relationships this week.

He responded almost immediately.

Good call.

Take that, Samantha.

"Okay, class, we read a different version of *Goldilocks and the Three Bears* yesterday. Who can tell me what was different about today's version?" I asked the class, smiling at the pure wonderment on their faces a few hours later. "It can be anything from their clothes, the scenery, the pacing—how fast the story moves. Who wants to share?"

Jessica Dowdy raised her hand in the air as high as she could, so I called on her. "My brother's birthday is in thirty-two days."

I waited a beat, digesting her words as they were so off topic, I had to blink away my surprise. "Wonderful, birthdays are so much fun. But what is different from the story from yesterday?"

Jessica scrunched her face together before smiling. "The food. Yesterday was porridge. This was soup."

"Well done!" I wrote her answer on the board and surveyed the class. "Jake?"

"The outfits."

"Nice!" I wrote down six more differences they provided and capped the red marker before picking up a third version of the fairy tale. "We are going to dive into a new one today. Who's excited?"

Choruses of me's echoed around the room, and my heart grew two sizes in my chest. This was why I did what I did. This passion and energy fueled my soul, and I wanted to hug them all. I refrained, as it would be weird and we didn't have time, but the thought remained as we read through the story. This version was my favorite because the illustrations were vivid. We got all the way through before a low-pitch noise sounded outside the school.

It was a sound from my nightmares, and my pulse pounded in my throat, making it difficult to speak. It wasn't even tornado season, but there was a cold front coming in, and it wasn't unheard of to have a strong storm in August. I glanced out the window and sucked in a breath at how dark it was for midday. *Damn.* "O-Okay class, that is the tornado siren. Did you ever have a tornado drill last year in kindergarten?"

"Tornaydough? Like play dough?"

"No." I put a hand over my chest and willed my heart to settle down. We had to act. This wasn't a drill—those were on Tuesday mornings. "Everyone, grab a book from your desk and get into your recess line."

They all jumped up and followed the directions, and I smiled through my own fear. Tornadoes scared the shit out of me, and I shoved my hands in my pockets to hide my trembling. There was a reason they'd named it Tornado Alley.

"We are going to go outside the classroom and line up against the wall and sit crisscross, okay? Once you sit crisscross, you're going to cover your head with the book."

They nodded.

One girl started crying, and I took her hand. "It's okay, Maureen. We are very safe."

"My brother says tornados eat people."

"They are dangerous, but they do not eat people." I squeezed her hand and led us out into the hallway, catching Maggie's eye across the way.

She looked grim, and a bright flash lit up the entire hallway as a terrifying loud boom of thunder followed. The windows at the end of the hall shook just a little bit, and I swallowed hard.

Shit.

"Okay, kiddos, keep going. Sit down like we practiced, okay?" I said, hating how my voice trembled. The last kid left the room, and I shut the door. If we were to get hit, the classrooms were lined with windows, and the thought of all the glass had my blood turning to ice. I gulped and slid onto the floor in front of the door, hearing the siren continue on an endless loop to let our county know a tornado was spotted.

It could be heading right for us. It could destroy the building and us in it. I swallowed hard as sweat dripped down my forehead, and I wiped it away with the sleeve of my rugby shirt. My hand shook, and I crossed my arms, hoping to hide it. The kids would freak out if they saw me worried, and I *had* to hide my fear better.

"You seem pale."

I didn't need to open my eyes to know it was Christopher. "Didn't get a lot of sun this summer."

"No. You're flushed." His voice got closer, and he sat on the ground next to me, our shoulders not quite touching together, but his body heat radiated toward me along with that damn cologne. "Gilly, open your eyes and take a deep breath."

I did, but only to check on the class, not to placate him. His face was inches from mine, and his unfairly long lashes danced across his cheek when he blinked. Beautiful bastard that he was, he had nice features. "Do you…have you heard…the storm?" I asked, willing the buzzing sound in my ears to go away.

"It's about ten miles southwest of here. We won't get hit unless the storm goes against nature and backtracks."

"Can that happen?"

"Not usually." He pulled up his phone and showed me the radar. "We're here. The tornado has already passed us, but it's still in the county so the alarms go off."

I sank into the brick wall and swore my legs turned to pure jelly in relief. "Grood. Good. Great. I meant great."

Christopher's face didn't look as mean and unhappy as it normally did, and a small part of me grieved the chance we would never have to be friends. Thankfully, a kid pulled my attention away from him, and I sent a small prayer for that. Thomas started crying, and I had him move to sit next to me. "Why are you sad, Thomas?"

"My dog is outside at home. He gets scared. What if he's wet?"

"Dogs love getting wet. Have you seen a dog swim before? They are so happy." I patted his hand. "Is there a tree or a cover in the backyard?"

"He has a doggy house."

"Oh, then he'll be totally safe!" I assured him. "Doggy houses are the best. They block the rain and wind. I bet he's cuddled up in there, smiling at the rain."

"And the tornado won't eat him?"

Ugh, my heart. That damn Maureen sharing that lie. "Nope. The tornado missed us so we'll be safe."

"Thanks, Ms. Carter." He leaned on my arm for a second, and I let him.

I felt Christopher's gaze, and I looked up to find him watching me with an odd expression. It wasn't quite a smile, and it certainly wasn't joy, but it also wasn't anger.

The fact he wasn't scowling at me was so unsettling.

I didn't get time to ask him why he was watching me because Dave came on the speakers and announced we had to wait another five minutes before returning to class. My legs shook as the adrenaline needed an escape, and I tapped my feet on the tile in a rhythmic beat.

"You're scared of storms."

I slid him a warning glance and jutted my chin at the kids sitting next to me. It was a major no-no to look scared in front of them because it would set them off. One time, I cried because my hormones were out of control, and it made four of the kids cry. They fed off my emotions.

I kicked him in the shin.

His mouth dropped in shock, and I snorted.

"You just…kicked me?" he said, his eyes wide as a stop sign. "What the…?"

"I'll do it again if you put my fears out in the open." I wiggled my foot in his direction again, and he moved his leg out of the way. "That's right. Fear me."

"You are too tiny to be feared, Martha Stewart."

And our little truce—if it was even a real one—was over. I masked my face and sat up straighter, giving him my back and zero of my attention. I'd rather count the individual bricks lining the walls than talk to a man who hated me as much as he did, and it was time I stopped caring.

"Ms. Carter, what is a cloud?"

"A cloud is a collection of tiny drops of water or ice crystals, Jimmy."

"What is rain?"

"Water that falls from the clouds."

"What are coconuts?"

I snorted.

A small chuckle came from the beautiful grump I was trying to ignore.

"Coconuts are from palm trees and are kind of like nuts."

"What are boobs?"

"Okay, question time is over for today!" I ignored Christopher's joy. Dave chose the perfect moment to come on the intercom, letting us go back to our rooms. I went rigid when a warm hand landed on my forearm. His hand was large and comforting, and *Christopher was touching me.*

"Can I stop by your room after school today? I have some questions."

I took my time sliding my gaze up his throat, over his full lips and day-old beard, and landed on his gorgeous eyes filled with warmth? What? No. Not warmth. That made no sense. Mirth?

"Questions? But you aren't a first-year teacher. Surely you can figure them out."

He ran his tongue over his bottom lip as he smiled. "Nice zing, Ms. Carter."

"Your appreciation is noted." I clapped and motioned my hands for the kids to keep moving. "Put your books under your desk and start thinking about fairy tales, little ones!"

"So will you be free?"

"As your *buddy* teacher, I have to be." I refused to look at his mouth again and focused on his forehead. "What is this in reference to?"

"Observation."

"Great," I said, not hiding my sarcasm. "Can't wait." And with that, I went back into my room and scanned the hallway to see where *she* was. There was no way having her reassigned to unload boxes deterred her plans, but there was no sign of her anywhere.

Good.

"See you then, *Gilly*."

The way he said my name made me snap my gaze in his direction. His answering smirk confused the hell out of me. He had to be playing at something. Maybe it was because my not-a-dime outfits were better than he thought or the fact he knew storms terrified me and he wanted to exploit my weakness. Either way, I had two hours to figure out what he wanted to talk about.

Chapter Seven

WEDNESDAY MORNING USUALLY MEANT A STUPID *HUMP* DAY JOKE from a colleague and shifting point in my lessons where I would make changes to meet the students where they were at. Instead, I woke up an hour early to get ready for my SPIRIT day.

The email announcement last night had changed *everything*. I wanted to beat Christopher just to throw it in his face and watch him cry, but now, the winners from each grade level went to a showdown and got to pick the professional development training at the end of the month. This was huge. Bigger than huge.

Christopher *couldn't* win because I refused to sit through a training on *how to teach without a personality* or *why white walls are best for inspiration*. No. I couldn't.

That was why I was light-headed from blowing up fifty balloons and taping and tying them on to strings and yardsticks. Nothing was purchased, so I was still following all his dumb rules, and I knew I was going to kick his ass.

Christopher could waltz in here with his rigid lack of fun, but he didn't know the staff like I did. He didn't know that Miranda's mom used to live with her until she relocated to Florida to live with her other daughter. He wouldn't know that she had a walker with tennis

balls at the end unless he was Snapchat friends with her—which I was
—so that was how I scored a walker to complete my outfit from the
movie *Up*, going as Mr. Fredricksen. She let me borrow it without
even bribing her with chocolate.

My brain felt fuzzy as I blew in the last balloon as Larissa walked
in and grinned so wide, I swore I saw every single individual tooth in
her mouth. "Holy cow, Gilly."

"Can you…help me get it ready?" I'd borrowed an old dollhouse
from the preschool attached to our building and taped all the balloons
so it looked like the house from *Up*. My classroom had tons of paint,
and I used every color I had. "Think this is creative enough?"

"Um, yes. You went far out." She clapped, looking adorable in her
Mrs. Incredible outfit, which would've cost forty dollars at the party
store. "I'm impressed. For real. You'll make the rest of us look bad,
but it's worth it. You see APD's email about the training?"

I nodded too hard and winced. "I'm not letting *him*"—I jutted my
thumb over my shoulder to point at Christopher's wall—"win. I'd
rather eat a tube of glitter glue."

"I don't know…the kids love him."

"Don't remind me." I huffed and adjusted the big clunky belt to
make my too-large corduroy pants—curtesy of Larissa's brother—stay
up. "Okay, fake glasses. You brought them with you?"

"Sure did." She handed them over and snapped a photo.
"Amazing."

"Keep the compliments coming. I need the confidence." I sighed
as she frowned at her phone. "What is it?"

"Helen wants to meet to work on our lessons for the week. This
observation thing the first full week back is killing me. Are we all doing
this crap? Why can't they let us do this later?"

"It's just for the new teachers to the school and second-year teachers." I agreed that the timing wasn't ideal, but I understood the need
to help model how to do anchor charts for classroom rules and poli-
cies. "Not all of them know how to adjust lessons into anchors."

"Fine. You're right." She rolled her eyes and groaned. "Can't wait
to hear the gossip about your outfit today. You'll be the talk of the
staff, for sure."

I winked as she left and lost myself in the lesson that Christopher was going to observe. It was only for thirty minutes since APD would cover his class so he could sit in mine, but it felt bigger than just a lesson. Like my student teaching experience but amplified. Which annoyed me.

I didn't care what he thought.

Okay, sure.

I had an hour to prepare and check my emails, so there wasn't time to worry or overthink about the fact he would be in my room, watching me, with my students. I wasn't going to waste it worrying about some guy.

Christopher was still not in my room as I stood outside my door and greeted all the students. His door was open, but Dave was in there, like it was planned, and my stomach tightened with nerves. Would he show up late to try to fluster me? Was this a trick to mess with my mind?

Either way, it was working. My poor nail was barely there from my constant nibbling, and just as I accepted he would ruin whatever I would do, his tall frame appeared at the end of the hall. He wore a dark jacket with a striped scarf and—*oh my gosh, is that a bald head piece?*

Were those…pillows in his jacket to make him look exactly like Gru from *Despicable Me*?

Oh, hell no.

He was mid-laugh with another male teacher when his gaze landed on me, and the appreciative glance he did up and down my body made my skin break out in goose bumps. *What the?* I was dressed like an old man. There was no way for him to look at me with interest in those eyes.

I cleared my throat at the lack of hatred coming from him and prepared for the worst when he approached my door. "Mr. Callahan, or should I say, Gru? Are you ready to join us for anchor charts?"

"Sure am, Mr. Fredricksen." He shoved his hands in his pockets, and one side of his mouth lifted on one side. It wasn't an entire smile, but it was at least a quarter of one, and there was no reason why I returned the same, almost visible smile back. It was because kids were around. That's the only explanation.

He walked into the room, and in the worst accent I had ever heard, he mimicked the character. "Gooooood morning, my minions."

"Mr. Callahan! Is that you? Where is your hair?"

"Your nose isn't big."

"You need eyebrows."

"Are you hot? It's August, and you have a scarf."

Excited and loud voices greeted our temporary guest, and my eye twitched a little bit at the way they all smiled at him. These were our kiddos, sure, but they liked me for me...not the flashy toys. I was almost sure.

"Okay, my intelligent, kind humans. We are going to do an anchor chart for how-tos. Who can tell me what *how to* means?"

Danny raised his hand and took a large breath. "Instructions."

"Yes, excellent." I grabbed a dry erase marker and drew a cartoon of a young student sitting crisscross on the board with one hand raised and the other in his lap. I wrote WHAT LISTENERS DO at the top of the board. "Okay, can someone tell me what this student is doing?"

"Sitting!"

"Raising a hand!"

"Tooting!"

I fought the urge to laugh and caught Christopher's eye for a split second. He, too, looked about ready to chuckle, and I forced myself to keep my face neutral. "Great observations!"

I wrote in big handwriting, *Raises hand to answer.* "Raises hand to answer. Can we all raise our hand and keep quiet, like good listeners?"

They all threw their hand up in the air.

"I want you all to talk for two seconds to the person next to you while I tell the class my favorite color, okay? Whoever can tell me what I say will get to take the lunch menu down to the office. How does that sound?"

They nodded, and I held up three fingers. "On the count of three. One...two...three."

Conversation exploded in the room as I said in my normal street voice, "*Blue.*"

"Okay, be good listeners!" I raised my hand and closed my mouth, waiting a good ten seconds for them to settle down. "Who was a good listener? Raise your hand if you heard my color."

Two students had their hand raised.

"Missy, what did I say?"

"Pink!"

"No," I said kindly. "Hank?"

"Red."

"No again." I smiled and pointed at the drawing. "Can you see why we have to raise our hands when we want to share something? It helps make sure we all can hear each other, and that's important." I paused and did a quick sweep of the room. They were all tuned into me.

"My favorite color is blue." I grinned, and a bunch of chatter started. "Ah, ah, good listeners, right? Now, what can you tell me about his face? Where are his eyes? Are they on his hands or staring forward, playing close attention to the speaker?"

We went through every part of the cartoon's actions. His feet position, his mouth, what he was thinking about, and by the time we were done, we went through practice on how to be good listeners. The twenty-minute lesson ended, and we moved to language arts as Christopher got up and made his way toward the front of the room.

"Can we all wave good-bye to Mr. Callahan, or shall I say, Gru?"

Twenty-four students laughed and waved at him as he bowed and used the same awful accent to say *gudbye*. I didn't have to fake a smile as I walked him to the door, the high of knowing the lesson went great despite the fact he was there, and I had a comment right on my tongue about how I didn't use a single prop besides a marker when he nodded at me.

"That was good."

"Wait, excuse me?" I said, blinking and making a real scene about clutching my chest and taking a few steps back. "What?"

He let out an annoyed breath but repeated it. "The lesson was good. Different from what I expected."

"Did you think I'd fly in on my hoverboard and use holograms? I'm saving those for next week."

Christopher barked out a laugh, giving me a real, genuine smile that made my toes curl into my old slippers. "Okay, Martha."

He waved one last time to the class before leaving into the hallway, and my students had zero chill and distracted me before I had any time to analyze his comment. It was for the best because there was no way he would start being nice to me.

Nothing had changed.

THE HIGH FROM THE MORNING ONLY LASTED UNTIL LUNCH, WHERE it exploded like a firework when I was midbite into my macaroni bowl. Helen stood up from her lunch table and cleared her throat before smoothing down her blue dress. "Today is the last day, y'all. If you don't have your money for the group brewery tour, I can't sign us up as a group. I hate to be that person, but I sent an email about this last week."

Last week, I had been trying not to have a panic attack that Samantha was here, and Helen emailed the whole staff too damn much, so I often skimmed. She called it a *group bonding,* and I forgot it was about the trip. Dang it. *I never gave her money.* My face burned so hot, I swore my skin was going to melt off. How could I forget to pay her, and now my money was tied up? Shit.

What was I going to do? I clenched my plastic fork tighter and tried to rationalize how I could get the money. It was fifty bucks, which wasn't insane, but not something I just had lying around.

"Did I pay you? I can't remember," Peter Dee said, scratching his head and scrunching his eyebrows together. Conversation seemed to stop in the teacher lunchroom. "My mind is just a blur this week."

Helen laughed. "I know, mine too. Let me check." She pulled out her phone and clicked her tongue until she nodded. "Okay, for *Hops and Hoops* get-together, I need Larissa, Gilly, and Maggie. Everyone else is good to go."

"Can we still sign up if we're interested? This sounds like fun," Christopher said, making my blood boil. The thought of him going to it with all the teachers who were my friends was my version of hell.

This was supposed to be fun, and seeing him on a Saturday, with the staff that I loved working with, was the opposite.

Helen, the angel, smiled softly at him. "Sorry, Christopher, unless someone doesn't give us their money, there isn't a spot. I can let you know at the end of the day if I have an opening or not."

He nodded, and his gaze flicked to me for one second. I looked at my plate and felt the sweat forming on my brow. Attending an outing at the brewery would be such a great way for all of us to relax and work out the back-to-school nerves, and knowing Christopher was ready to take my spot made it so much worse. He could turn everyone against me.

Fritz. I would call my brother, and he'd lend me the cash, especially if it was for school. I couldn't feel too bad about asking when it was to further my professional relationships, right? That was work-related. It was important.

Larissa and Maggie excused themselves to go to their classroom to get their checks, and while conversation picked back up again, my heart beat pounded so loud I couldn't make out the words. I couldn't finish the salad, so I tossed it into the trash and went into the hallway. My fingers shook a little when I called my brother, hating that I forgot about this cost. This was my own damn fault, and this stupid *one-month* challenge was biting me in the ass.

"Hey, Gil, what's going on?" he asked, his playful tone a good sign.

"I need to borrow fifty bucks."

"Um, no."

"Please, it's for this school thing, and it's due to today and I forgot about it when I did my budgeting. It's important, Fritz," I said, almost on the verge of begging.

"Gil, no. We agreed for one month. You need to figure this shit out on your own. If it's not a life-or-death emergency, then you gotta figure it out. This is what you wanted, okay? I'm not trying to be a dick about it."

His words were true, but it still upset me. "Fine, yeah, I'll figure it out."

"Don't pout," he said in a stronger voice. "You can do this, Gil."

"Yeah, bye." I hung up and knew my anger wasn't really at Fritz, more at myself. How could I forget about the payment? I pinched the bridge of my nose and tried to think of any way to get that by the end of the day. The only options I could think of were to pawn something or drop clothes off at a consignment shop or sell something online. It would only work if Helen accepted the payment later in the afternoon though. Swallowing down my pride, I tried to sneak into the workroom without making noise, and I approached Helen at the copy machine. "Can I send it to you later this afternoon?"

"The payment?"

"Yes," I said, hating how I could feel *him* staring at me. It was like there was a specific jerk detector on my skin that prickled whenever he was around. "I forgot, honestly, and need to get the money. I will though."

"Okay, Gilly." She smiled. "If I don't have it by five, it'll to go Christopher though."

"Right, fair. Totally understand," I said through gritted teeth. "I'll have it by then."

"I hope so. We were looking forward to you joining us," she said, her words soft and sincere. She didn't speak loud by any means, but that didn't stop Samantha from snorting at the table nearest the copier. Her little laugh sent ice into my veins, and before I did something stupid, I had to get out of there.

I forced a smile and went back to my classroom. *Okay, what could I sell?* What if it went to Christopher? God, that would eat me up. I had a dull headache and no answers, but it didn't matter—there wasn't time to think about a solution when lunch ended and twenty-four little pairs of feet bounced back into my room.

That was the one thing I could almost always count on. My students. They could distract me from whatever mess my life was in, and I was thankful.

THE REALIZATION THAT I HAD A SPENDING PROBLEM STUNG. Knowing the owners of Bonny's Boutiques had its perks for many reasons. Getting notified when vintage purses and dresses arrived tended to make my day, but now, it was reversed. She told me if I ever wanted to sell part of my vinyl collection to them, she would happily take them. I rushed home to do just that. I got my Beatles albums that my dad gave me and carefully placed them in the back of my car. She squealed when I handed them to her. Before I could change my mind, I accepted the fifty dollars Bonny offered me and rushed out.

My lower back sweat more than I was comfortable with, but now I could hang with the other teachers for a few hours. I parked a little too fast, my tires over the painted lines, and hustled into the school. I didn't have much time to drop it off before heading to the tutoring place, so I booked it toward Helen's room. There were quite a few staff members there at the late hour, but it wasn't uncommon during the first week or two back. I smiled at Maggie, who was on the phone, before I turned down the hall leading to the upper level classes.

I got three steps closer toward her door when Samantha appeared like a black cat, quiet and menacing. Not a good sign. Her eyes even seemed to glow when she looked me up and down. I sucked in a breath when she crossed her arms, arched a brow, and smiled like she knew all my secrets. "Excuse me, I need to drop this off and head out."

"Oh, is this the *money* you said was tied up for a month? Interesting." She stepped closer to me, keeping that creepy smile on her face, and eyed my hand. "I'm hungry and want the cash. So give it to me, or I'm calling Fritz. It's your choice, really."

"Samantha, this is for the *Hops and Hoops* trip. This is beyond you and me and my brother. Please." Panic had my heart beating so fast it hurt, and my eyes stung a bit. It would be *so* unfair if my spot went to Christopher, who started this whole thing in the first place. Seeing him friend everyone would slowly kill me. It was the social event of the semester. Missing that would be awful. They'd bond and have inside jokes for the whole year. Last year, we went to an escape room, and we stilled talked about it. I gritted my teeth as I clenched the envelope tighter. Agreeing to this challenge was all Christopher's fault. If he weren't such an ass, I wouldn't have accepted the *not-a-dime* crap.

No. It's mine. I shouldn't have paid her. I shook the thought out of my head when she ran her tongue over the side of her mouth and grinned.

"I don't give a shit if it's for neglected puppies. None of that matters. Give me the cash." Her voice took on a dark tone, and my stomach dropped. She took her time getting her phone out of her pocket and sliding her fingers over the device. "*Hey, Fritz, it's Samantha. We have a lot to talk about. I left because your sister——*"

"Fine, fine." I shoved the money at her. "Take it. *Don't* text my brother, please."

She grinned like a Cheshire cat, winked, and patted my hand. "I always love when we get together, don't you? It would've been *so* fun being your sister." Then she walked off, swaying her hips.

My spot would go to Christopher, and everyone would wonder why I couldn't pay—that sucked, but protecting Fritz was more important right now. It would always be the most important, and this was my penance for helping him. With a brief moment to feel bad for myself, I straightened and told Helen I was out.

Now, I had to hustle to get to tutoring on time and try not to cry.

Chapter Eight

My body sagged with exhaustion as I loaded my *Up* costume into my car and was glad to slip into a pair of jeans and a green blouse that had a high neckline after the mess of a day. Whenever I went to the literacy center, I spent most of the time bending over or on the ground helping, and it got annoying to always make sure my cleavage wasn't on display, so now I made sure I never had any.

I shoved my costume into a bag and grabbed my stuff before locking my classroom door and heading toward my car. Scanning the area for Samantha sent another wave of irritation through me, making my skin itch. That stunt she pulled, demanding the cash and threatening to text my brother…it caused a sharp pang in my chest. She had the unique ability to send a spike of anxiety crashing through me, and I hated not feeling confident and prepared. The only other person who could throw me off my game was the infuriating, handsome man who taught next door to me.

Speaking of…Christopher stood next to his beat-up car—a Honda that was at least ten years old—and was on the phone. I didn't mean to eavesdrop, but his tone was sharp and *loud*. The fact it wasn't directed at me gave me pause.

"*Then use your brain*," he said, putting one hand on his hip and glaring at the playground. "We're left picking up the pieces from your mess. Figure it out yourself." He muttered a cuss word before snapping his gaze to me, and a fire brewed behind his blue eyes as he clenched his jaw so hard, it made my own teeth hurt to see it.

"I wasn't listening," I blurted out, fumbling with my keys in my hand and looking down.

"Stop lying. I'm getting sick of the act," he snapped, the dark edge I hadn't heard from him all day back in full force.

"What? I'm not...okay, I didn't mean to listen. And it was only the last part."

"No, you know what I'm talking about." He clenched his teeth and shook his head at me, like I was the most disappointing person in the world. "Cut the shit, okay? I'm over it."

I ran my teeth over my bottom lip as my stomach bottomed out with dread. "Cut...what shit?"

"Christ, I don't have time for your crap." He opened his car door with a loud squeak that showcased how old his car was, and how new mine was, and he slammed it when he got in.

"Okay then," I mumbled, wishing I waited another thirty seconds before leaving so this showdown wouldn't have to happen. Things had been uneventful, and this untimely conversation gave me a headache. Samantha and then him. The worst duo. I unlocked my door and tossed my materials in the back seat, and without a glance, I got in and drove out of the parking lot. Christopher sat there, watching me drive away, still in his stupid Gru outfit, and his expression only darkened.

He was back to hating me, so that was great. It still blew my mind that this was the man who laughed and was kind and considerate—and giving—in bed all those months ago. It was like that entire night was a figment of my imagination.

It sucked. Totally, sucked.

My phone rang over my car speakers, and I answered without looking at who it was. "Hello?"

"She's back in town."

Shit.

My brother's voice was low and *pissed*, and there was only one she who he was referring to. Samantha.

"What do you mean?" I squeezed my grip on the wheel as my mouth dried up from the guilt. I knew she was back, and I was the reason, but Fritz could never know that. Ever. I'd rather lose a limb.

"She followed me on Insta and posted a picture not too far from your school." He exhaled so hard it caused a static sound in the phone.

No. Please, no. I swallowed, the gesture causing a ball of pain, and blew out a breath. "Has she…tried talking to you?"

"Nope."

"Are you going to…reach out to her?" I froze as I waited for his answer. If he did, it would throw off her plan and could send her into a different direction. One where Fritz got hurt, again.

"What would I have to say? I'm not saying shit to her. She walked out of my life six months ago without a fucking word. God, I do not need this shit right now." He groaned, and my heart broke into two for him. "This case is kicking my ass, and I can't afford distractions. Did she follow me to mess with me, or does she want to talk?"

She wants money.

"Probably to mess with you," I said, keeping my voice even despite the absolute terror and turmoil going on in my mind. My overconfident, overly flirty brother was broken from her. She had damaged his sunny outlook, and it got me pissed all over again. "Look, I'm volunteering at the literacy center for a few hours. Want to grab dinner after? We can talk crap about her or avoid it. I can fill you in on this dumb competition at work. You should see my outfit today, Fritz. I was amazing."

He let out a forced chuckle. "Yes to dinner. Don't wanna go out though. Just come here when you're done. I'll order Chinese."

"You're my favorite brother," I said, using our typical joke but hoping he knew the weight of the words.

"Yeah, yeah, I know. You're mine too. Bye, Gil."

He ended the call, and I used the remainder of the drive to figure out how I could get Samantha to go away, avoid Fritz getting hurt again, and to still win this competition at work. My poor brain was working overtime, and when I pulled into the parking lot of the literacy center, I was met with a sense of relief. This would be the perfect two-hour distraction, and that's exactly what I needed.

I walked into the bricked building, signed the visitor form and put on a name tag, and practically skipped toward the tutoring room where students who struggled with reading were grouped by skill. There were six- to twelve-year-olds in this room, where the other room focused on high school-aged students. Working here the past two years had been one of the best joys. Our parents always encouraged us to volunteer in areas we were passionate about. They said it was necessary for all humans to give back, but that since we had wealth, it meant we had to do more. So I tutored two days a week for the fall semester each year and always donated money to the center for the holidays. It was always anonymous, and it would remain that way.

"Ms. Carter! Hello! Welcome back." Paige Martinez, the director of the literacy center, smiled wide at me and handed me a clipboard. "Here is a list of students with their Lexile scores. I'm thrilled you're joining us again this semester."

"Wouldn't miss it." I returned the smile and studied the list of kiddos I would work with on Wednesday and Thursday afternoons. "Okay, this looks good."

"Did you recruit someone else for us?"

"Hm?" I tilted my head and moved my gaze to her face. She focused on another clipboard that had Mountain Elementary in bright-red letters on the top right corner of the page. "Oh, is someone else from my school working here?"

The hairs on the back of my neck tickled, and it was like he had the unique power to make the particles in the room shift around me. With a nervous breath, I spun and found Christopher Callahan standing at the edge of the room, his gaze filled with curiosity. *At least it wasn't hate.*

"You must be Mr. Callahan! Welcome! I was just telling Ms. Carter that we are thrilled another teacher from Mountain Elementary is joining us here. She's been here what, three years now?"

"Yes," I said, my tone growing stronger as his gaze swept over my face. "It's absolutely wonderful spending a few hours here."

He didn't get a chance to respond before a student I worked with the year before, Leticia Romano, walked into the room and smiled so wide she looked a little crazy. "Ms. Carter!"

"Leticia! Look how big you are!" I bent down when she ran up to me, and I gave her a huge hug. "Wow, you're so tall. How old are you again? Forty? Fifty?"

"No!" She giggled. "Six. You know this."

"Of course. It's so good to see you. Want to get started?" I ignored Paige, and Christopher for that matter, and followed Leticia to one of the round tables so we could work on her phonics. Her parents spoke Spanish at home, and Paige had us read up on one of the most challenging parts of being raised in a bilingual household —that kids often skated by with minimal skills in both languages, instead of making them successful at both. If I could rule the world, I would have all schools dual-language where students left fifth grade being fluent in two languages. It was so cool students could learn two languages at the same time. They were incredible sponges, and it upset me when adults underestimated children's potential.

"Okay, let's see what your teacher has you doing today," I said, grinning as she rushed to get out her materials.

She had her folder and pencil on the table as another student, Marco, joined us. We went through their homework, where they felt they struggled the most, and took our time going over the expectations. When they had some independent time, I used the moment to reapply lip balm because all the talking had made my lips chapped. As I swiped my finger across my bottom lip, I caught Christopher staring at me.

There wasn't fury or rage or anything in his expression beyond curiosity. My body seemed to shiver with awareness, like it remembered how it felt to have his skin on mine, but I shoved the unwarranted attraction away. The sting of his words from not an hour ago hadn't left, and I wasn't in the mood to figure out what his problem was or why he was so complicated and uptight, so I ignored him. He wasn't worth the little energy I had left. Focusing on the kids and seeing their skills grow was better.

Between questions and working one-on-one, two hours flew by, and I got up from the small chair and stretched my hands over my head. My bones cracked, and another wave of tiredness hit me. Dinner with Fritz would have to be short so I could plan my outfit for the next day and go to bed early. Paige was on the phone when I walked toward the exit, and she waved with a smile. I'd be back the next day with the same group of students, and without even looking to see if *he* was still there, I exited the building into the hot August sun.

"You've volunteered here the past three years?"

And I guess he was there. Damn.

"Yes," I said, not bothering to look at him as I walked toward my car. If he was going to follow me and talk, that was fine.

"Why?"

Excuse me? I stopped in my tracks and glared at him. "You're asking me *why* I've volunteered at a literacy center for three years?"

"Yes." He crossed his arms and took a long breath as he stared at me. It was the same sharp gaze with questions swirling behind his eyes. "Why do you do it?"

"Why do you?" I fired back, sounding really mature.

He narrowed his eyes before speaking. "Because when I taught inner-city students, reading was the best way to help them. Working on their core skills without all the trinkets and tools and newest toy in the education world was best. They didn't need the toys to learn. They needed fundamentals and a caring adult."

"That's what you see yourself as."

"Yes. I care about them without all the flair. So I ask again, Gilly, why do you volunteer here? Is it for show? Is it some mandated requirement? I'm having a hard time understanding why *you* would willingly do this."

He might as well have slapped my face from his insinuation. "You know what? Screw you. I've done nothing to make you hate me, yet it's the same every day. I volunteer here because literacy is important to me. So is giving back to the community. If I can spend four hours a week to help young learners better their skills and grow into independent thinkers, workers, and citizens, then I feel good about myself, okay? That's it. That's why. Did you see the way Leticia hugged me and thanked me? I'm helping make a difference in her life, and that matters to me."

He blinked slowly. That was his response to me.

He was the most frustrating and infuriating man, and I was done. I unlocked my car and got in, desperate for a glass of wine and to forget about him. If I could go back three months and not enjoy a night with him, maybe this all wouldn't bother me so much. He'd be just another asshole.

It was the fact I knew he could be kind, but chose not to be to me and only me.

It was a hard pill to swallow, and if it was even possible, the urge to win the competition grew stronger. Two more days of creative and cheap costumes, and I had to win.

Chapter Nine

Thursday flew by in a blur, and Samantha never showed her face on campus. I texted Fritz a stupid amount of times to double-check she wasn't seeing him, but he assured me he hadn't heard a thing from her since the Instagram follow. I even stalked my brother's accounts to make sure...I didn't trust that woman, and her silence on my end made me nervous. She was the type of bully you wanted visible. *Keep your friends close, and your enemies closer.*

It was easier to see her flirt with Christopher or have her make dumb comments to me rather than having no idea what she was up to. But it didn't matter. The longer she stayed out of my life, the better. My limit on my funds was up in a month, and if she were still sniffing around, I could pay her off. Maybe she'd get bored and find a new target. One could only hope.

It was finally Friday. The final day of the SPIRITS competition. The day we had a school-wide assembly where students would vote for the most creative teachers. Our tie-dye SPIRIT day the day before was probably my least favorite, but that was okay. My heart beat twice as hard that morning when I woke up, and even now, with class starting, the adrenaline kicked in an hour before the assembly started.

One of us would win today, and not only get to pick a training for our team, but also get major bragging rights. I would throw it in his face so hard, he wouldn't be able to look at me for a week. My competitive drive scared me a little bit, but I was rolling with it. Athletics weren't my thing, but winning SPIRIT weeks most definitely were. I'd put this on my résumé and wear the badge proudly.

"Good morning, Ms. Carter," one of my students, Emily, said as she walked into my room. "Did you know that Mr. Callahan is funny and had a fish growing up? I have a fish too. Do you? Fish are my favorite."

"That is super cool!" I said, making my voice remain positive. "What's your fish's name?"

"Ted Red." She smiled, and her eyes widened at Christopher standing outside his door. "Mr. C! Mr. C! I did the thing you told me to with my homework, and I got it. You are the best!"

"High five, Little E." He bent down and held out his hand when she went up and high-fived him.

She never smiled at me like that, with awe and wonder and grati-tude, and my stomach clenched. When did I care about being the favorite? It was selfish. Kids should have an adult they trusted and liked in their life, and that wasn't always going to be me. I knew this and was a million percent okay with it.

But why him?

The conflicting emotions hurt my soul. When Emily came back to my class, I forced a smile. The great part about swapping students for certain subjects was to expose them to different teaching styles. I loved that, but it meant Christopher and I shared the same students, and one of us would eventually be favored over the other. He took all things science, and I focused on ELA activities.

"Can I sit on your bouncy ball today for class?" Emily asked, the harsh reminder that my class had the three evil Ts: things, toys, and trinkets. "I want to try them, please!"

"Right, of course." I nodded at her as I felt Christopher's gaze digging into my back. Today's theme was school spirit, and I wore every yellow-and-blue item of clothing I had, from shoes to knee-high socks, to a skirt and leggings and a tank top over a long-sleeve shirt with gloves, face paint, and a hat. Christopher looked okay, but since he was new and couldn't spend a dime per his own rules, he didn't have Mountain Elementary swag like I did.

Karma serves him right.

"Nervous about the assembly, Gilly?" he asked, his tone softer than normal. Like he was the wolf trying to be nice to the lamb to trick them. He wasn't fooling me though.

I puffed out my chest and pursed my lips. "Not really. It'll be nice to finally win this thing and be done with you. I've spent far too much time ensuring I don't spend a *dime.*"

His lips quirked up on one side, but the smile faded when Samantha came out of Marisa's room and headed toward his. She wore a skintight blue body suit and a yellow dress over it. It was tacky and not that appropriate for a school setting, and I had no doubt Larissa would roll her eyes and mumble something under her breath about it. While her outfit made me cringe, her presence didn't. Seeing her caused relief and my anxiety to spike. It was a horrible combination. But if she was here at the school, she wasn't with Fritz.

"Christopher, hey you." She swayed her hips when she went up to him and ran her fingers over his forearms. "You didn't call me back last night."

He has her number. Go figure.

He chose not to call me after our one-night stand but had already exchanged numbers with Samantha. Disappointment weighed me down. God, this sucked. I hated how I cared when there were a million reasons why I shouldn't. He was rude and awful to me. So why did his opinion matter at all?

I walked into my room to escape their exchange and was thankful to see Timmy frowning at his backpack. I needed to stay distracted from the unwanted thoughts plaguing my mind. "What's wrong, little man?"

"It's stuck." He tried pulling it apart again and groaned. "My big brother said I'm weak and small and stupid."

"Oh, Timmy. You are none of those things." I got on one knee and showed him how some of the material got stuck in the zipper. "When this happens, you kinda have to pull the material out so it's free. See?" I pulled, got it free from the metal zipper, and smiled. "I have a big brother, too, and he used to call me mean names."

"Really?"

"Yes. I was so mad, but I told him it hurt my feelings and that I loved him."

"Was he nice?"

"We're best friends now."

He smiled for a second before looking at the ground again.

"Hey, Timmy, you are going to grow and get stronger and bigger every day, so he might be bigger now, but that doesn't mean you're weak or stupid, okay?"

He nodded a few times and sniffed, and without warning, he jumped to give me a hug. I patted his back just as Christopher poked his head into my room, and I swore, for one second, his gaze softened at me.

"Ms. Carter, can I have a word?"

"Sure." I let go of Timmy and took hesitant steps toward my enemy. "What is it?"

"Clarissa is having a really hard time today because her dog died last night. She's in my room crying right now. Can she just stay with me until the assembly?"

Oh, my heart broke. "Yes, of course." I put a hand on my chest and frowned. "Is there anything I can do to help?"

"I'll let you know." He ran a hand over his jaw and held my gaze for one, two, three seconds. He opened his mouth, closed it, and finally said, "She likes me because her older brother is named Cal, and my name reminds her of him. It makes no sense, but that's why she's in my room. It's not anything more than that."

"No, I'm glad she has you to help. I won't mark her absent. Let me know if we need to call her parents or the counselor."

"Right." His lips curved up on one side of his mouth for half a second before he left, and the rapid pace of my heart had nothing to do with the competition or our past or the assembly and everything to do with the fact he was *such* a good teacher. He didn't have the budget I did or the pretty walls or colorful posters. He cared, and his students knew that after one week.

I turned my attention back to the littles in my room and clapped my hands.

"Okay, let's review our anchor chart for rules and get ready for the assembly!"

Cheers echoed around my room, and I threw myself into the lesson, ignoring Samantha and my brother and the fact Christopher was a good teacher who just hated me.

"Let's hear a howl!" APD hollered into the microphone so loud, there was an awkward feedback sound over the speaker system. Hundreds of kids put their hands over their ears and winced. "Sorry! Let's try that again. On three, I want you all to howl for our first assembly of the year!"

"One, two, three!"

Howls and screams carried over the gym and seemed to bounce off the walls as students got excited. Dave was a tough, mean-looking guy, but he had the biggest heart and loved making school a fun place for everyone. He was decked out in a bright-blue suit with a yellow tie and shoes, and anyone else would've looked ridiculous, but he pulled it off. "Good morning, Mountain Elementary! We are so excited to have you help us select our staff winners for the SPIRITS competition!"

There were cheers, and Larissa winked at me from three rows down. I wiggled my brows at her and searched for Christopher just to send him a mean look. He sat on the opposite end of the same bleacher section, and his gaze was *on* me. It was unnerving and almost too intense—bringing me back to that night at the bar when he looked at me like I was special.

He hates me.

He needed to stop looking at me like that if we were going to continue to be enemies. That was for damn sure.

"Kindergarten staff, get on down here please." Dave clapped his hands as the group of four got up from the bleachers and went to stand in the middle of the gym. They always dressed up as a group each year, not wanting to compete with each other, and it was adorable. Dave rolled his eyes and held up a sheet of paper. "I need you all to clap as loud as you can for this amazing group of ladies. They worked together so well, they are going to get free donuts for all their classes. Does that make you excited?"

It didn't matter that fifth graders wouldn't get the donuts. Every kid cheered, and excitement seemed to spur more excitement. It was contagious. My nerves made my stomach do flip-flops as the kinder teachers went back to their seats. First grade was next.

"Okay, first graders. Please welcome your all-stars!"

Marisa, Maggie, Maria, Christopher, and I moved toward the center of the gym, and every muscle in my body tensed. I plastered on a fake smile because no matter what happened, I would not upset the kids. This was about me and Christopher and our weird past and challenge.

He caught my gaze again and raised his brows, leaning down to whisper to me, "Don't be upset when you lose."

"I'm going to kick your ass, Callahan."

He chuckled and straightened, making our height difference more apparent as we stood shoulder to shoulder. He was a good ten inches taller than me, so I stood as tall as I could and even thought about going on my tiptoes.

Dave got a couple of paper certificates and handed them to the three Ms before thanking them for their participation. He stared at me and Christopher before bringing up three students. "You all know each year that admin scores the teachers on their SPIRIT with a rubric. Well, we have our first ever tie, and we need you all to help us choose who was more creative and innovative. Those are our foundations at Mountain Elementary, so we are going to have three students choose who they think won."

I gulped and made a fist and hid it in my pocket, still forcing a smile as everyone watched the two of us. This tie-breaker business was new. We never had that the past three years, and Larissa met my eyes and frowned. I glanced at Christopher and enjoyed the absolute look of shock on his face. He thought he had it in the bag, and he didn't. It felt *really* good to see him suffer. Now, I just had to win to bring it home.

Dave called three students up toward the center of the gym and handed the mic to a student both Christopher and I shared. Max. Dave bent low and smiled. "Okay, Max, tell us who you think should win. Who was creative and innovative?"

"I think," he said, taking a long breath and shifting his weight onto his feet. "I think Ms. Carter should win because she always comes up with new ideas to help me with my art. I never stay in the lines, and she says that's okay. She makes me feel smart."

Don't cry. Don't cry. My eyes stung as I bent down and pulled Max into a hug. He squeezed me as tight as he could with his little arms, and Dave moved to the next student. There was a light cheer in the gym, but I was so happy at Max's response, it filled my whole heart with joy.

"Emily, what do you think?" Dave asked, moving on to the second student standing near us.

I let go of Max and patted him on the shoulder before watching Emily.

She let out a loud *hmm* for a full ten seconds, making everyone laugh. She grinned wide and stared right at me. "I like Ms. Carter because she's safe and reminds me of my mom when she tells me she cares for me and helps me when I'm confused."

Okay, tears for real now. I pulled Emily into a hug and didn't care about the cheers or the competition anymore. It was stupid to get caught up in Christopher's crap when this was the reason I taught. For this. The relationships and trust and sense of family. "You're the best, Emily."

She beamed at me and hugged my leg as Dave walked toward the final student. Henry was shy and wore glasses that were a little too large for his face. Dave repeated the question.

Henry took the mic and mumbled into it in his small voice, looking straight at the ground. "Uh, I think Ms. Carter is creative because she always lets us try things and doesn't yell if we mess up."

"Well, there you have it, Mountains. Ms. Carter is the winner for first grade!" Dave said, the gym clapping again for me as he held out a fist.

I bumped mine against his and didn't care that I had tears on my face. My heart was three sizes too big for my chest, and I didn't pay attention to the rest of the assembly. I didn't even look at Christopher once because my whole reason for being was validated. My job was my life, and all the doubt Christopher put into my mind evaporated. I kept thinking about what the students said, why they liked me. They never once mentioned the *things* I had in the room or the tools or treats I brought them. It was about how they felt in my classroom, and it was what I tried to emulate every day. A safe, fun, creative place for students to learn and create memories for a lifetime.

I was more than my flash and colors, and it was good to remember that.

"Hey."

A voice pulled me from my roller coaster of emotion, and I blinked a few times before turning to see Christopher moving to sit down right next to me on the bleachers. He didn't leave more than two inches between our legs, and I had the urge to scoot over.

"I don't want to hear a word unless it's *nice job, Ms. Carter.* Don't ruin this for me, please. I needed it today." I took a breath, and my throat felt heavy, like the air was peanut butter and I was trying to breathe it in. "If you're worried about the training I'll select, don't worry. It won't be about how to decorate a classroom or bribe your students into liking you."

He winced, like I wanted him to, and it was the first time he looked ashamed of himself. His face paled, and his lips parted an inch before he sighed. "You'll pick something about literacy, won't you?"

"Yes, because that is something I'm passionate about. Now, excuse me." I got up, leaving him sitting there with a confused look stretched across his face. I thought winning would feel better after seeing Christopher, but it didn't. My body was weighed down in disappointment in the fact that the student's answers shocked him so much. So it couldn't possibly be true.

I clapped for the rest of the assembly and didn't have to fake my smile when I went back to my class to finish day. The students were thrilled for me and let me know all day, and my dark cloud left the longer I was around them. It wasn't until the last student got on the bus for the day that Samantha stood next to me outside, the closest person to us at least twenty yards away.

"I'll see you Monday, Gilly. Better figure out some solution for me. You are so *innovative* and *creative*, right? You'll figure it out, dear, Ms. Carter." She curved her pink lips into a menacing grin and winked before strutting in the other direction.

I had two and a half days to figure out what the hell I was going to do.

Chapter Ten

I FELT A LITTLE LIGHT-HEADED AS I STOOD ON THE EDGE OF THE
football field where Grace watched the sophomore football team practice on a Saturday afternoon. Normally, I ate breakfast, but nerves got
the best of me that morning and I went with only tea. I liked to join
her on weekends sometimes, but especially now that I felt unsettled. It
was hot as hell outside, and my black shirt stuck to my back, but I
didn't care. I craved vitamin D *and* the warmth. I hadn't been able to
calm down since Samantha's threat, and it was a secret that was
eating me up inside. I wasn't sure if my shivers were nerves or the fact
my condo was always kept cold. Either way, I was a mess.

Did I tell Grace and see what she thought? Or would she judge
me? Would she yell and not understand? Would she tell me to disclose
everything to Fritz?

She yelled at two of the athletes being idiots before coming over to
me and rolling her eyes. "Boys act like doofuses at every age."

"True." My mind went to my infuriating hot buddy teacher for a
second. "You look good on the field though, G. Like you belong."

She flashed a grin as a teenage girl wearing a school shirt and
black athletic shorts walked up to us. "Mrs. Anderson, can I, uh, ask a
question?"

"Of course," she said, looking at me for a second. "She's in my advisory and in my sports med program, so we see a lot of each other. You don't mind, do you?"

"Oh, not at all. Please, ignore me." I smiled and took a few steps back to let them talk in something that resembled privacy. I got my phone out to scroll through emails, but her voice carried over.

"I'm not sure what to do. Peter cheated on me, and he's in our advisory and texted everyone I'm easy and a slut, and I just...I'm so embarrassed, and he plays on the team and..." She sniffed and looked over the field with her heart in her eyes, and it brought me back to the heartbreak of high school. The pain was so sharp and real and horrible as a teenager that I wanted to hug the girl myself.

Peter was an asshole, and I already hated him.

Grace's face softened as she turned her attention on the girl, and pride flushed through my body seeing my best friend turn into a mentor. "Kayla, you are intelligent and have so much going for you. One teenage boy is not going to ruin that for you because he made a dumb decision. If you're about to tell me you're quitting my program to avoid him, we will have words. You are fantastic and—"

"Anderson, we have blood," a coach yelled in our direction, and Grace almost growled.

"I'm sorry, Kayla. I have to go, but we are not done with this conversation."

"I understand." The blond girl sighed and pushed her hair out of her face. She looked so heartbroken and sad, I couldn't stop myself from walking toward her. She wiped under her eyes before her very blue eyes landed on me. She flushed with embarrassment, and I held up a hand.

"I'm Gilly. Grace...uh, Mrs. Anderson's best friend." I smiled, and the girl nodded. "I'm so sorry—I wasn't trying to eavesdrop. It just kinda happened, and I'm going through something similar to you. I work with someone who is awful, but I refuse to let his actions dictate what I want out of life."

"Really? Did he...ruin your reputation?"

"No," I said, tilting my head to the side. "But he makes me doubt myself a lot."

"Yeah, Peter made me feel gross and dirty. We never did more than kiss, and he said all this stuff…it's just not true! People believe him, and it makes me so pissed."

"You know the truth though. Your friends know. The people who matter know the truth, and sometimes, that's all you need." I thought of Fritz and Grace and Larissa, ignored the guilt seeping in about Samantha, and focused on Kayla. "It's really hard, and I wish I could say this stuff doesn't happen out of high school, but it does. You just learn how you deal with it better."

"What are you going to do about this guy at work?"

"I'm going to keep doing what I love—which is teaching. Do you love the sports med program with Mrs. Anderson? Does it make you happy being on the field and treating injuries?"

She nodded and pulled on the hem of her shirt. "I would love to do what Mrs. Anderson does when I grow up. Being a teacher was always something I liked, but doing sports medicine with it would be cool."

"Then you work hard at it. Ignore this Peter dude. The best revenge is being happy. Have you heard that before?"

"No, but I like it." She smiled a bit. "Be happy."

"Yes. He did that stuff to get a reaction out of you, to hurt you. There's no other reason besides that, so him seeing you happy will be like a kick to the shin." I nodded a few times and found myself following my own advice. Being happy and continuing doing what I love—teaching—would block out the weird and confusing feelings about Christopher. "People are going to hurt you. This guy…really misjudged me, like Peter did to you, and it hurt. It still does, honestly."

She exhaled and stood up a little straighter. "Thanks for being honest with me. There are a lot of teachers or adults that think being seventeen means we need kid gloves or something. That's why I like Mrs. Anderson so much."

"Yeah, she's always been pretty real with people. I met her when I was just out of high school."

Kayla smiled as Grace waved her over, but before she started jogging, she thanked me again. "I hope your work situation gets better."

"And you, I can't wait for Mrs. Anderson to tell me you're kicking butt."

She joined Grace, and the weight in my chest felt lighter. Samantha would keep coming back if I paid her again, and Christopher would continue to upset me if I let him.

I needed to take a stance...I just wasn't sure how.

MONTHLY SUNDAY BRUNCH AND BAGS WAS A DUMB YET IMPORTANT tradition as we all moved on from college and started our lives. We never missed it, and it was the promise to each other to always stay in each other's lives. Since Grace and Brock had a house, we tended to meet in their backyard where we grilled out, had a few mimosas, and caught up. Grace and Fritz were midargument about the rules of Bags while Brock stood at the grill watching his wife with the same soft look that conflicted with his grumpy exterior. Seeing them together always caused a weird combination of joy and jealousy. He was so good to her, for her, and I would always be thankful they found each other.

"Stop cheating, you dumbass," Grace yelled at Fritz as he tried to argue that you could bounce the bag of rice off the grass and onto the board. "Brock, tell him he's wrong."

"Fritz, you're wrong."

"Oh, beat me up, big guy," he fired back, earning a middle finger from Brock.

I laughed, seeing the people I loved most in the world hang out, and enjoyed a nice long sip of orange juice and champagne.

"You still refusing to date anyone, or can I set you up with this adorable teacher at my school? She's your type, Fritz, I swear," Grace said.

"No." His tone darkened, and just like that, the momentary bliss I felt evaporated like an ice cube in the Midwest summer.

"No, as in you are interested in someone else?"

"No, as in I'm not dating." His jaw tightened, and I had to set my drink on the armrest to place my hands on my legs to hide the tremble. "Samantha sent me a message last night."

"*What?*" Grace yelled, causing Brock to frown. Even the grump knew about the hell Fritz went through.

"Yeah. It said, *hey you.*" Every line on my brother's face hardened, and I hated this woman even more.

"Did you respond? You can't. Gilly, did you know this? Why now?" Grace said so fast, she didn't breathe between statements. Her gaze moved to me.

I shrugged. "He told me."

"I'm not responding. There's nothing to say." He took off his sunglasses and ran his hand over his face. "I shouldn't have said anything. I can feel the anger off both of you. Let's just…play bags and eat. I'm not in the mood to have you two analyze my emotional scars today."

Grace snorted. "Fair enough. I will try to analyze you later though."

Fritz grinned, and it eased the sudden tension for everyone else. Not me. I got up and excused myself. "I think I left something in my car. Be right back."

They didn't pay me any attention as I got up and used their side gate to move into the front yard. I needed to get it together. Like now. With a shaky breath, I moved my limbs like I was stretching before a game, and when I was done, I gasped at the vision in front of me.

Christopher was there. Shirtless and sweating and ten feet to my right. He took a long swig of water and some of it splashed on his very muscular chest, and my entire body tightened with need. He was so damn hot and *oh my God.* His body wasn't even fair. Broad shoulders and defined biceps that made my toes curl into my sandals. He was effortlessly handsome and took care of himself, and *shit.* His attention moved to me and widened with the same panic mirroring my own reaction.

Time seemed to freeze for what could've been a minute, or maybe two hours. I wasn't sure I cared. With his wet skin shining in the sunlight, I couldn't look away. His gaze traveled from my face, down my body, stopping at my cleavage before moving to my legs, lingering there.

What is happening? Why is he next door? Where is his shirt? Can I take a picture?

His mouth parted, and despite the fact we didn't get along, memories from *that* night flushed through me. The way he used his hands, his mouth, his teeth. How defined his chest was and how hard his body felt when I explored every inch of it. He hid his body at work, and it was easy to ignore my attraction with all those sweaters and goofy outfits, but now...I shifted my weight back and forth between my feet the longer we stared at each other. Was he trying to remember why he hated me, too? Because if he told me to touch him right now, I would.

"No way!"

A young girl's voice broke the moment, and I shook my head, blinking away my unwanted lust, and my eyes about bugged out of my head.

"Kayla?"

"Wait, you know *my sister?*" Christopher almost yelled as Kayla walked down the front porch and over the driveway toward me in ripped jeans and a large shirt.

"Yes! This is the woman I was telling you about yesterday. The one who has an awful coworker who really upset her." Kayla beamed at me as my entire body turned red. She had no idea that her brother was the person I was referring to, but her brother definitely did.

I watched as he swallowed, hard. So hard I heard the click of his throat, and he had the gall to look at the ground.

"Do you live next door? That would be awesome!" she said, jumping up and down a bit. "This guy is my brother. Sorry, he's in a bad mood because he and my dad were fighting about money, again."

"*Kayla,*" Christopher snapped, making us both stand a little taller. "Will you check on Dad for a second? He was trying to install a microwave on his own. Stop him."

"Ugh." She rolled her eyes. "Fine. But Gilly, why are you here?"

"Mrs. Anderson lives here." I jerked my thumb over my shoulder. "I'm visiting her."

"No way!" She grinned. "Okay, I'll come say hi after I save my dad from himself. He's a wonderful idiot most of the time."

She waved and practically bounced inside her house, leaving me with my inappropriate thoughts of her shirtless brother. His stare was intense again, making me a little breathless because I had no idea what was going to come out of his mouth.

An apology? An insult? An invitation to his bed? If I had to pick, I wasn't sure which one I would've preferred.

He put his hands on his trim hips and pressed his lips together as he scanned my outfit again, this time, his gaze heating. "I feel like we should...talk."

"Talk?" I repeated, not even caring that I let the word fluctuate, bordering on flirting. I hated how this guy made me feel, yet...here I was.

"Yeah." He cleared his throat and rubbed the back of his neck, which only made every muscle of the front of his body move with the movement, and I sucked in a sharp breath. He was the last guy I was with, and while it never bothered me before, it did now.

Why did I wait so long?

"I'm not sure we do." I closed my eyes, hoping that not seeing him would help the lust overtaking my rational thoughts. "I should—"

"Gilly, get your ass back here. We have a bet going on about your *not-a-dime* situation," Fritz said, leaning over the gate with a curious expression on his face. "Uh, did I interrupt something?"

"No. *No.*" I took three steps back, like standing ten feet from Christopher would give everything I was feeling away. "This is..." I froze, unsure what to say. They all knew who this guy was. They heard me complain about him the last two weeks. But a part of me was petty, and a grin stretched across my face. "My buddy teacher."

"No shit." Fritz laughed, hard. "Grace, get over here. Looks like your neighbor might be Gilly's *buddy teacher.*"

"Shut up!" Grace joined Fritz at the gate, and her eyes widened. "That's the guy?"

I scoffed and went back to my friends. "He's not worth introducing."

"I disagree. I'm Christopher Callahan." He followed me toward the gate and held out a hand to Fritz. "I know she probably hasn't used the term *buddy teacher* in any good instances, hm?"

"Not a single one, dude." Fritz shook his hand. "I'm her brother, but I gotta say, the not-a-dime challenge was hilarious. Really challenged her, which was fun. She got all worked up over it."

"Is that so?" Christopher's gaze warmed as it landed on my face before shaking Grace's hand. "You must be Mrs. Anderson. My sister, Kayla, loves you."

"Oh, what a small world! You gotta meet my husband. Brock, come be social."

"No," he grunted from the grill, and I had never loved my friend's husband more.

I snorted and put my hands on my hips this time and tried to look tough. "Well, this has been…fun, but we're hanging out, and you should go help your family move in."

"He can have a beer, Gil. Chill out. Seriously, he deserves one. He teaches kids. Little humans. Just hearing you talk about it makes me tired." Fritz opened the gate and ushered him in. "If you have time, you can join us."

"I think I will."

"Fritz, you're my brother. Side with me, damn it." I almost stomped my foot at how weird the situation was becoming—my enemy was in the backyard with my friends…shirtless and being goofy?

What the hell was happening?

"Yeah, no shit, Gil. But the fact he got you, the most high-maintenance person I know, to stop your funds for a week is incredible."

"*Fritz*," I yelled, using a tone I rarely used. Everyone stilled, and my brother finally got the fucking message. I glared at my idiot brother as Christopher's sister appeared at the gate.

"Dad needs help, Chris. He swore he didn't need to read the directions, but you know how that goes. Oh, hi, Mrs. Anderson." Kayla smiled again, and her eyes got wide when they landed on Brock. I understood the feeling. Brock was as intimidating as he was handsome, and it flustered me the first couple of times too.

"Rain check on the beer." He nodded to Fritz and jutted his chin to me. "Walk me out, hm?"

"Rather not."

"Wasn't a question." He placed his large hand on my elbow and raised his brows. "Please."

Maybe it was because his skin was on mine, or the fact his chest was inches away from my face, but I sighed and let him lead me toward the gate. He smelled like soap and sweat, and heat seemed to radiate off his very delicious body. Warmth spread through my body at how my hormones seemed to completely forget he was awful to me. I could feel my friends' stares on my back, but I didn't care.

"What are you doing?" I whispered, glad Kayla moved back toward her house.

"What did your brother mean?"

"Why were you fighting with your dad?" I fired back, playing the exact same game he was.

His chest heaved as he let go of my arm and stared down at me. He studied my lips for a full thirty seconds before he smiled. "You blushed like this that night too."

Good lord. His tone was dark and secretive and hot. My stomach swooped at the first mention of our night together, but I didn't get a chance to respond. His dad came out, and he gave me one last pointed stare. "We have a lot to talk about, and I know exactly how to make it happen."

"Hm?"

"Gotta go. I'll see you tomorrow, *Gilly*." He said my name like a promise and winked.

Okay, what the hell just happened?

Chapter Eleven

Things were *different* at work that day, and I still couldn't wrap my mind around it. Christopher flirted with me. I was absolutely sure of it, unless I was totally off my game, but my face warmed thinking about the look he gave me before I walked to my car. *Stop. We hate him.*

Do I though? Do I hate him anymore?

I groaned and gripped the steering wheel tighter as I drove to Fritz's place. There was too much going on for me to worry about feelings for a guy who had been a total jerk to me. Not when Samantha was sneaking around and threatening to come back into our lives. She should have my focus, and that was how I convinced myself to not think about Christopher. Fritz was still in a funk, and it was my duty as his sister and best friend to help him out of it.

I parked my silver BMW outside his condo, locked the doors, and made my way upstairs to find him in *a mood.* "Dude, why are you grumpy?"

He frowned at me before plopping back down on the couch with his tie undone and his face set in hard lines. "Six months. She walked away without more than a *this is over* text and disappears for six months. Why is she liking my posts now? Why is she in town *now?* I don't fucking understand, and I hate it. I thought I was doing fine, but as soon as I see her liking my shit online, it all comes back."

My stomach churned like I'd ridden a roller coaster a million times, and I forced my face to remain neutral as guilt made speaking almost impossible. I cleared my throat and grabbed a pillow to hug it against my chest. "Do you...still love her?"

"No." His eyes were hard and dark, and his jaw was tight. "I don't, but I was going to propose to her and pictured the rest of my life with her. That is still raw and makes me never want to try again. It's hard enough to find someone as is, but once they find out about our money, it's even worse. Thank God our court case was out of town. I can't even imagine living here and having every fucking person know about our wealth." He rubbed the back of his neck.

It was like a thousand-pound weight had formed in my stomach and held me down. The sadness, six months later, was exactly why I couldn't do love. It's why dating and having flings were safer, easier, than ever falling for someone. Our money would always attract the wrong people.

Especially when Samantha fooled both of us so damn well when it was a con the whole time.

Would it hurt worse for him to know it was all about money? That he was a job? Or would it help him move on? My throat hurt at my lack of response, and I took a deep breath. "You can't...let her ruin any chance at happiness."

He scoffed. "Forgive me for not trusting someone anytime soon. God, she just ghosted me. No reason why after telling me she loved me. I just...it fucking hurts, and I thought I'd be okay by now."

I have to help him. I had done this, and it was my duty to help him.

"Okay, new plan." I got my phone out and started searching for free singles events in the area. Larissa always talked about this *buddy* night at a swanky brewery where people went to make friends, but they also had singles night. "We are going out tonight," I said, using my sternest voice. "You will not argue with me."

"But what about your budget, Gil?" he fired back, smirking like he'd one-upped me.

"How dare you insinuate I can't flirt for free drinks? I still have some charm."

He laughed, and the sound calmed me down and reassured me that maybe paying off Samantha, twice now, wouldn't send me straight to hell. "Fine, whatever. Maybe it's better to get out of this place. I swear all I've done is work, see you, or pout. I'm sick of myself."

"Fritz, you will be okay and find love again."

He rolled his eyes. "I'm not looking for love again. It's not for me. I don't like the dependency or the power it gives someone to destroy you. So hard pass, thanks. But a fling? Yeah. I could do that. Relive my college days."

I forced a tight smile. It was one thing that I felt that way, but for him…no, that wouldn't do. He had the biggest heart and deserved all the happiness in the world. He had been my, and Grace's, rock for years, and despite his insistence on being carefree, Fritz loved *hard*. Samantha couldn't ruin that for him. "Fix your tie. I found a thing to go to."

"A thing?"

"Yes, I'll tell you once we're there."

He narrowed his eyes at me. "Your tone tells me I won't like this *thing*."

"Don't care if you do or not. You're going." I stood up and dragged his ass to my car where I drove him to the brewery about two miles from his place downtown.

His only reaction to the singles night was a long sigh, and the fact he didn't fight me had to be a good sign. He ran his hands over his thighs, and if I had to guess, my brother was nervous. It made my chest tight seeing him without his over-the-top confidence.

I parked, and two beautiful women walked arm in arm into the large wooden doors.

Fritz sat up straighter, and the playful expression I had seen way too many times in college returned. "The only reason I'm not bolting out of this car is because I wanted to try this place out."

"Uh-huh, it had nothing to do with those babes."

"Not a thing." He smirked and got out, the tight feeling in my chest loosening at seeing him be playful again. He was always the goofy, overprotective flirt around Grace and me. He was always there for us and in a good mood and looking for a good time, and I missed this version of him, where I was torn between rolling my eyes or elbowing him in the side.

I joined him inside, where we signed our names on a clipboard and got a red wristband. It let others know we were there for the event and not just the beer. A handsome man with tattoos and long hair played the guitar in the corner, and couples lined both sides of the beer hall.

"I'm going to find that hot ass—*lovely* woman I saw walk in."

"I knew it," I said, smiling as he winked.

He smoothed down his shirt and headed toward the pair of women and I sighed, suddenly feeling nervous. This was about Fritz and now that he was occupied, I realized I would be required to talk and flirt too. It'd be great to have a distraction, but the last time I was at a bar, in a mood to flirt, I left with Christopher, which for whatever reason made him hate me.

How would he act if we never had that night together? Would we be friends? Flirt? I frowned, imagining a world where we got along and how good that sounded.

"Okay, singles! We're going to do some pairing up and start some convos." A soft female voice rang out over the portable speaker, and everyone seemed to stop talking at the same time. "First thing—raise your hand, and the first person you make eye contact is your partner for this activity. Once you see someone, high-five them!"

I fought the urge to roll my eyes because this felt like a classroom thing, but I did as told and met the gaze of a man who was about my height and had bright-red hair. "Hi, I'm Gilly."

"Steven," he said, shaking my hand with a very sweaty palm. He blushed from head to toe, and a part of me felt a little bad for him. "You're beautiful."

"Oh, thank you." I smiled, feeling ten shades of awkward, and wanted this round to be over. The emcee gave us the prompt, and I went first. "I teach first grade, my favorite activity on the weekends is to read or hang out with friends, and I drink tea every day."

"Wow, a teacher, yes, you look like one. Uh, I work in finance, I like hanging out, and I love beer and coffee. Yes." He gulped and looked over his right shoulder to another guy who seemed to be hamming it up with a woman.

"Okay, we're going to do this activity again, but this time, you're going to share three fun facts about yourself and what you look for in a partner."

We lifted our hands in the air, and I turned to my left, thankful to be rid of Steven, and as I spun, my skin tingled and my heart beat twice as fast as I stared into a pair of very blue eyes. *Christopher.* Excitement and lust combined into weird hyperadrenaline, and we both seemed to walk faster to each other. He grabbed my hand in a high five and didn't let go as our arms came down.

"Hey," I said, smiling and feeling nervous as hell. Which was stupid. I saw him all the damn time.

"Hey yourself," he said, his gaze warm and tender as he stared at my face. "This is a fun coincidence."

"Why are you here?" I asked, not caring that it was none of my business.

"Well, my buddy got out of a bad divorce and needed a pick-me-up. Thought this was a good place to have him try. You?"

He *still* held my hand, and I focused on his mouth instead of how good a simple hand-holding felt. It was sweet and nice, and the way he dragged his thumb over the outside of my hand made my toes curl into my shoes. "Uh, well, my brother. He's been in a funk, and I thought…this would help him."

"Ah, small world then." He smiled again, letting his gaze drop to my mouth for a beat. "We should follow the prompts and be good participants, don't you think?"

"Right, of course."

His answering grin made my face get hot because oh baby, his smile lit up his face and made him a million times more attractive. Not that he wasn't handsome, because he was, but the joy on his face felt special, and I could only stare at him when he looked at me like that. "What? You have this weird expression right now."

"Your smile makes you *beautiful*," I said, not caring that I sounded dorky. My face turned into an inferno, and I shifted my weight back and forth and looked at the ground. "Anyway, before I say something embarrassing, three fun facts about me...uh...I like tea over coffee, I've always wanted a tattoo of an apple, but every time I try to get it, I chicken out, and I once won artist of the month in third grade."

Christopher let out a deep chuckle, *still* holding my hand, and said, "The next part of the question."

"What was that?"

"What do you look for in a partner?"

"Oh." I studied him for a bit, taking in his long lashes and strong cheekbones. This felt too personal for me, for us, for the moment, and panic clawed its way down my body. I didn't want to be serious or intense, I wanted a distraction. "Size. Size definitely matters to me."

His brows drew together for a second before he burst out laughing. "Size of their heart, right?"

"Exactly what I was referring to," I teased, absolutely loving this new playful side of him that I finally got to witness. "What else could I have meant?"

"Size of their bank account, size of their feet, you know, the usual."

We smiled at each other for a full minute, my stomach swooping out of control with the heated look from him, and I nudged him with my free hand because he *still* held on to my other one. "Your turn."

"Hm, okay. Fun facts. I would usually go with I'm a teacher, I have a younger sister, and I'm a diehard Cubs fan, but you seem to know all those."

"Yeah, I shared original ones, you didn't."

"Not so original. I already knew you liked tea because I smell the citrus flavor every time you walk by me. I can't smell an orange and not think of you." One side of his mouth quirked up, and the slow way he said it made my chest feel funny.

"Oh."

"You need to give me a new one if we're going to be original."

"Fair," I said, blowing out a breath because the harder I tried to be fun and flirty, he kept making it *more*. "I don't like dinner dates."

He froze and lines appeared on his forehead. "Why?"

"Nope. Your turn." I removed my hand from his and placed mine on my hips. "Don't avoid it."

He rubbed the back of his neck as someone bumped into him, and a beautiful brunette put a hand on his forearm and apologized, and he didn't do more than glance at her for a second. "It's all right," he said, moving his intense gaze back on me, and it sent a weird thrill through me.

I arched one brow and pretended to look at my wrist. "Time's ticking, Callahan."

"Fun facts about me. I think barbeque is overrated, I won the spelling bee in junior high two years in a row, and I once lost a bet with a buddy and have a tattoo showcasing it."

"No way! Where is it?"

"Ah, that will have to be for another time." He stepped closer to me, and I sucked in a breath, smelling his subtle cologne and forgetting all the reasons why I disliked him. "Family is important to me, and I need to be with someone who understands that, who will do anything to help their family out." His gaze moved from me to Fritz in the corner, and while we both cared for our family, guilt made my stomach cramp at exactly how far I would go to help Fritz.

"I agree," I said, my voice a little unsteady as I placed a hand on his chest. He was so *hard* and warm and close. He took a deep breath and his nostrils flared, the look in his eyes mirroring the heat coursing throughout my body.

"Okay, we're switching partners! Hands up, people. Hands up!" the emcee said, making me jump a foot away from Christopher. His answering smirk unsettled me.

Was he enjoying this game? Was this a joke for him to get me worked up? I wasn't sure, and I pushed my hair behind my ears and stood up taller. "Best of luck tonight," I said, winking to try to balance the scales. "I hope you *really* find a connection."

"I'll let you walk away this time, Carter," he said, not looking put-off by my comment. If anything, he lit up and smiled wider at me. He ran his tongue over his bottom lip, and I trailed the movement for a second before slamming my eyes shut.

Attraction didn't mean trust, and trust didn't mean safety. Fritz's laughter carried over from where he chatted with two different women, and his situation with Samantha was the dose of reality I needed. Love wasn't for everyone, and I never wanted to be in his position—ever.

I just needed to ignore this *zing* with Christopher. That was all.

Chapter Twelve

My stomach flip-flopped more than normal walking into work the next morning. I couldn't stop myself from searching for his broad shoulders and messy brown hair that stood out in our narrow hallways. Carrying my tea and teacher bag, I went into the teacher's lounge and checked my mailbox like I did every morning. There was nothing in my box, which wasn't a cause for alarm, but it was unusual, and I shrugged.

"Good morning, Gilly." APD walked in with a mug of coffee that was far too large for any human being. "I'm glad I found you. The junior high and high school want to team up with you again for National Honor Society for the teaching grant. You still okay to head that up? I know you're busy, but you've done great work with all the fundraisers."

"Right, yes. Of course." I hit my forehead with my free hand. "I loved the program last year."

"Great. I'll give the go-ahead for it, but I know you're swamped with everything else going on so far. They have announcements going out next week, but are you *sure* you can collect the funds for our school? I can find someone else."

"Yes, I really don't mind." The grant with NHS went to a high school senior who was planning on being a teacher and helped them with college funds. The year before, our school raised a thousand dollars for it, and combining it with the junior high and high school, the student received enough to help cover tuition for a semester at state school. It was amazing and something I held close to my heart.

No one needed to know how much I donated or how much I made Fritz put in. It was our secret, and one way we could give back without credit. I smiled, hoping to ease APD's worried face. "This grant is important to me, okay? I'll handle it just fine. Let me know when donations can start coming in, so I can arrange with the bank for the separate account."

"Perfect. Okay, I can check this off my list. Thanks, Gil. Oh—that conference in Chicago? The literacy one you emailed me about? It was full, but I got you booked. All the information is in an email. Counting on you to bring back all the information and share it with staff."

"Got it. Thanks, APD."

He moved on to another teacher in the lounge and started talking about the IEP meeting that afternoon, and I took that as my time to leave.

Butterflies sent a weird manic energy through me as I headed toward my classroom and found Christopher leaving his room, wearing a fitted navy sweater and gray slacks that fit him *so* well.

He stopped midstride and gave me the widest smile I had seen from him. "Hey, Gilly," he said, his gaze moving down to my bright-purple flats. "I got your mail for you and was about to drop it on your desk."

"Thanks?" I chewed on the side of my mouth as he followed me into my room.

He smelled so good, like laundry and leather, and the tension from last night was still there. He waited as I set my bag on my chair and faced him, and my breath caught in my throat at how he looked at me.

He had no business doing this at work, making me flustered and confused.

"So, my mail?"

"Right." He blushed and passed a stack over to me. "There was an article in *Education Magazine* that I thought you might like. I added it to your pile. Just recycle it if you don't want to read it."

"I'll look at it," I said, running my finger over the desk. When I looked up at him, he stood close and his eyes were heated.

Oh damn. My mouth dried up, and I took a sip of tea to take a moment. My question was answered though—the sexual tension was very much still alive. We stared at each other, the air seeming to thicken between us when Larissa poked her head in.

"Heyo, Gilly, how was the single—oh my, am I interrupting?"

"Absolutely not," I said, embarrassed at the thoughts I was having at seven thirty in the morning at my *job.* I was always professional. *Until* Christopher showed up. "We were talking about mail and, uh, a conference," I lied.

"Right," Christopher said, narrowing his eyes at me a bit as confusion swirled in those blue orbs. "Tell me, Larissa. Don't you think it would be more beneficial if we both went to a literacy training instead of just her? I think it would be great to bring back the knowledge for our students, and we could each work with the rest of the staff."

"He's right. The few I've been to were so rich and intense, my brain spiraled out of control, and I only attended half the sessions. Two or three people would be better." She shrugged, giving me an apologetic smile.

"Exactly." Christopher looked smug, and while they were both right, I wasn't ready to agree to a conference with him when it was highly unlikely he could attend. APD said he had to pull strings to get just me.

"Dang it," Larissa said, eyeing her smart watch. "My mom has called three times, and that's never a good sign. Talk to you later, Gil. I want to hear about the singles night. I hope you have some good stories for me." She pointed a finger at me and gave me a hard look before leaving and shutting the door after her.

That left the two of us alone in my room.

"Have a great day, Ms. Carter," he said, giving me another playful smile before heading toward the door. The immediate departure caught me off guard again, but before I could say anything, he paused at the door frame. "I'll see you at lunch."

"Lunch?"

"Buddy teachers meet on Tuesdays." His eyes flashed with amusement. "I can't believe you forgot." He shook his head in mock disappointment and put a hand over his heart before walking out.

THE MORNING EXHAUSTED ME IN THE BEST SORT OF WAY. I LOVED the beautiful chaos of teaching and loud voices and endless questions, but sometimes, I wanted to insert an IV of caffeine to get through the day. It was one of those days, and after getting more tea with the highest amount of caffeine, I got my salad and went to Christopher's room. Buddy teachers were supposed to meet in their buddy's room to make them feel at home and more comfortable, but being in his room meant he had more power.

Yes, his walls were boring and bare, and that had zero reflection of how good of a teacher he was or how much his kids liked him, but it still annoyed me.

"One day I'm going to come in here and spray paint everything hot pink," I said as my greeting. He looked up from his laptop and rolled his eyes. "I'll do it."

"You won't." He jutted his chin to the chair next to him, not the one on the other side of his desk. "I want to show you something I've been working on and get your feedback."

"Right, of course." I blinked at the irrational thoughts I was having, like he was going to touch me or tease me or do something inappropriate at work. Flirting was confusing.

He grinned, like he knew exactly what was going on in my mind, and I sat, carefully setting my food and drink on his desk. His already-eaten burrito was in the trash, and his jaw moved as he chewed gum.

I hated how much I loved his jawline. It was stupid to admire it, but I couldn't seem to stop myself. It tensed with each bite. He frowned when he caught me staring at him. "Uh, sorry."

"You seem…flustered today. You all right?" he asked, his voice a little lower than normal. He somehow moved the chair closer to me, so our thighs brushed together, delivering an explosion of lust.

"Gilly?"

"Yes, I'm fine." I cleared my throat and crossed one leg over the other to not touch him, but the movement caused a lot of skin to show, and he was not subtle as he stared at my calf. His jaw went slack, and he swallowed, hard, and thoughts I bottled up from all the months ago came back without mercy.

How he kissed without hurry to the point it drove me mad.

The way he touched every part of my body like he had all the time in the world.

His strong arms and legs and toned muscles that came from taking care of himself.

I took a shaky breath as our gaze met, charged with want, and I was about to do something stupid. So stupid, I didn't think about it when I leaned an inch closer to him. He seemed to have the same idea when he licked his bottom lip.

"Hey, Chris!" A loud, *familiar* voice destroyed the moment, and we both jumped as Samantha walked into his room with wide, evil eyes. Her gaze moved from him to me and back to him, a dark glint entering her eyes before she plastered on her fake smile. "Aw, sorry, are y'all working? Chris, I wanted to cash in on that rain check to help me with the spreadsheet budget we talked about."

Chris?

Budget?

My nails dug into my palm as she pretended to look innocent, batting her long lashes.

He blinked fast and pulled away from me. "We were working on some questions for the buddy program."

"I can come back later," I said, needing to put distance between us, *now*. Samantha was there, her gaze on Christopher, and I didn't need to give her any ammunition to mess with him.

"I hate to interrupt, Gilly." She had puppy-dog eyes, and I couldn't look to see if Christopher bought it. If he did…I wouldn't be able to handle it, and I ducked my head and grabbed my food.

"I'll talk to you later, Christopher," I said, keeping my voice neutral even though the flash of anger caught me off guard. We were talking. There was no reason to get nervous.

"Gilly, wait, we can finish this," he said, his voice sounding a bit worried.

I shook my head and got out of there, the rock in my stomach doubling in size. How foolish was I? Forgetting she was always around and would be back for more? God. I crashed into my chair and rubbed my temples, completely lost at what to do. She would be around until the end of the month, and if I couldn't figure out what to do then, she'd find another way to get what she wanted.

I just wanted her to leave Fritz and Christopher alone. I took a long breath as I went back into my classroom, confused at how I could figure out a solution where she didn't hurt anyone, but nothing came to mind.

My door squeaked before I could even take a bite of my food, and she walked in, her eyes lit up like a kid at Christmas. This was not a good sign. Not at all.

"Do you think you'd *actually* have a shot with him if he knew what a spoiled, entitled princess you are? God, you paid me *ten thousand dollars* to dump your brother." She laughed, loud, and put her hands on her hips. "You really are leading a double life, aren't ya, Gil? You're not the sweet, morally superior school teacher they all think you are."

"*What* do you want, Samantha?" I sat up straight and put my hands in my lap to hide the trembling. "You got my fifty bucks last week."

She pursed her lips and gave me a condescending look. "I need your car."

"Excuse me?"

"I spoke English. Unless you want your hot neighbor over there"—she canted her head in the direction of Christopher's room —"to know the truth about you, then I need your car for the week."

"I'm not *giving you* my car."

"Fine, then I guess it's fine to tell him everything, hm? Think the guy who drives a beat-up, piece-of-shit car is going to take it well that you're a rich heiress? Everyone will know the truth and question you.

The award, how you got the job, all the *grants* I hear you spend hours writing to get all the fun things in your classroom. Oh, I listen to how they talk. But it's your choice."

My eyes stung as the reality of what she'd said washed over me. The questions, the doubt, the fact I lied the past two years…no. This was the place no one cared that I came from money. Christopher wouldn't understand, not that I wanted him to, but…my reputation would be ruined. My friendships would never be the same. Money changed everything. My throat tightened as I fought the combination of anger and absolute disgust at myself. "One week. I need it back Sunday. If I don't have it, I will report it stolen."

"Oh, testy." She wiggled her brows and clapped her hands. "Seems like I hit a sore spot." She walked toward my desk and held out her hand. "Keys, please."

I hated myself in that moment more than I had in a long time. It wasn't pleasant to know I caused this, that my actions made her keep coming back. I got my car key and took it off the key ring, placing it in her palm as my stomach churned. There was no way I could eat now. "*Get* out, you have it."

"You are too easy. God, this is fun." She pocketed the key and sat on the edge of my desk, getting all in my space and leaning down to talk to me. "I guess I better get back to Chris's room, where he's showing me all about budgeting. Little does he know he's going to set me up from the money you'll give me. It'd be fun to tell him, but I think this key will keep my mouth shut for now. He thinks all this money I'm talking about is from me working really hard to save every penny. It's adorable."

She didn't give me time to respond before getting up and walking out of my room, leaving me in a pile of unhelpful thoughts and regrets. Before I spiraled into a dark place, my email pinged with a link to an article titled "Why Too Many Wall Decorations Distract Kids."

Just in case you forgot—C

I snorted, thankful at the reminder that things were changing between us, and if I didn't want it to be ruined before I had a chance to explore it, I had to handle Samantha.

Chapter Thirteen

Twenty-four hours later, Samantha still had my car, and she hadn't shown up at school. I hesitated reporting it stolen because this could be a game for her, but she wasn't the total idiot I mistook her for. She texted me she was out of town and would be back by Sunday, along with a countdown until the end of the month.

My options were simple—tell Fritz what happened and know he might not forgive me for it, tell Christopher the truth and ruin any chance we might have, or continue this cat-and-mouse game with Samantha.

I couldn't talk to anyone about it, and the lack of what the right thing to do was eating me up every second I wasn't distracted. The second school got out, I was glad to have the literacy center to keep me busy because going back to my apartment alone, pretending everything was fine, was less than ideal.

I could try to convince Grace to grab a drink after too, maybe try to tell her what I'd done, what I had caused. She wouldn't hate me for it, but she could judge me, and I wasn't sure I was ready for that. But better with her than Fritz. I sighed, hating how this year knocked my normal confidence to shreds. My professional life was my safe space, where Grace and Fritz were my family. Samantha coming into our lives ruined the entire balance, and I would never forgive her for it.

"Hey," Christopher said, pulling me from my self-pity and leaning against my door frame. He wore a dark-green button-down shirt and khakis that fit him well. His heated looks at our staff meeting that morning made my belly do a roller coaster, and the sparkle in his eyes gave me hope. "I have after-school duty, but I noticed your car isn't here. Is it at the shop?"

Yes, that makes the most sense. I nodded.

"Want a ride to the lit center?" He spoke so nonchalantly, like it was no big deal for us to be in the same car together.

"Yeah, that'd be…great."

"Perfect. I'll come get you when I'm done watching the littles get picked up." He took a step off the door and gave me another soft look. "I've decided that the rainbow is your color."

"What do you mean?"

"It doesn't matter what color you wear, you look fantastic." He assessed me from head to toe before leaving, his compliment warming me inside out.

His change in attitude toward me had to be fueled by something, and with the two of us getting dinner, I would figure it out. Now, I had to keep my nerves at bay until then, something that was becoming more and more difficult as my life seemed to implode around me.

The email from Dave sat in my inbox, asking me about preferences for the conference next weekend. It was all about data and how we could use it effectively—not just talk about it. His assistant needed my meal preferences and basic information to make a reservation at the hotel. A part of me felt bad I got to go and not Christopher. He'd love something like this, but I won and was chosen to go. It would be such a learning experience, and it would be foolish to pass up because of my uncertain feelings toward my buddy teacher.

The email sent with a swoosh, and a smile broke out as I thought about escaping for a few days. I could shop on Michigan Avenue and treat myself—shit. My funds wouldn't be lifted by the time the conference came around, and it dulled the spark of hope that retail therapy offered me.

I put on some lotion, a new layer of lip gloss, and got my lesson plans and materials ready for the next day and was about to head out into the hall when Christopher walked back in. We stood a foot apart, just inside my classroom, and his gaze dropped to my mouth and stayed there for a few seconds, so much that his attention made me squirm.

He cleared his throat. "Ready?"

"Uh-huh." I swallowed and followed him out of my room toward the parking lot.

He looked back at me, the sun hitting his face at the perfect angle to see a light dusting of freckles on his nose, and he was so good-looking, it was distracting. The urge to kiss him threatened to make me say to hell with my reservations. His full lips curved up, and his white teeth were a hair crooked, and I was smitten.

"How long will your car be in the shop? Hope it's not anything too bad. The last time I had to take this there it was like a grand." He winced and unlocked the passenger side door with his key before moving to his side.

The lie fell off my tongue with an ease that worried me. "A week."

"Well, I can give you a ride to the lit center tomorrow if you'd like." He gave me a large grin before he got in on his side, and the urge to tell him the truth was right there—this was the moment. I took a deep breath and got into the car, noting the creaky door and the weathered look. His car was old but very clean.

"Thanks. Yeah, I'd appreciate a ride again if it's no trouble."

"Not at all. Gives me an excuse to see you outside work."

"Looking for reasons for that?"

"Perhaps." He slid me a look before backing out of his spot and getting on the road. "Starting to wonder more and more about you, Gilly."

"Like what?"

He got onto Main Street and tapped his fingers against the wheel like he didn't have a care in the world. "What makes you laugh, are you always so nice to everyone, that sorta thing."

"I laugh at dumb movies and great jokes, *and* I'm usually nice to everyone. There are always exceptions."

"Like former hookups who acted like an ass for a few weeks?"

I snapped my gaze to him, but he stared straight ahead, hands on ten and two on the wheel. "That's one *very* specific example, yes."

He sighed and turned onto the road that led to the literacy center, and I swore tension fell off him when he said, "I'm doing this all wrong, but I can't seem to stop myself."

"Doing what wrong?"

He cracked his knuckles with one hand before glancing at me with torment in his eyes. "We need to talk and I owe you an explanation, but all I can think about is kissing you. Even now, when you look confused and probably a little annoyed with me, your pink lips are driving me crazy."

My body hummed at his comment, and I flipped my hair over one shoulder, needing to busy my hands with something. It validated my own thoughts of that night, kissing him, but his words were also like a bucket of cold water. He did owe me an explanation. "Then I guess don't look at my mouth when we're in the center."

"I'll do my best," he teased, and the tension disappeared. He pulled into the parking lot, and we got out, his gaze landing on me with a small smile. "After this. We'll talk."

"And you'll explain why you were a total ass to me the past few weeks?"

"Yes, Gilly, I will." He nodded toward the double doors. "As soon as we're done, I'll tell you how I thought you were a con artist."

"Wait, *what?*"

"Come on, we'll be late, and we can't have that." He grinned as I tried to have him explain his comment, but he just walked in the door.

Thank God working with kids was distracting because *what the hell* did he mean?

THE SUN STARTED TO SET WHEN WE WALKED OUT OF THE CENTER, and as soon as we got out of the building, Christopher took my hand in his and intertwined our fingers. "Ready to grab some food?"

"No, and I refuse to go anywhere until you explain that *very* insane comment." I yanked my hand out of his, and he laughed. The dang man laughed. "Is this funny to you? I'd like to get to the bottom of it right now."

"I know, but you're cute when you're annoyed."

"I'm annoyed because I keep thinking about you, but I shouldn't. I should wait to hear your explanation, but my body doesn't seem to get the memo."

There, I said it. It was the truth, and I refused to feel stupid for saying it.

He moved *fast*. One second we were a foot apart in front of the passenger door, the next, Christopher had one hand on my neck, the other digging into my hip as he pressed me against the car. "Damnit, why are you making this so hard?"

"Making what hard?" I said, my pulse pounding at our position. He just had to bend down an inch to connect our mouths. We could kiss now, talk later. I was sure of it.

My heart pounded against my ribs so hard it hurt. His minty breath hit my face, and my legs trembled when he dragged a thumb over my bottom lip. I *needed* him to kiss me, and I gripped his waist, telling him without words to do it. *Close the distance.*

His chest moved faster under my hand, and as he bent down, a car door slammed, making him jump back a foot. His eyes went wide, his face tight, and he wiped a hand over it. "Shit," he said, letting out a groan, making me feel all sorts of stupid.

He wanted to kiss me. I felt it, yet he stared at me like this was *my fault.*

He shook his head, wet his bottom lip, and walked over and opened the door for me. "Sorry, let's uh…talk."

I got in and waited for him to walk to his side of the car, and he slid in with a twisted expression on his face.

He didn't appear like a man who had almost kissed me. He seemed *ashamed*. His face paled, and he scrubbed a hand over his face before he leveled his gaze with me. He started the car and turned the air on, but rested his hands on his thighs as he swallowed hard a few times. His jaw was so tight, it looked painful, and his eyes looked tortured when he glanced at me and said, "All those months ago, I

thought you stole from me. I thought you had conned me. My dad…
he trusted the wrong people. Kayla's college fund is gone, and my
parents won't be able to retire for another two decades because of a
con. I had worked for *months* to save money to help my parents out,
and it went missing after that night with you."

"Christopher…" I trailed off as it felt like someone fisted my heart
and squeezed it. "I didn't…I didn't take your money."

"I know. I *know* you didn't. Money is a really sore subject for me."
He blew out a breath and looked so sad, so apologetic, I just listened.
My lips still tingled from the lack of a kiss, but that didn't matter.

"I admire you, Gilly, how you spend your teacher's paycheck on
your students. I misread you. This has been weighing on me for a
while, and I'm glad I can finally say it. I know we don't see things the
same way when it comes to teaching, but I understand you weren't
using materialistic things as a crutch. You're a phenomenal teacher."

Oh God. His words were like a hug and a fire that couldn't be put
out. Hearing this from him meant so damn much even though his
evaluation was partly a lie. I pressed my lips together before I said
something stupid. I took a few seconds to digest his words and knew I
had to tell him. Even if it sucked.

"Look—"

"That buddy that I brought to that event Monday? His ex-wife
already had a ton of money from her inheritance, and she still
dragged him through court and took every penny he had." He hissed
and clenched a fist at his thigh. "Entitled people with so much money
they don't know what to do with it…" He shook his head. "I just
would hate to go through what my dad did, what my buddy did,
where money destroyed their shot at happiness. I know you can't
always protect the people you love, but knowing money had something to do with it makes me bitter."

The truth was right there, but then he reached over and squeezed
my hand. "With both of us being teachers, I feel like I'm on level
ground with you."

No. I couldn't tell him, not yet. Not at the way he looked at me and
said those words. My response evaporated, and I nodded, unable to
look him in the eye.

He tilted my chin up and spoke softly. "I'm sorry for misjudging you."

"I understand why you would." I gave him a small smile, my lie making me feel all sorts of awful.

"All right, let's head out. Want to stop for a quick burger on the way?"

"Yeah, sure."

He flashed a grin, this one not holding the lingering hesitation he often threw my way. It felt like an elephant sat on my chest the longer I remained quiet about my truth, my background, but things were finally better between us. A selfish part of me wanted it to last.

Chapter Fourteen

Lying to *just* Fritz was hard to live with, but keeping the truth from Christopher now that we weren't enemies anymore made my stomach twist with guilt to the point I gave into it. I'd talk to Grace. She'd tell me it wasn't the worst thing in the world and help me figure out how to get my life back together. We'd been each other's rocks far too many times for it to be weird, so I called her after work on Thursday as I sat in my classroom after everyone else had left. Two days since the almost kiss and Christopher's confession.

"Hey, Gil, what's up?" she answered, her cheery voice making me almost change my mind. She would not agree with it. I knew it in my bones, but I needed to tell someone before I burst.

"Can we grab a drink or something tonight?"

"Yeah, for sure. Brock has to be at the stadium late. Wanna come over and we can make margaritas and binge-watch reality TV?"

"Yes." I sighed and cracked my neck to each side to relieve some tension. "What time are you off?"

"Five. I have my assistant working the sophomore game tonight, thank God." She said something over the phone, and hearing her boss teenagers around made me smile. "Sorry about that. Yeah, head over there soon. I'll be there in an hour."

"Well, could you do me a favor? I might need a ride. I'm still at school," I said, chewing my hangnail off my thumb. "Don't have my car."

"Oh, is it in the shop?"

"Something like that."

"Hm, okay. Yeah, I can get you. You better tell me what's going on. I don't like the weirdness in your voice."

"I will, G." My voice almost trembled, a dead giveaway that I was struggling. "Let me know when you're here."

She hung up, leaving me an hour to kill, and I busied myself cleaning the room three times and reorganizing everything. It didn't help the tension growing at the base of my stomach, and by the time Grace arrived and let me know with a text, I hurried out and got into her passenger side door and blurted it out. "I paid Samantha ten thousand dollars to leave Fritz."

She blinked, gripped the wheel for a second, then put the car in park, and faced me. "What?"

"I caught Samantha talking to some dude at a bar. She was kissing him, all over him, and when I got up the courage to confront her for cheating, I overheard them. She was waiting until Fritz proposed so she could get joint checking accounts. She checked his search history, knew it was coming, and that once she had access, she'd take everything, and she and this guy would leave."

Grace made a raspberry with her lips and ran a hand over her forehead. "Jesus."

"I wrote her a check then and there for ten thousand dollars. Told her I wouldn't say a word if she broke up with him and left. She did. Hadn't heard a word from her until she *showed up at my school.*"

Grace paled, and I faced the parking lot instead of her, already imagining the things she'd say about what I did.

"Fritz doesn't know."

"No. And she's back, threatening to tell him if I don't give her more money."

"Fuck, Gilly." Grace groaned and leaned back into her seat, the light squeak of her seat stabbing the silent air. "Have you given her more?"

"About fifty bucks and my car."

She sucked in a breath and didn't say a word. Nothing for a full minute before she said, "I love you and I understand why you did what you did, but you need to tell Fritz."

"I know. I just…" Tears stung my eyes at shame and regret. It proved their point about my money and how I used it to solve everything. "He'll hate me."

"Keeping this from him is worse." She tapped her fingers on the wheel, hard, and shook her head. "Tell him. I mean it. She is extorting you and is going to do worse. That's how people like her work. Fritz will be pissed, Gil, but he'll forgive you with time. You must know that."

I twisted my fingers together so tight they hurt as the severity of her words sank in. She was right. It was due time, and I owed my brother the truth. "Yeah."

"Tonight."

"What?"

"You gave her your car, Gilly. What the hell? You need to tell him tonight." She narrowed her eyes at me and jutted her chin to my phone. "Now."

"I didn't give her my car. She's borrowing it until the weekend."

"Oh, okay. You're arguing small details that don't matter?"

Her anger fueled my guilt, and I texted him to head to the Anderson's. He agreed, and the drive to their house—right next to Christopher's parents—sent my thoughts into a whirlwind of varying levels of awful.

Fritz could hate me. What if he never forgave me and cut me out of his life?

What if he didn't believe me and went back to her? *Oh God.*

I closed my eyes and exhaled, trying to figure out the right way of how to do it. Did I lead up to it? Just blurt it out?

"I'm sorry this happened," Grace said as she parked in her driveway and reached over to squeeze my forearm. "I'm not *mad at you.* I'll support you until the grave, Gil, but this is too big to keep from Fritz."

"I know," I said, sighing and letting my gaze shift over to Christopher's parents. His car was outside, and a small blip of hope blossomed at maybe seeing him, but it extinguished knowing he too was a part of my inner turmoil.

"I'll make the margaritas. You think about what you're going to say."

We went into their house, and I sat in my usual spot on the La-Z-Boy. She had a pitcher made when Fritz walked in. He raised his brows in greeting to me before heading straight into the kitchen. Normally, seeing him walk in made me happy, as we were our own little family of four, but not now.

"Grace, my girl, I need *shots.*"

"Oh, okay." Grace frowned and met my eyes, wordlessly saying, *what the hell?*

Fritz poured two shots of whiskey and took them back to back, wiping the back of his hand over his mouth, and he had a sad, almost feral look about him. "Samantha."

"Wh-what about her?" I asked, Grace's penetrating stare pinned on me.

"She texted me: *hey Fritz, miss you.*" He got a glass of the margarita and took a long sip. So long in fact, he'd be drunk pretty soon. "Miss you. She left me without a goddamn word and messed with my head so much, and this happens as soon as I think I'm over it."

Grace's eye twitched as he got another shot, and she took the bottle away from him. "No more, Fritz. It's Thursday."

"It's not a school night for me, Grace," he fired back, wincing at the end. "Shit, I'm sorry. Come here." He went up to her and pulled her into a tight hug. "My anger is not at you. Either of you. I love the shit out of both of you. Even Brock. Don't tell him though."

Grace forced a tight smile, and I had to excuse myself to the bathroom. Tonight wasn't the night. Not when he was in a mood. We needed to support him. I did my business and washed my hands, only to find Grace outside the door. "He's going to get hammered."

"I can't drive him home. Can he crash here?" I asked, my eyes filling with tears. "I can't tell him today, Grace. Look at him."

"I know." She gave me such a sad smile, I pulled her into a hug and buried my face in her neck. She patted my back a few times and said, "It'll be okay. I promise."

"I'm not so sure," I said, pulling back and wiping my nose. "I need to pull it together. He'll know something's wrong."

"I'm going to make tacos, and we're going to chill for a while. He can crash here, but you *need* to tell him this weekend." She gave me a pointed stare.

I nodded. "I will."

Two hours later, Fritz was stupid drunk as we watched YouTube videos of people falling—his idea, not ours—but it made him laugh, so it was worth it. I excused myself to leave for the night and was going to call an Uber, using the PayPal account I still had access to. It wouldn't set me over budget, and it wouldn't clue Fritz in on my car dilemma. I hugged him good-bye and kept it together as I walked out the front door and sat on the edge of the curb. It'd be at least ten minutes before one got here, and I called for it just as the door shut at Christopher's parents'.

"Yeah, good night," he said, his voice carrying over toward me, and I recognized his footsteps. That's how in tune I was with him. His gait had a certain rhythm to it, and it stopped when he approached his car. "Gilly?"

"Hey," I said, hoping my face wasn't giving away my absolute mess of emotions. "How's your parents' new place?"

"It's okay. Don't love how they financed it without telling me, but it's their business, I guess." He shoved his hands in his pockets, and his lips quirked up on both sides. "We seem to run into each other a lot, don't we?"

"Yeah."

"What's wrong?" He moved closer to me, and his brows drew together as he eyed me from head to toe. "Your posture is off."

"No, it's…I did something to help my brother without telling him, and it's eating at me."

"Ah," he said, glancing down the street and at his car. "Are you waiting for a ride? Your car is still in the shop, right? I didn't see it at school."

"I still don't have it," I said, careful not to lie because that's all I did now. "There's an Uber coming."

"Cancel it. Come on, I'll drive you home. You can talk to me about your brother. My sister and I...we've had our moments too." He held out a hand to help me up, and I placed my damp palm in his, and it was stupid how my stomach fluttered.

"You sure?"

"Yes," he said, smiling and moving his hand to open up the passenger side door of his car. I hesitated for a second, and he narrowed his eyes. "Get in."

He still wore his work clothes, and his polo fit his shoulders so well. No one had muscles like that without hard work. I gulped when he got into his car.

Maybe it was my emotions going out of control, but the car seemed smaller. His soap-and-leather scent tickled my nose, and I sighed, exhausted from everything.

He reached over and placed his hand on my thigh, just above my knee, and squeezed. "Siblings fight. It's part of being a family. You'll get through it."

He removed his touch and put the car in drive, totally unaware how that simple gesture sent a shot of heat through me. My toes curled into my flats against his dirty mat, and I chewed on my lip. He looked completely unaffected by how close we were, again, in his car. I could lean over the console and crawl into his lap in one movement.

But would he want that?

"Tell me what happened," he said, glancing at me as we hit a red light.

"I made a decision for him, without consulting him or telling him about it. If I tell him now, he'll never forgive me."

"Okay, what was the decision?"

I paused, unable to complete the sentence as I squeezed my eyes tight. "Uh, well," I started, but he waved a hand in the air, cutting me off.

"Kayla was sneaking out with this guy who was just an asshole. Used her, said the right things, but they were lies. He'd try to convince her to do all this stuff she didn't want to, and one night, when I knew he was coming over to sneak her out, I waited. I scared the shit out of this kid, threatening him and warning him it would not end well for him if he ever did it again. She refused to talk to me for two months, but that guy? He got another girl pregnant a month later. Not saying that would've been Kayla, but I don't regret doing that."

I sucked in a breath through closed teeth and nodded. "Looking out for her."

"I thought so, yeah. She was fourteen. This guy had a motorcycle, and yeah, not my baby sister." He barked out a laugh, turning onto the street that led to my modest apartment complex. It might not look flashy on the outside, but no one knew it had a doorman and extra security. It let me live in my illusion a little longer, where he had no idea of my wealth.

I was such an asshole.

"We do things for the people we love," I said, my voice coming out less strong than I'd intended.

"We can't protect them forever, but every once in a while, we can. It's part of the sibling handbook." He flashed a grin, and the force of his full smile made my stomach flip over. He seemed so at ease, so comfortable, that I watched him.

The hard angle of his jaw, the strong muscles of his arms, the full, gorgeous hair that curled around his ear. He was so attractive it wasn't even fair. His car made a shaky sound as we neared the street by my place, and he put the car in park, undid his seat belt, and let out a long sigh. "You want to talk about it more? Would that make you feel better?"

Shit. He was being considerate, and for whatever reason, that question got me all warm inside. Warm enough for my voice to get raspy. "No. I don't want to talk."

His gaze dropped to my mouth and trailed the movement when I licked my bottom lip. The car shrank ten times smaller, and I knew exactly what I wanted to do to help me forget my situation with my brother. It involved Christopher's mouth on mine.

His nostrils flared twice, and he drew in a shaky breath. "You're biting that lip, and it's making it real hard to be a gentleman right now."

"That's not what I want, *right now.*"

His eyes got wider, heavier with lust, and he ran a hand over his jaw a few times as he struggled. I wasn't sure who I was anymore—teasing my coworker in a car, thinking about making out with him until my brain was numb and my lips tingled. I could blame the stress of Fritz and Samantha, but that would be a lie.

This man might've thought I stole money from him, but we had chemistry, and I wanted to explore it again. Now.

"Christopher," I said, my voice sounding like I'd just woke up.

He sat up straighter when I said his name, and his chest moved up and down a little faster. Then, he snapped.

It was incredible to witness the uptight, controlled buddy teacher lose rationale. He grabbed the back of my head, pulled me toward him, and dropped his mouth to mine in a soul-searing, hot-as-hell kiss.

Yes. His full lips were like I remembered. Soft and demanding. He groaned as I parted my mouth, letting him slide his tongue inside, and it was nothing but wet, noisy kisses in the car. He pulled at my bottom lip with his teeth, and I arched my back, needing to get closer to him. He tasted like mint and smelled like sweat and soap, and when he lifted me off my seat and into his lap, I almost whimpered. It felt so good being near him, finally touching him and feeling his lips on me. My heart hammered against my ribs, and my skin tingled from head to toe at the fierce way he kissed me back—like he, too, thought he might die if we didn't kiss harder.

"Gilly, my God," he said, lifting me onto his lap and spreading my legs so I straddled him in his front seat. He onto my hip with one hand, the other running through my hair as he kissed me harder. He tilted my neck to gain better access, and I moaned at the pleasure of it.

We were making out. *Hard.*

I couldn't get enough. I ran my hands over his strong shoulders and neck, over his chest and underneath the collar of his shirt. His warm skin seared my hands, and I rocked against him. He stilled for a beat, making me open my eyes, and his blue orbs were liquid water, different shades of blue, filled with promise and seduction.

"I like seeing your mouth wet from me," he said, running a hand along my neck, over my collarbone and down my side. "You're beautiful, Gilly."

I swallowed at the emotion in my throat and bent lower again, taking his mouth in mine and taking control. I didn't want feelings or doubts or my brain to get involved. Just his kisses. We made out again for what felt like an hour before he groaned and pulled back. "What's wrong?"

He rested a hand on either of my thighs and looked up at me with regret all over his face. That expression sobered me up fast, and I propelled myself off him. He couldn't kiss me like that and regret it seconds after, right? My chest got tight and my breathing faltered with hurt. "Th-thanks for the ride," I said, my shaky voice barely contained as I awkwardly tried to get back into my seat.

He reached over and grabbed my wrist with gentle fingers. "Uh, hold on. Hold on. Where you going?"

I slammed my eyes shut. "Inside."

"I can read your face pretty well, Gil. Did I upset you? I stopped because we're in my crappy car, outside, and my control was slipping. I'm trying to be a good man here and not do this like we're teenagers." He sounded uneasy, and I snuck a glance at him.

His face was flushed, there was an evident bulge in his pants, and he stared at me like he *wanted* me. "I didn't stop because I wasn't into it, if that's what you're worried about."

"Okay," I said, relieved more than I cared to admit. "Yeah, maybe not…in your car."

"Another time. In a bed."

"Yes."

He grinned, his swollen lips and flushed cheeks making him so damn handsome, and he cleared his throat. "Let me at least walk you to your door."

"Don't want to come in?"

"Not tonight. Soon, but not tonight."

He got out and kept his hand on my lower back as he walked me to the front of my building. Letting him inside would show the security features, and I wasn't ready for that discussion, so I stopped us.

"Thank you," I said, standing on my tiptoes and using his shoulder to balance my height as I kissed him. "For the ride."

"Any time," he said, cupping my chin. "I'll see you tomorrow."

I nodded, blushing from head to toe at the promise in his voice, and watched him get into his car and wave before pulling off the curb. My mind barely understood the array of emotions I had within that hour, and I wanted nothing more than to take a bath and analyze it. But the second I had my fingers on the door handle, someone said my name.

That high-pitched voice.

"Oh, hello, Gilly."

Samantha.

Chapter Fifteen

My spine turned to steel. The woman had the unique ability to show up at the worst moments, and all the leftover adrenaline from Christopher flowed through my body, making my hands shake as I spun around to face her.

She wore cutoff jeans and a skintight red tank top, but it wasn't her outfit that worried me. It was her expression. It was pure malice.

"It's Thursday. Back early?" I said, needing to not let her see my fear. I crossed my arms and made my face go hard, like when I had to discipline a kid even though they were cute.

"Yes. I'm sick of waiting for your bullshit month to end. I need ten thousand sooner than the end of the month." She mirrored my stance and arched a brow. "I'm starting to think I should've kept in the game with your brother. Ten thousand is pocket change compared to what you two have. He showed me his bank statements, the idiot."

My lip curled up at the mention of Fritz, and my voice came out stronger than I intended. "Stay the fuck away from him. You made your choice—you chose cash. Deal with it."

Damnit. Her eyes lit up, and I played right into her hands.

"Okay, you're right. I want two thousand by Monday."

"I don't have access. It doesn't matter what you say or do. I literally cannot get the money until the end of the month, so threaten me all you want. I don't have it." I took a steady breath and stared her down. Samantha was a bully, a con woman, and an asshole, and the warning in the back of my mind blared.

I just had to tell Fritz, and then I'd be done with her, for good.

Samantha didn't like my response. She licked her lips and grinned at me like an evil, psycho Cheshire cat and got her phone out of her pocket. She clicked her tongue a few times and held up the screen, showing me a photo.

It was me, on top of Christopher, in his car. Only you couldn't see him at all.

"How would Mountain Elementary like to see photos of Ms. Carter being a slut in a car? You think this would change their mind about you? The rich heiress who fucks anywhere."

"Samantha," I warned, the white-hot fear making my thoughts blur together.

She swiped to the left, and another photo was there, me with large hands at my ass, and it was like she punched me in the gut. I looked racy as hell. Kissing Christopher had consumed me, and it was obvious I paid no attention to my surroundings.

"You can't...why? Why take these? I already told you I'd give you what you wanted."

"First off, I don't believe you." She laughed and showed me a third picture. This one was when he picked me up and moved me onto his lap. My dress came up in the move, and if this photo got out, I could lose everything. My reputation, my anonymity, my job. Samantha giggled and put the phone in her pocket again. "I already sent copies to my guy Devin, so if you're trying to think of ways to get my phone, it won't work. Think of the parent groups online. What would they say? How far would they go to get you fired? Would it go to the Board? Would it be public knowledge? God, it makes me giddy thinking about it."

"I can't...I can't get my funds, Samantha. I swear." My eyes watered at this point, and my misery seemed to feed into her energy. She bounced on her heels and tilted her head to the side, studying me.

"Any dumb tricks or excuses, and these go public. You hear me?

The second you fucking get access, I want a check." A crazed look crossed her face, like her eyes went unfocused, and a part of me wondered if she was on drugs.

A loud engine made me jump, and Samantha grinned at the driver before pinning me with one last stare. "Ten thousand dollars, Gilly, or your precious little life is over."

She took about ten steps before tossing my car keys at me. I let them fall to the ground and watched with panic coursing through my body as she got into the black car with music so loud it shook the earth. Then I got my keys, went into my apartment, and cried.

THE NEXT MORNING WAS LIKE ANY OTHER, BESIDES THE FACT I HAD Samantha's threats to worry about, the lie to Christopher, and the fact I paid my brother's girlfriend to dump him. Other than that, it was a normal Friday at school where the students had a different energy about them. Fridays in the fall were so much fun—the football team played at the high school, everyone wore school colors, and weekend plans were shared between lessons.

I forced a smile through all the chatter about camping and bonfires and had two extra cups of tea to keep my pep in my step. Even Christopher's little smile he threw my way wasn't enough to shake the storm cloud over my mind.

It was lunchtime, and while I always ate in the teacher workroom, I stayed in my class with the excuse to catch up on stuff. It wasn't entirely unheard of—we all did it from time to time—but Christopher seemed to think it was an invitation, and he joined me a minute later.

"Oh, did we have a buddy meeting?" I asked, my unanswered text to Fritz leaving a hole in my heart. I asked if we could talk this weekend. Nothing more or less than that.

"Nope. Just wanted to eat lunch with you." He sat in one of the chairs on the other side of my desk. The folder with all the information for the conference the next weekend was there, and he picked it up. "This one looks fantastic. Hillary Jones is one of the keynotes. Her passion for differentiation is incredible."

My heart clenched at the longing in his voice. I was excited about the conference, but not in the same way he spoke about it. "Are you a fan of Hillary Jones?"

"Yes. I've read all her books and got to hear her speak when I lived in Chicago. She's inspiring and data driven. There are too many gurus who are focused on the emotional piece, which is important, for sure, or those who are all numbers and data. Hillary Jones, though, she uses both." He took a bite of his sandwich with one hand and set the information sheet down on my desk. "You'll have to tell me all about it. Maybe get a photo with her and let me see it? I could use a new desktop background."

I snorted, really needing the humor, and we shared a smile for a beat. The eye contact, the slight curve of his lips, and his foot resting under my desk, an inch from mine, brought me back to the car where his lips were on mine and his hands on my body. I cleared my throat, refusing to let my mind go there at work. "Yeah," I said, shaking my head a little bit. "I'll get a picture, sure."

"Great." He smiled again and studied the wall behind my desk. His attention stopped at a photo of Grace, Fritz, and me with our arms around each other and covered from head to toe in mud. "You three are close, huh?"

"Yes." The guilt crept back in, and I checked my phone. Fritz still hadn't answered me, and I hated to think Samantha was the reason. If he found out from her, there would be irreparable damage done to our relationship. At least if I told him the truth, there was a sliver of hope. "Grace forced us to do this mud run. It was awful, honestly."

He laughed. "You look happy in the photo."

"Because we were done."

His amusement warmed my face, and I tried eating a bite of my salad. I loved homemade dressings with oil and vinegar, but it tasted off. Everything had tasted off since Samantha had visited the night before, and I forced myself to swallow. My phone buzzed, and my heart leapt into my throat. My brother had finally texted me back.

Fritz: Is it an emergency or can it wait? Need to go out of town. Camping with some colleagues.

Gilly: Oh, good. When you get back then.

Fritz: Deal.

There went my plan to tell him soon.

"Things not better with your brother?" he asked, reminding me that he saw right through my emotions. His soft and kind voice was the same one he used on students, and a part of me wanted to crawl into his lap and have him tell me it'd be okay.

But that wasn't his job, and I'd caused this mess.

"Not yet. He's going out of town this weekend, so we'll have to talk after that. It's just eating away at me."

"I get it. If it's one of those conversations that needs to be in person, it's hard to wait, but it's the right thing to do. You clearly love each other, so I know he'll forgive you. Try not to be so hard on yourself, Gil."

Gil.

The stupid, one-syllable nickname that everyone called me should not have elicited a full body shiver, but it did. My face heated, and I bit my lip to prevent a smile. He would not be calling me that or being so nice if he knew the truth about what I did, or what I kept from him, but that was filed into a *later* folder. "I appreciate you saying that," I said, meeting his warm gaze. "Thank you."

He shrugged and dived into his food again, repositioning himself so his foot rested against mine, and instead of moving, I kept it there. His large foot and my small one, sitting side by side, felt intimate. "What are you doing this weekend?" he asked after we ate in silence for a few minutes. "My college roommate has this bro bachelor party up in the city for the weekend. Food trucks, paintballing, the beach. I've been saving up for it for a while, and I'm excited to be back up there."

"You miss living there?"

"Yes and no. I moved here to be with family, and I have a few friends from here, actually. It's a different lifestyle for sure. Everyone drives everywhere, and the nightlife isn't nearly as fun, but it's homey. I want a family someday, and this is the kind of town perfect for that."

It was undeniably sexy to hear a man say he wanted a family and be upfront about it. Too many crappy dates or horror stories from Larissa clouded my mind when it came to the opposite sex. The fact he said it all, just like that, made me like him even more, and that was dangerous.

"This is a great town for a family. I loved growing up here and only going to college a short drive away." I took another flavorless bite and felt his stare like a caress. "Um, your weekend sounds fun."

"I don't do it often enough, so I'm excited. But, I gotta admit, it's been nice running into you after school."

"It has been…nice," I said, letting the word hang between us. It was more than nice, and if I thought about him, about us too much, it'd mess with my already muddled brain.

He grinned, like he knew my mind was a hot mess when it came to him, and he finished his sandwich. "All good with your car? Hopefully it didn't cost an arm and a leg."

"Yeah, it's…good." I forced a tight smile, but he didn't notice. He gave me a lazy grin that made me think of his lips on mine, and I looked down. Someone knocked on my door, making us both look up, and APD was there.

"Gilly, got a minute?" he asked, his voice serious as he clutched a folder to his chest. He rarely wore smiles, so nothing should've raised the hair on the back of my neck.

What if those are the photos?

"Yeah." My teeth ground together and I stood up way too fast, earning a frown from Christopher, but I ignored him. I marched toward APD and went into the hall with him. Not another great sign.

If this were good news, he'd have said it in my room in front of Christopher. *What is the punishment for those photos? Suspension?* "What's going on, Dave?"

"Wanted to give you a heads-up about the conference next weekend." He sighed, and an annoyed look crossed his face. "The board will want an update from what you learned. You know how they feel about us spending money on *teachers* instead of students."

"Oh," I said, my limbs relaxing. That's what had him all worked up. It was almost laughable compared to being blackmailed with racy photos. "Georgia?"

"Yes, you know her passion for literacy." He ran a hand over his face, and just the mention of literacy made me think of him, about how excited he was about Hilary Jones.

"I think Christopher should go instead of me."

"Wait—why?" Dave narrowed his eyes and tilted his head to the side.

"He's passionate about the topic and was fangirling over Hillary Jones. I'll have other opportunities."

He ran his square teeth over his lip as his brows drew together, and he eyed my classroom door for a beat. "You sure?"

"Yes. He should go," I said, knowing this was the right move. I'd have to tell Fritz the truth then, and it would be best to be here. "He'd be a great teacher to go soak up all the info and bring it back to us." I nodded to further prove my point. "Change it to him, I insist."

"If you're sure, I can see if I can change the reservation."

"Thank you," I said, smiling for real this time because even though my life was a hot mess right now, Christopher's wasn't. He deserved to go to a conference in his favorite city. I did not.

I had to deal with my brother, and lord knew I'd need the weekend to prepare for it. Once I told Fritz, then I'd tell Christopher the truth.

Chapter Sixteen

Eating Tums was becoming second nature, and I was shocked I didn't have an ulcer at this point. Grace was annoyed with me, refusing to talk until I told Fritz, but he didn't have time after taking a couple days off work. That gave me plenty of moments to stew about telling him the truth, about Samantha's possession of photos that might or might not ruin my job, and the fact Christopher and I hadn't talked about that make-out session once.

Not once.

A week went by, and besides a few heated smiles, it was like that never happened. *Kinda like we never talked about the fact we slept together.* I pushed my hair behind my ears as the end-of-the-day laughter carried over the halls. We were finishing our unit on weather, and it was wonderfully exhausting. My kids learned so much and had fun while doing it, and normally it gave me a high, but not now.

I was just tired.

My phone buzzed, and with a quick glance to see Grace's name, I prepared for her rational dig.

Grace: This weekend. This isn't you. MY BEST FRIEND ISN'T A LIAR.

And my guilt level rose three degrees, making the acid churn in my stomach even more. I rubbed my forehead and thought about asking Larissa to grab a drink because a large margarita was what I wanted. I barely got my texts open before male voices caught my attention. APD's stern and deep voice was unmistakable, and Christopher's timbre always perked my interest. He was excited, talking too fast, and I smiled.

"I get to go to this conference, the one Gilly was supposed to attend, with Hilary Jones," he said, excitement teasing his tone and making him sound like a kid on Christmas, and not the grown man who frowned at rainbows.

"Correct. Here's the information for your hotel room, for the conference. My assistant got you set up."

"I don't understand why. Is she not going?"

My face flushed. It wasn't with embarrassment, but if Dave told him the truth, then it felt like exposure—which wasn't something I was ready for as he still hadn't talked about that make-out session. This was just a professional move, the right decision for my buddy teacher. I could go to a conference any time, really. Christopher couldn't. He worked hard and deserved to go. End of story. But every part of my body tensed, desperate to hear the reply.

"I'm waiting to hear back if I can get her in. The hotel is sold out, but having two of you go would be fantastic," Dave said.

"Get her in?" Christopher repeated in his deep voice.

"Gilly wanted you to go instead, so we've been making changes."

Christopher's silence felt like Thor's hammer pounding into my rib cage over and over. It was like the air shifted with the truth, and I could picture his furrowed brows, his full lips rubbing together as he digested this information.

"Give her my hotel room if that's the issue. I have friends I can stay with."

"Christ, not sure if I can rearrange all this again." Dave sighed and shifted his feet, his loafers always clicking on the tile. "Email my admin assistant, Addy, about it. She's the one getting this all set up. Just tell me when it's finalized."

"You got it."

I waited, my pen frozen in my hand in the middle of writing my to-do list. Would he come in here? See my face and realize that I caught a few feelings for him? Would we talk about that kiss and what the hell it meant?

But a minute went by, then another, and I cracked my already tense knuckles to relieve the pressure. He was not coming into my room, and I exhaled, calming my erratic heart rate. This was fine. Totally fine.

I shouldn't be worrying about him or what we were, or weren't.

I packed my bag and made sure everything was set up for the next day, my normal routine soothing me. I got my broom and dustpan and got the leftover pieces of scraps on the floor and did a quick wipe down of handles. Content with my classroom being organized, I put my bag over my shoulder and turned off the lights.

Then I ran right into Christopher's very large and broad chest. "Oof," I said, groaning as the impact rocked my balance. He steadied me with one hand on my hip, and God, I felt the warmth all the way between my thighs and to my toes. "Christopher."

He sucked in a breath and his lips parted, his face inches from mine, and my skin tingled with awareness. Awareness of how tall he was, how soft his touch was, how good he kissed, how his full lips feasted on mine in his car. He swallowed, loudly, to the point it clicked in the back of his throat, and his gaze moved to my lips.

It didn't matter we were at school. I needed to feel his lips on me again, to get lost in the feel of them, of *him*, and I gripped the collar of his shirt, pulling him toward me to close the distance. His lips barely grazed mine when clicked footsteps neared us, and I stepped back, almost panting with want, and stared at him with wild eyes.

While I didn't get what I wanted, his mouth on mine, the frantic look in his eyes matched the fire in my gut. Dave stopped just outside the door and smiled. "You tell her?"

"Just about to," Christopher said, his voice a shade too deep. He cleared his throat, making me smile at his attempt to hide his reaction.

"Tell me what?"

"We're both going to the conference," my stupidly hot buddy teacher said, his grin stretching ear-to-ear. "We leave tomorrow."

"Wait, Dave…how?"

"Buddy from college is on their committee. Charmed him. Plus this kid gave up his hotel room. I got subs coming in tomorrow so make sure they are ready. Georgia will be there tomorrow. Please play nice with her."

"You got it," I said, unsure if I was more excited about going with Christopher, about escaping the town for the weekend and avoiding Fritz for three more days, or the combination of everything. "This is excellent!"

"Glad you're happy." Dave nodded at us and moved farther down the hall, where Samantha stood chatting with Marisa like they were best friends. I didn't even have it in me to care. Not with the way Christopher looked at me, his gaze softening and the lines around his eyes relaxing.

"You gave me your spot," he said, dragging out the words like they were a poem made for me. His jaw was a little slack, and he shook his head back and forth a few times, like he couldn't believe it. His incredulous expression had my face even hotter. "Gilly," he said, reaching out for a second before letting his hand fall at his side.

"It's no big deal," I gushed, shrugging and attempting to hide the absolute mess going on in my mind. "Really."

"It is," he said, his voice getting husky, and I squeezed my thighs together. My physical reaction to him was out of my control, and it was like he knew. He moved closed, trailed his teeth over his lip, and smiled. "Let's drive up together."

"Yeah?"

"Yes." He pursed his lips and sucked in a breath as he studied my face, neck, and body for a full minute. "This is going to be fun. You and me, in the city."

"You made that sound...dirty," I whispered, my voice shaking at all the scenarios in my head. Just the two of us together, in a car, at a hotel, decompressing with a drink.

"Oh, it is." This time, he reached over to tuck a piece of hair behind my ear, sending goose bumps all the way down my body to the point I shivered. "Tomorrow can't get here fast enough.

"Holy crap!" I said, smiling to wide my face almost split in two. The conference was incredible. So many upbeat teachers and laughter all around us, and Christopher stood *right* next to me as we checked in. Posters of speakers were everywhere, and I pointed to one, Heather Smith, and squealed. "Oh my God, she's my idol. I know you're a boring traditionalist, but her work on flexible seating is my teaching bible."

"Not boring."

"Eh, a little bit," I teased, adding a wink on the end.

He rolled his eyes, and we made our way to the large table organized alphabetically.

"Hi, Mountain Elementary. Gilly Carter and Christopher Callahan."

Christopher's chest hit my back as we waited for our lanyards and conference information, and that slight touch alone got me hot. We'd taken my car since it had fewer miles on it, and it *just got out of the shop* and took turns driving. It was amazing how fast the two-hour drive went with all our talking.

No kisses though. Just an accidental brush of the hand or this, where he stood close to me, and it was making me desperate for more. He told me all about his family, and I shared stories about Fritz and Grace from college. It was wonderful to chat and get to know him more.

"You have some time to check into your room before the welcoming session starts, so take your time. Meet down in the foyer around seven. Enjoy!" the woman said, her own smile making mine get bigger.

This was so cool.

"Care if I drop my stuff off in your room until I can head to my buddy's place later?" he asked, a heated look entering his eyes.

"Yeah, of course," I said, trying really hard not to think about just the two of us in a hotel room alone…with a few hours to kill. "I want to set this suitcase up there."

We headed toward the elevator, and we had to wait a good ten minutes before we could get on. It was that busy. The doors dinged, and we moved inside, the crowd of everyone trying to get in with their friends making us stand even closer. This time, we were chest to chest.

I looked up, my face even with his chest, and his parted lips and flared nostrils made my stomach squirm with need. He smelled like laundry and soap, and when he dragged his tongue over his bottom lip, I squeezed my eyes shut. Was he trying to kill me with lust?

Was that what this was?

I groaned, and as soon as the sound left my mouth, Christopher tensed and sucked in a hard breath. I peeked one eye open at him, and he looked seconds away from snapping. *About damn time.*

The journey to the eighth floor took a few minutes, and each chime meant we were that much closer until we would be alone— which was sounding better and better. Would we kiss again? Like the car? Did I want to do more? Yeah. I did. I wanted his body on mine, his rough kisses and desperate touches. Shit, I was way too turned on to be at an education conference.

The doors opened, and we squeezed our way through the crowd, walking out with another group of teachers who giggled and head the opposite way down the hall. My room was 8456, and I frowned, studying the sign that let us know which way to go.

"On the left, Gilly. Move," he demanded, and holy shit, it got me *hot.*

He yanked my suitcase out of my hands and sped toward the door, his chin jutting to the keycard in my hand. "Get inside that room."

"Or what?" I fired back, absolutely loving the desperation on his face.

He did not like my answer. He growled, took the key from my hand, opened the door, and pulled me and the bags inside. I barely got a foot in before he slammed his mouth onto mine in a hot, wet, *soul-marking* kiss.

"Oh," I said, melting into him as he gripped my waist with two hands and sucked my tongue into his mouth in a filthy, manic move. The scruff on his face burned my skin but in the best way ever. I moaned into his mouth and about cried when he picked me up, wrapped my legs around him, and slammed my back into the wall. It was *everything* I wanted.

"Goddamn, Gilly," he said, pulling back for a second before he kissed me harder. It was all teeth and tongue and sloppy kisses. I ground into him, making him lose more control as my body flushed with heat. There was no more rigid or uptight Mr. Callahan. This was my version of him, and I loved it.

I could get drunk off Christopher Callahan losing his cool.

He gripped my ass under my dress, kneading his strong fingers into my cheeks, and he moved from my mouth to my jaw, nibbling on the sensitive skin as he trailed his fingers between my thighs.

"Can't get you out of my damn head, woman," he muttered, biting on my earlobe as he pushed my panties to the side. "Christ, you're wet."

"Have been since last week."

He slammed his mouth on mine again as he slid a finger inside me, curling up at the end before sliding in another. He let out a deep, sexy sigh that I felt in my core, and he thrust his digits in and out. He wasn't gentle or smooth—he was rough and moved fast, but each thrust sent a ripple of pleasure through me. It had been months since we were together, and feeling his body heat, the way he looked at me, it felt so damn right. A whimper escaped at how good it felt, and before I could grind against him, he moved us to the bed where he tossed me down. "Strip."

Oh, bossy Christopher was my favorite.

My body felt more alive than it had in months as I shimmied out of my dress and threw it on the floor. He ripped off his shirt and was undoing his belt as his eyes took me in. His chest puffed out, and his breathing faltered when I undid my bra. His attention felt like a caress as his jaw tightened as he stared at me. His gaze started at my face, moving toward my bare breasts, and he groaned when I parted my thighs for him, the only barrier my thin lace panties. I liked sex, a lot, but this look on his face felt empowering as hell.

"Fuck," he said, his voice just above a whisper. "Better than I remembered."

He kicked his discarded pants to the side and hovered over me on the bed, stopping me from removing my panties, and he traced one of my pebbled nipples with his tongue in a slow, torturous circle, before biting down and sucking it into his mouth.

"Oh!" I arched my back, but he pushed me down and pinched my other nipple with his thumb and finger.

He cupped both breasts in his hands, burying his face between them before letting out a deep, satisfied moan. It turned me on to see him struggle, and I brought my hands up toward his shoulders and chest and felt all of him I could.

His muscles tensed, and he covered my body. The only material between us was my lacy black panties, and he cupped my neck before kissing me hard again. Heat prickled along my skin and down my spine when he grabbed his pants, reached into his pocket, and got out a condom.

"Yes," I said, not wanting to stop kissing him. Kissing him was better than anything I'd ever done, and I wanted more of it. His rough whiskers, his greedy tongue, the clash of his teeth. "God, I need you inside me, Christopher."

He grinned wide as he sheathed the condom on, yanked my panties off my legs, and stared at my thighs spread wide. "I could just eat you all night."

"Later."

He growled again and pulled me down to the edge of the bed so my legs went up onto his shoulders and his hand rested just above my clit. He massaged the swollen nerve with his thumb as he thrust into me. I squirmed in a delicious, painfully hot way. I was so needy. My pulse pounded between my legs, and the release I craved was so close.

Christopher started slow with careful, patient thrusts of his dick into me. I got used to him after a few strokes, and he picked up the pace—not just with his thrusts, but with his fingers giving me the right pressure.

We weren't kissing. Just watching.

His greedy eyes focused with a fascinated haze as he pumped into me, my bare pussy on display for him, and I watched him study me. It was the hottest thing ever, to see him be so captivated by us having sex, and the orgasm got closer. He held on to me tight, like he too wanted this to last as long as possible, and I knew one time wouldn't be enough. I wanted to lick every line and ridge on his defined chest, taste his skin, and drive him wild.

My skin tingled, and my muscles clenched as I watched him. "More, please," I begged, arching my hips to get the pressure just right, and he snapped.

Christopher held on to my waist with one hand, massaged my clit with the other, and fucked me *hard*. It was rough and sweaty. Slapping skin and grunts and whines. I gripped the bedsheets on either side of me as the pleasure exploded in white-hot bursts at the base of my spine, sinking into my veins like a drug.

"*Yes, oh my God*," I cried out, tightening around him as his legs stiffened.

"Gilly, God." He held on to my waist, his two large hands splayed over my stomach as he bit down on his lip and let out the sexiest, longest groan as he came. He panted, his gorgeous chest heaving as he pulled out and fell on the bed next to me. "So damn good," he said, his breathing coming out heavy and his face full of soft angles and an easy smile.

"Agreed."

"I swear, that wasn't my intent. You kept chewing on that damn lip in the elevator and…"

"I've been thinking about this since the car last week, Callahan," I said, rolling to my side and smiling at him as a deeply satisfying sigh escaped my chest. This was the distraction I needed. The touching and kissing and orgasm.

His eyes flared, and he studied his bags inside the door. "I'm not saying it's the best idea, but we could do this all weekend?"

"You inviting yourself to stay in my hotel room?"

"Absolutely." He grinned again, pushing up onto his side and running his hand from my neck all the way to my hip. "Learning and bickering with you all day, then coming back here at night."

My stomach swooped at sharing a room with him all weekend. It would be intimate and erase any chance of us going back to being just colleagues. Maybe it was the way he stared at me, like I mattered to him, or how I felt safe with him. Or maybe I was selfish and convinced myself this was an escape from the mess with Samantha. Or maybe…it was because I knew I had feelings for him, and if this was the only time I got with him, I was going to enjoy every sexy second of it.

I nodded. "Yeah, I'm in."

Chapter Seventeen

There was something electric in the air as Christopher and I navigated our way through the vendor section of the conference. So many tables, smiles, and free stuff. It was a weakness. Free pens, stress balls, key chains, and stickers. There was a competition going on—if you could get your *conference passport* stamped by visiting all the vendors, you could enter it for a new iPad.

Christopher was not into it at first, but once I made a bet with him, it was game on.

"I can't believe you talked me into this crap," he said, rubbing the back of his neck as we approached a table all about cybersecurity. We had no say in purchasing anything like that for our school, but we needed their stamp. "I hate small talk."

"It'll be worth it though," I said, winking at the end and getting a warm thrill up my body when his gaze heated. His jaw tightened, and his gaze moved to my mouth before he gave a resigned nod. All the bickering made the sex explosive, and we had the entire weekend together. I was beyond excited.

His grumpy sigh made me giggle, and we moved on to three tables where we chatted up the vendor and asked for the stamp. Christopher's posture rivaled a steel pole, but he did it anyway, and I liked him even more. My uptight, adorable buddy teacher was talking to a vendor named Kirk about the Chicago weather. There was nothing sexy or remotely admirable about it, but seeing him try made my chest twist with emotion.

"Why're you looking at me like that?" he asked as we moved to another table.

"Oh, no reason. You're just cute." I shrugged and pursed my lips, moving my attention to a stack of books all about flexible seating and implementing technology with young students. Heather Smith talked about how to not shy away from introducing technology in an authentic way to promote twenty-first-century learning, and disappointment weighed me down as I picked up the paperback book and eyed the price. Thirty dollars.

Before I made the challenge with myself, I would've bought a copy for my entire team and told them I won a raffle. The fact I couldn't, even though I had the money in an account, ate at me. God, I hated that I'd handed over all my credit cards to Grace so I wouldn't be tempted.

Like right now.

My fingers twitched along the book, and the urge to just fold, to do it, had my heart rate speed up. I followed Heather Smith, a flexible-seating guru, on all social media, watched her YouTube speeches, and had her book in my hands. But Grace's and Fritz's words repeated in my mind.

I was high maintenance and used my money too easily. I couldn't even keep a promise to them, to myself, that I could live without frivolous spending. My transgressions all came back in full force, and with a heavy heart, I set the book back on the table. I hated that I fought with myself. It wouldn't hurt to purchase it, and I could lie about it, but I was full of lies. Why add another? I was so lost in thought I didn't hear Christopher approach me. He reached over and ran his thumb over my forehead, making me frown in his direction. "Any reason you're touching my forehead?"

"You look sad and had a little wrinkle there." His gaze moved to the book I'd set down and back to me. "Are you mad I'm going to beat you with the passport competition?"

"Yeah, right, ain't happening, buddy."

He pulled on the end of my ponytail in a gesture that felt so easy, like we did that all the time, and he guided us toward another area of the conference. There were breakout sessions that lasted thirty minutes where we could either buddy up or go to separate ones to get as much information as possible.

We decided to split off. I went to using data in the classroom, and he went to scaffolding reading to help bridge the gap of beginning English learners. My instructor talked about the kick-ass session that would be that afternoon, with Heather Smith, and how it would be one of the best keynotes of the whole weekend. My palms sweated, and I itched to sign up as soon as the break out was over. I even packed my bag up with five minutes to spare before bolting up from the chair and racing toward the table where people could sign up last minute.

But when I got there, they were putting up a sign that said FULL. My heart sank to my knees. I missed the deadline, and while it would be fine, disappointment hit hard. There were other events for the afternoon that would be beneficial, but seeing Heather Smith speak, hearing her preach about things that meant so much to me, would've been everything.

I sighed, adjusted my hair, and opened the event app on my phone to search for another event to occupy the afternoon. There was nothing that stood out, and I sat on a bench just off the hallway where Christopher had gone to attend his sessions. I tapped my yellow flats on the white tile and checked my texts every couple of minutes. He should've been here ten minutes ago, and I imagined him talking to a presenter and getting into the nerdy details about having bare walls in the classroom. The thought made me snort, and I relaxed, still hesitant to believe this weekend was happening. Him and me.

I swore the air shifted when he approached me with a sneaky grin five minutes later. My pulse sped up at the look on his face, and I stood, anxious to see what joke he'd share. It had to be something funny because his eyes were lit up. "Good sessions?"

"Pretty useful." He stopped right in front of me, one brow arched as he looked at the busy foyer. "Any ideas for this afternoon?"

"You know how much I wanted to see Heather Smith, but they were full, so I'm game for whatever you want to do. When is your girl, Hillary Jones, talking?"

"She's tomorrow. Don't worry, I'll camp out and sleep outside the lecture doors if that's what it takes."

I snorted, and we shared a smile.

He narrowed his eyes and had a half smile on his face when he said, "There's a session over there about all the reasons why posters can distract students, and I think it would be best for you to attend and learn." He licked his bottom lip and laughed when I rolled my eyes. "Actually, follow me."

"Hm, okay?" I said, following his lead and admiring the way his jeans fit him. They were worn and faded in the pockets, and paired with his black polo, he looked gorgeous and dangerous. We hadn't talked about what this weekend meant, but I didn't care. Living in this bubble for another day was fine by me.

Christopher wove through the crowd, toward the three sets of double doors that I knew led to the arena-like area where Heather Smith was going to speak. Was he going to try to get us in? I reached out and grabbed his elbow, stopping him with a small smile. "It's full. I tried already."

He grinned wider and pulled out two small sheets of paper and handed them to the stern-looking woman wearing a dark-navy blazer at the entrance. The woman took the papers and waved us in, and for a moment, I was dumb struck.

Did he bribe her to get us in? Did he know her? How in the...? People chatted loudly in every direction as seats were filling up, fast. The stage was lit up with lights, and loud music played as a projection showed a countdown from five minutes. "Wait. What were those papers, Callahan? This was full. Totally full. Like we shouldn't be in here."

"You wanted to see Heather Smith speak, right?" he asked, crossing his arms over his large chest and looking all sorts of smug with raised brows and his eyes dancing with amusement. "You were talking about it the *entire* drive up."

"Yes, she's one of my favorites, but how?"

"I asked about it yesterday and got us spots."

"I could kiss you on the mouth, right now," I said, jumping up a little bit and letting the shock wear off. "Holy shit, Christopher. This is…thank you."

"You're welcome, Gilly."

My heart about burst in my chest with excitement and appreciation and awe. He did this yesterday. Before we slept together. Before things changed. I grinned up at him and said to hell with it. I grabbed his collar and pulled him down to plant a wet, loud kiss right on his lips. "This is amazing. I can't believe you did this. I just…let's get seats!"

He laughed and held my hand—which sent an entirely different array of butterflies through my gut—and we got seats in the center of the tenth row. It was perfect, and large crowds never bothered me. Our thighs touched, and we leaned into each other, and even though it was a conference for teachers, it felt like a date…almost. He smelled like a freshly sharped pencil and my favorite season—fall—and I scooted closer as the lights dimmed and Heather Smith got onto the stage. It was the best damn day, ever.

HOURS LATER, WE SAT AT THE HOTEL RESTAURANT, AND Christopher chewed his lip as he studied the menu. We were on a strict budget per diem from the school, and while we had our meals paid for, we couldn't really get the steak dinner.

"I think I'm going to do the chicken. That's simple yet filling," he said, setting the paper down and giving me his full attention. Clear-blue eyes, long lashes that fanned them, and a coy smile always teasing his lips. "What about you?"

"Chicken Caesar salad. I know it sounds dumb, but that is one of my favorite meals."

"Okay, super-important question. If you could only eat one food for the rest of your life, what would it be? It'd be day and night, forever."

"Um, what?" I said, laughing and tilting my head as I considered my answer. "Where did that come from?"

"One of my students asked me that before we left, and it's been on my mind. I said pizza because you could change the toppings each time, but now I'm wondering if I should've chosen tacos."

"It is a difficult question. That's for sure." I ran my finger tip over the rim of my water. "Peanut butter and jelly. That'd be mine. Protein, carbs, a little sweet. It fills you up, and it tastes good."

His gaze softened at me, and he bent over to his bag on the floor and hesitated, his expression suddenly appearing nervous. His muscles tightened, and he narrowed his eyes at me for a beat. "I got something for you."

"What?" My pulse raced again. "You getting us into that event was the highlight of my month, Christopher. Seriously." I blushed, hard, and frowned as he pulled out something rectangle from his bag. "No. You don't need to get me a thing."

"I saw you eyeing this with a really sad expression on your face, and I figured...I wanted to give this to you as a thank-you."

"I didn't do anything."

"You're my buddy teacher, and you remained positive even when I was acting like a shit. You also could've come here alone but wanted me to experience it. So please, take this. I want you to have it." He held it out and waited for me to take it. It was heavy, and my throat got tight when I undid the very light layer of tissue paper.

Heather's book sat in my hands with a signature in Sharpie on the cover. "It's *signed?*" I shouted, making a few people look over at us. "Oh my God!"

He grinned, wide, and nodded. "Sure is. You like it?"

It should not have made my eyes sting, but damn...I blinked back emotion and held the book tight against my chest. "Thank you."

"You're welcome, Gilly. It's my pleasure, really."

I sighed, the need to tell him the truth right on the edge of my tongue when his phone went off and his expression tightened. He flexed his jaw and blew out a long breath. I didn't want to pry, so I waited to see if he wanted to share whatever he just read.

He sipped his water and put his phone in his pocket. "That was

Kayla. She is working on scholarship on a Saturday night instead of going out and being a dumb teenager like she should be."

"Um, didn't you say you hated when she was dumb and dated dangerous boys, Mr. Older Brother?"

"Yes," he said, shaking his head when I called him out. "It's just… my dad had this fund for her for college. About thirty thousand, which would be enough to help her out, get her started. Then he had this buddy start a business that my dad swore would make it. He wanted to get in on the ground up and invested all of it. All of it." Christopher wiped his hands over his face. "He also did this without telling my mom or me. Dealing with that mess, seeing how desperate our family got…it turned me into this frugal, uptight person. I mean, I didn't have to worry about college, but my sister? She's so talented and deserves to have that option if she wants it. I can be an asshole about money sometimes. You might already know this."

"Oh, I do," I said, hoping my teasing tone would help the somewhat gloomy mood.

He gave me that half smile for a second. "He lost it all and tried to make up for it through other half-assed attempts at making lots of money fast. His *buddy* turned out to be a con artist and is in jail for faking checks. I didn't have to worry about this stuff when I was in high school, and I hate that Kayla has to. She has charts with all the scholarships she can apply for, like the left-handed one, but hey, a grand is a grand."

"Wait—she wants to be a teacher, right?"

"Yes, why?"

"There's this future-teacher scholarship the NHS does each year! It's like three grand! We could get a last-minute application in if she does it, like first thing Monday." I got my phone out and searched the URL with all the information and texted it to him. "She can totally apply. I'll tell my best friend, who teaches her, to write a letter of recommendation."

"How do you know about this?" he asked, his voice tight with excitement.

"I collect funds for it at our school. I worked with the NHS sponsors at the junior high and high school. The deadline was this weekend, but I can see if we can pull some strings, see if we can get it in Monday. It's honestly one of my favorite projects. Teachers played such an important role to me growing up. My...uh...parents took us on these work trips all the time, like work all day and have a schedule, and I'd go to bed tired as hell, so school was my favorite thing in the world. Anyway, the winner last year got to visit my classroom for the day, and it was just the best. She's kicking ass in college right now too."

"This is awesome," he said, his fingers flying over his phone. "I'm texting it to her right now. Thank you."

"Of course. I'll send any more your way if I find them." I smiled and admired his love for his sister. The way he looked out for her reminded me of Fritz. "We can even work on the application together when we get back."

"Really?"

"Yes." I reached over and ran my fingers over his strong forearm and squeezed. "We could have a scholarship night. Put on music, eat, and write all the annoying introduction letters."

His jaw tightened, and the look in his eyes sent a shiver all the way through my body. It wasn't lust, but something more. Something that I couldn't put a word on, but I felt it too—the fact that maybe we were good together.

Now I just have to tell him the truth about me.

Would it last?

Chapter Eighteen

"I *LOVE* YOUR DRESS. OH MY GOD, AND IT HAS POCKETS?" KAYLA said, two days later as she stood inside my classroom with her purple backpack hanging off her shoulder. She had the wide-eyed look of a teenager who still had their life ahead of them, and it made me smile.

I hoped she never lost that joy and wonder.

"Yes, pockets are a must. I keep everything in there when I'm walking around," I said, laughing and finishing up the organization of projects. With the deadline looming for the grant, Christopher wanted to do it first thing when we got back, and if it meant helping him out, I would be a fool to pass up on that. There was something sexy and charming seeing how he looked out for his sister.

"Noted." Kayla walked around my classroom and eyed the walls. "Your room is so different than my brother's. I love your colors. This is, like, the classroom of my Pinterest dreams."

"Thank you," I said, grinning when Christopher walked in, and his gaze seemed to go straight into my chest and wrap around my heart in a caress. "I want school to be a safe, fun, and creative place for students. I never got to go to the beach growing up or play ghost in the graveyard or anything like that, but school? My teachers? Their rooms became home away from home, and if kids remember anything about me, or my class, I want it to be that they were safe, loved, and inspired."

"Wow, I love that," she said, just as her brother leaned against the door with an unreadable look on his face.

His soft blue gaze lingered on me for a beat before he pushed off the frame and headed toward his sister. "You getting started? We need to leave within an hour to get you to your swimming practice."

"We're about to. She was admiring how wonderful my classroom is compared to your boring one. That's all," I said, trying to lighten the mood. I'd gone too deep talking about my past and wanted to act like I hadn't shared a deep part of who I was with the Callahan siblings.

"It's true," Kayla said, shrugging and sitting down at one of the chairs and getting her laptop out.

Christopher rolled his eyes and joined her at the table before taking out a notebook and going over her application. It was the absolute cutest thing.

"Is there anything you can tell me about the process on how they select winners?" Kayla asked.

"Mm, I'm not sure, but I think they are looking at the whole student. The person who is applying, not just all the stats. How are you a leader? How do you help others? How are you, Kayla, going to make a difference in the world? Show them who you are, not what you think they want to hear."

She nodded and chewed on her lip for a second. "Right, yeah."

Christopher tapped his fingers on the desk. "You were a manager at the church camp for two years—that's leadership. Then you're captain of your swim team too."

Kayla's face lit up at her brother commenting on her leadership like it was a big deal. It was, and it felt weird listening to them work in my room. I didn't want to be caught listening like a creep with a major crush, so I got out my own laptop and started a chat with Grace to see if she was done with the letter of recommendation.

Grace: call me

I frowned as worry took root. Maybe she didn't have time or couldn't do it. I excused myself to go into the hallway and dialed her number with my stomach in a knot. It rang three times before she answered. "Hey, Grace."

"Ah, sorry. I'm doing a million things at once and couldn't chat. I have the letter done. Just need to scan it. Could it wait fifteen minutes? I'm in the middle of dealing with practice."

"Of course, yes," I said, hearing the sounds of others shouting in the background. "Thank you. We're filling out the application now."

"Are you seeing your brother later?"

Her question sent ice in my veins. Her tone was direct and more than annoyed, and I swallowed, eyeing up and down the hallway a few times to make sure no one was there. *Like Samantha.* "I, uh, don't have plans to."

"Gilly, this isn't like you," she said, disappointment clogging her voice and making me feel as small as an ant. "You're lying to Fritz, and Christopher, and that's not you. You need to be yourself. Your *real* self. Money doesn't define you, Gil. Never has. You have too big of a heart, but if what you told me about your weekend with Christopher is true, you owe him the full truth. Not the lies."

"I know, Grace," I snapped, pinching the bridge of my nose. "Fritz was camping, then I had that conference, and I have like ten days left of this challenge."

"I think it's time to let that go. Money is a huge part of your life. You can't deny that. You have millions in a bank, and letting Christopher think you don't is cruel, especially after what he shared with you about his family. It doesn't have to be a big deal, but it will be the longer you keep this charade up. And don't get me started on the fact you paid Fritz's girlfriend to leave. I'm just...not understanding why you're continuing the keep it from them. Tell Fritz, tell Samantha to piss off, and tell the guy you're crushing on the truth."

My eyes stung a bit, and I *hated* the truth to her words. My best friend was pissed at me, and this was all my fault. Not Samantha's, Fritz's, or Christopher's. Mine. "I-I will. Soon. What if it ruins everything though?"

"I've seen you yell at people three times your size in college. You helped me deal with the loss of my mom. You can handle this, Gilly. Fritz will forgive you, and Christopher is into you because of *you*, not your lack of money. Plus, why would you want a relationship with someone who liked a fake version of you? That's not real. That's not a genuine relationship."

"I'll tell Fritz."

"I love you, Gil. I really do. But as your best friend, it is my job to tell you when you're being an ass, and you are. But you have the power to fix it. Money is a part of you. Be honest about it. Stop the dumb challenge. You were only doing that to prove it to Fritz and me, and honestly, I think it's made you a little crazy. I gotta go. I'll send the letter in a bit."

Money is a part of you.

Her words repeated in my mind, and I hated the way it made me feel. I didn't want my money to define me.

I paced in the hallway, struggling with pulling myself together. The urge to cry hit me hard, but it wasn't so much in pity as it was frustration. The challenge to live off a teacher's salary was supposed to be fun and to prove that I could live without all the funds. Something fiery went into my veins. It was like the time Fritz told me I couldn't juggle, and I spent all summer before seventh grade learning so I could prove him wrong. He didn't even care when I showed him, but I did. I'd learned it to prove to myself.

With a resigned sigh, I nodded to no one in the hall. The challenge for the month was to prove to myself that I could do it.

Screw Fritz and Grace. I didn't want money to be a part of who I was or how someone saw me. Christopher was not Samantha, using me for money, but he would be affected. He might not want to see me, be with me, or want anything to do with me if he learned the truth. That was my reality.

Was it selfish to want to hold on to what we had a little longer? To see him look at me with warm eyes and like I mattered to him? Probably. But I made a priority list in my mind.

I had to tell Fritz about Samantha first. I owed him that.

Then confront Samantha and tell her to get lost. That bitch wouldn't get a dime from me.

Finally, I'd tell Christopher the truth about my inheritance and hope to God we could still be what we were. Which I wasn't even sure if we had defined it. We spent the whole weekend together, either learning and talking shop, or getting naked. It was an actual dream to be on the same page with someone on everything. Even when we fought about different teaching styles, it was a good discussion because we pushed each other to be better.

Shit. I rubbed my temples and made my way back into the room. Christopher looked up when I entered, a slight smirk on his face, and he winked. God, the gesture made me fumble like a total idiot. "Uh, Mrs. Anderson will send the letter soon."

"Perfect! I think we have the essay done! I can use this for other scholarships too." Kayla shared a smile with her brother and nudged her shoulder into his. "Chrissy has been awesome helping me with all this stuff. My parents mean well, but they get so stressed out even thinking about college for me."

"Chrissy told me a little about it, so I'm glad you're able to find scholarships like these," I said, loving how his eyes flared at using his sister's nickname for him. "I have a brother who I'm close with too, and it's great having someone who is always on your team." As soon as I said the words, my stomach tightened.

Would Fritz realize that I was always on his team? I sure hoped so.

The Callahan siblings worked for another hour, and I helped with the phrasing on some of her essay questions before they called it a night. Kayla put her stuff in her bag and hands on her hips. "They'll let people know next week, right?"

"Yes." I smiled, so thankful I was able to work with the high school sponsor to get her application in last minute. I loved and respected deadlines for adults, but for kids? It took some greasing, but I got her in. "We have most of the funds collected, and the committee is chosen. It all depends on the number of applicants who applied. Last year it took two weeks for them to decide, but the year before, it was two days."

"I hope I get it. I want to be a teacher so bad."

"Fingers crossed."

Christopher put his arm around his sister and led her to the hallway, making my chest get all warm and fuzzy seeing them together, but he didn't walk out with her. He came back into my room and walked right up to me. I barely had time to react before he cupped the back of my head and kissed me. Warm, wet lips greeted mine, and he traced his thumb over my cheek in the most heart-shatteringly gentle way. "Thank you," he said, his voice thick and smooth as he stared down at me. "She means the world to me, and I appreciate your help."

"Anytime, Chrissy," I teased, blushing from head to toe, and he bent down and nipped at my bottom lip. "Hey."

"We spent the weekend together, and it doesn't seem like enough time. Let me take you out."

"Like a date-date?" I asked, my heart racing at the seriousness on his face. He looked determined—the same way he had before our SPIRIT competition.

"Exactly like a date-date." He pushed my hair behind my ear as one side of his mouth curved up on the side like he knew a punchline to a joke. "Thursday night."

"Are you asking me if I'm free then or demanding?"

"It's the soonest night I have available, forgive me for being impatient." He trailed his fingers over my jaw, making goose bumps break out all down my neck and tingling in the best kind of way.

"I am free then, yes."

"Good," he said, letting out a long breath and pressing one more kiss to my mouth. "See you tomorrow, Gilly."

"Yeah," I said, breathless and excited and guilty all combining into one hot mess of emotions.

He winked again before heading to the door, but he stopped, put a hand on his hip, and narrowed his eyes in a teasing way. "Also, Kayla told me all about this *awful* coworker. She has yet to realize that it was me."

"I'll make sure she has all the details, Chrissy."

His eyes flared, but we shared a heated smile before he left. God, my heart swelled around him, and I could only hope that it lasted. I picked up my room and got everything into my bag before heading out toward my car.

Gilly: can I come over?

Fritz: I'm going on a date tonight. Date two, Gil. You and G would freak out.

Gilly: WHO IS SHE
Fritz: don't worry about it. You won't meet her until date 10
Gilly: Fritz. How dare you keep this from us?

I cringed at the double standard but held my ground. If he was going on a second date, tonight wouldn't be the night I told him. I couldn't remind him of all Samantha's bullshit and destroy a chance at him being happy. Not when this was the first time in half a year that he showed interest in dating at all. It would be horrible to dampen his mood. Grace would understand.

My car, undamaged from Samantha, reflected in the sun that remained, and I reached into my bag and groaned. *My damn car keys were in my classroom.* I was too damn distracted by Christopher that I forgot my car keys.

My classroom keys were in my pocket. I *never* forgot those. But ugh. I made the trek back to the building. The creaking sounds of a large empty building always sent a weird chill down my neck. It wasn't unsafe but eerie. Especially when most people were gone.

I got to the first-grade hallway and stopped in my tracks. Samantha was tiptoeing out of my room. *That bitch.* How did she get into my room? My heart lurched in my chest, and I waited until she was out of sight before running as quiet as I could to my room. *Did she take something? Destroy my stuff? Put a hidden mic?*

I unlocked the door, grabbed my car keys, and searched for anything that was missing. My laptop was there, my lesson plans. The scholarship donation sheet sat on the top of my desk. Nothing out of place that would've indicated why she was there.

I spent another ten minutes trying to find a single hair out of place but couldn't. I hated that she could fluster me like this. She had no business breaking into my room unless it was to mess with me. I gritted my teeth together as anger lit me up. It was time to end this shit with her. No more money. No more blackmail. This monster was going to be cut out of my life—I just had to make sure Fritz and Christopher heard it from me first.

Chapter Nineteen

"Red dress, for sure," Grace said over FaceTime three days later.

It was our date night, and we hadn't kissed since he was in my classroom with his sister. It was a special form of torture seeing his smirk and heated eyes every day, but tonight, it was us.

"It's flirty and fun and hot, Gilly. Make him pine for you. I think he deserves it since he thought you *conned* him." She snorted over the phone, and I was so glad she wasn't vocal about being disappointed in me.

We both agreed it wouldn't be right to tell Fritz now, not when he was just getting back into dating. It would crush his newly found spirit, and we needed to see how it went this next week before I told him. Knowing my brother, it would send him into a binge-drinking weekend where he was pissed at the world.

I couldn't have that, and the relief at hearing Grace agree with me made breathing easier again. I missed this with her—the talking before a date, the ways she used to laugh at my horrible dating life. It was back to normal between us, even if it was temporary, and it felt good.

"I forgave him for being an ass about all that con stuff after seeing him with his sister and family," I said, the twinge of guilt appearing in my gut. "Plus, he'll see it's even more absurd when I tell him the truth."

"Which will be…when?" she asked oh-so-casually.

"Soon." My mouth dried up. "We agreed I had to tell Fritz first."

"Hm," she said, her distaste from my reasoning clear through the phone. "So, red dress, right? You'll have him putty in your hands. Maybe that'll help distract him from the fact you are Ms. Moneybags."

Her attempt at humor made me feel better and less like I was awful. "When did you become such a little tease, Grace Anderson?"

"Since I married a grumpy softie." She beamed back at me, and I waved at Brock in the background. He shook his head at us and kept walking. Typical Brock.

I tried the red sundress on. It had tiny straps, fit my chest nicely, and hugged my hips until it flared out at the end. It did great things for my curves, and I felt confident in it. "Yes, this is it."

"You still have my shoes you stole?"

"You mean, the ones *you* stole from me that you now claim as your own?" I fired back, digging through my closet for the black strappy sandals that had just an inch of a heel. I slipped them on and grinned. "They work."

"You look incredible, Gil. For real." Grace repositioned the phone so she could on her stomach. Her goofy smile was just enough for me to share my inner turmoil. She was the perfect pre-date distraction.

"G, I'm nervous," I said, the scandal with Samantha and Fritz in the back of my mind. My stomach was in a constant state of knots knowing how much I liked him, how much I was into him. I was in unchartered territory and my poor body couldn't handle the nerves. Sex with him might've changed our physical part but a date night?

I couldn't remember the last date night I had. Years ago. Things were heavier. More serious. More risky.

"Why?" she asked, her brows coming together like I told her I was an alien.

"Because I like the guy." There, I'd said it. He cared for his family and his students, and he was respectful and loyal. Even though his misunderstanding made him be an ass, I understood his behavior. He was confident and knew what he wanted, and I was that person, for now at least.

"And you're nervous because he isn't just a hookup or a fling?" She tilted her head to the side and clicked her tongue—a sure sign she was deep in thought.

"He's different. What if the date sucks or what if he decides nope, not worth it? I guess I wouldn't have to tell him the truth then." I asked the question that kept me up at night. "The stakes feel higher with him."

Like the fact he didn't know about my money or what I did with Samantha. I could fall for him, and he could walk away once I told him the truth.

"Since you're invested, you have more to gain and lose. It makes sense," Grace said, frowning as she studied me through the phone screen. "Don't worry about all the ways it could go wrong. Think about all the right ways. I know we hated him for a hot minute in the beginning, but he challenged you, Gil. Not many people will go head-to-head with you on things, and he did. That's admirable."

I smiled. She spoke the truth.

"Now, put on a sexy pair of underwear and stop worrying." She looked behind her shoulder and scoffed. "Brock thinks we're talking dirty."

"Such a boy."

"That he is." She sighed, her eyes going all dreamy, and I swallowed back the twinge of envy. Grace got serious again. "Have fun. You deserve it."

"I'm gonna have a glass of wine before he gets here. That'll settle me down."

"Good call."

She hung up, leaving me with my anxieties and nerves. But excitement was in there too. My makeup was perfect, my hair curled and hung around my shoulders, and I slipped on my favorite black lace boy shorts. I wasn't sure if he would be seeing them, but I would not be caught without sexy underwear.

5:45 p.m.

Jesus, fifteen minutes. I paced the apartment and sipped a small glass of white wine. It did its job, and I kept looking out the window for his car. One minute passed. Then another.

I sprayed perfume and dabbed it on my neck and reapplied a pink lipstick. It wasn't so heavy that if we kissed it would end up all over him, but it accentuated the curve of my top lip. *5:55 p.m.*

I gulped and grabbed my purse, my phone, and lip gloss and set them on the side table. I should clean. Yes. Wiping the counters down would be a great idea. I got the paper towel ready when the buzzer from the main door went off. *It's him!*

"Yes?" I said, responding back just in case it wasn't my date.

"You gonna let me up or make me work for it? The doorman won't let me in."

Oh, that was Christopher. *The doorman!* Shit. I needed to think of something that would explain how having a doorman wasn't super extravagant.

I pushed the button and said, "Send him on up." I waited at the door with my heart hammering in my chest. It was like a movie scene when his fist pounded outside my door. My fingers shook a little when I opened it, getting a look at him in his dark-navy jacket, gray slacks, and white button-down. Handsome was too lame of a word. Delicious. Sexy. Perfect.

"Wow, Gilly."

He stepped into my place, placed a warm hand on my back, and pulled me into him. He didn't ask before bringing his lips to mine, probing them with ease. His minty taste burned my tongue as he slid his inside, tilting my head back to kiss me deeper. I reached up and fisted my hands in his collar, my panties dampening when he moved his hand from my back to my ass. He lingered on my mouth, pressing one, two, three more kisses before pulling back, his blue eyes sparkling at me.

"Hi."

"You kiss me like that, and all you say is hi?"

"That's as much as my brain can work right now." He dug his fingers into the spot right above my ass and closed his eyes. "You look beautiful."

He grinned down at me and gave a slight tilt of his head before putting distance between our bodies. I immediately missed his warmth and wanted to touch him again. A little pout left my lips, and he arched a brow. "Don't look at me like that," he said, his voice tense and husky.

"What do you mean?"

"All doe-eyed and hungry. I need to be respectful of you, and if you look at me like that and touch me, I'll forget to behave."

"Christopher, I'm so worked up, I don't want you to behave."

He pinched the bridge of his nose. "We have plans."

"You sound snippy."

"Gilly, I swear to God." He licked his bottom lip, and his gaze dropped to my chest. He groaned. My beaded nipples were on full display due to not wearing a bra with the dress and how turned on that kiss got me. He took a deep breath and brought his eyes back to mine. "I forgot I brought you something."

"Like flowers?"

"No. You don't strike me as the *flowers* type of girl." His cocky grin returned, and he reached into his pocket and pulled out a stack of sharpies, all tied with a rubber band. "Here's a bouquet more your style. All pinks and greens."

"Wow, this is a first." I took the markers, smiling way too wide, and stopped caring that this guy had the power to break my heart. "Let me put them in a vase."

He snorted when I grabbed an empty glass and put them caps down. I wanted all the ink to flow down. "No one has ever given me markers before."

"Good."

"You look proud of yourself."

"I am." He reached out and took my hand, pulling me to him like before, only this time softer. "You ready for our on-a-budget date?"

"Yes." My voice shook more than I thought it would, and I cleared my throat. "Are you?"

"Always have to get the last word in." He chuckled before reaching out with his thumb and wiping under my lip. "You had some lip stuff there."

"Is it all fixed?"

He studied my mouth for a full ten seconds, nostrils flaring and breaths coming out harder, and he nodded. "It's perfect. Now, come on."

It was like I was transported back to high school and I was going on my first date. That was how anxious I felt locking up my door and taking his hand as he walked us to the main area of the building. He narrowed his eyes as I waved at the doorman, and with a nervous flutter in my gut, I said, "My parents wanted me to live in a safe place since I live alone."

"Ah, yes, I can see that."

"They helped with…that."

He nodded, like my sentence made sense to him. It was a partial truth. My parents did insist on me living somewhere safe and recommended this place because their buddy owned the complex, but it didn't seem like Christopher cared that I had a doorman. He squeezed my hand and walked faster as we got outside. He smelled like fresh laundry and soap and gave me a hesitant smile before opening the door for me.

"I got creative tonight," he said, watching me get into the car and buckle in. His voice was deep again, toe-curlingly deep, and I squirmed at the intensity of his stare. "The goal is to not spend more than twenty dollars."

"Oh?" I said, finding it hard to breathe when he leaned over me, distracting all my senses with his body. He cupped my chin and lifted my face toward him, his thumb tracing my bottom lip and sending a lightning bolt of desire to my core.

"Yup. There are three parts of this date."

"Is one of them ending back up at my place?" I teased, hoping to fluster him or have him feel even a little off-balanced like I did.

He sucked in a sharp breath and shook his head. "Behave," he said, grinning ear to ear before shutting my door and walking around the car to get in on his side. While he didn't answer my question, he did look a little on edge.

He turned on the radio to an alternative station, and I recognized the band—Arctic Monkeys. He smiled when I sang along to one of the songs for a few seconds, and the pure lust and joy on his face made my chest swell. This wasn't just a big deal for me—he was into this too.

That should've reassured me, but the lack of truth on my part was getting bigger. I could enjoy the night with him to show him I wasn't defined by my money. Then, when the time was right, I'd tell him.

"Where are we going for the first part of this date?"

"The library." He looked pleased with himself and turned onto the main road that led to the downtown area. Restaurants, quirky shops, and the library all sat on the same road, and he eased into a parking spot. I hated to admit I wasn't sure I had been there in years, and a nostalgic feeling took over as we got out of the car.

He held out his hand again, and I took it, his entire face warming at me to the point my throat got tight again. *I like this guy. A lot.* The words were like a neon sign in my heart, lighting up in different colors and flashing to get all my attention. That was passion, and we certainly had chemistry. This other side, the soft one, was dangerous.

"What I was thinking—and we can change if you think it's stupid, okay?—but I wanted us each to pick out a book for the other person to read. Clearly reading is important to both of us, so I thought...I don't know. I started talking and you're giving me wide eyes, and now I feel weird."

"Oh, no, I *love* it," I said, my voice thick with emotion. His plan was so thought out and sweet. Like the surprise at the conference when he got us into the lecture and got me the book. Or the fact he brought me my favorite tea that morning. He was thoughtful as hell. "Yes, I'm in. We pick out a book for the other to read."

"You sure?" He frowned, and a slight blush appeared on his cheeks.

I had to kiss him.

I let go of his hand and placed my hands on his shoulders, stood on my tippy-toes, and pressed my lips against his. He melted against me, and I lingered for an extra beat or two. We were in public so I didn't use any tongue, but the kiss worked.

He smiled against my mouth.

"I love your plan, Callahan."

"Feel free to kiss me anytime you want." He dropped his hands to my hips and grinned down at me. "How much time do you need to pick out a book for me?"

"What is the criteria? A book we love? A book we want the other to read?" I asked, almost sighing as he rubbed his thumbs over my hips, like he didn't even know he was massaging me.

"Hm, how about one of your favorite books? Any genre, for any reason."

"Okay. Deal." I let go of him and took a few steps away. It was best for us *not* to touch at a library because the more his hands were on me, the more I wanted to take him back to my place. "See you in ten minutes."

He winked, and I took off toward the fiction section of the library. I loved reading and had way too many books at home and on my Kindle—all books I had bought. I never once thought about coming here to get them, and it was a brief, sharp reminder how different I was from what Christopher believed. I dragged my fingers over the backs of some spines and focused on my task. A book I wanted him to read.

I loved thrillers and romance and true crime and kid books. It was quite a range, but the most recent book I read that I still thought about was *The Devil in the White City.* It was realistic fiction based on true events and bordered on being creepy while still informative. I learned while the book freaked me out, and whenever I experienced a mixture of emotions, I knew it was a good book. I found the book and hid it behind my back, trying to search for where my date was.

His tall frame would stand out. I searched a couple of aisles in the back, hoping to surprise him. He wasn't there. My neck tingled for a second before he appeared right before me, pushing me into the back wall as he dropped his mouth on mine. He slid his tongue right in, moving his hand to grip my head, and oh wow, he kissed me, hard. Like he could barely control himself, and it made my legs go weak.

"Christopher," I muttered between kisses. "What are you...? We're in public."

He traced my lip with his tongue while he stared down at me, and the moment felt *intimate.* His eyes were an open book and full of lust, and I almost whimpered. "No one can see us now, and your lips drive me crazy."

"This is a new side of you," I said, letting go of the book I still held onto. It fell to the floor. He didn't even glance at it. He pulled me tighter against him, and I felt every hard ridge of his chest. "What about behaving?"

"Overrated. It was a great plan until I saw you in this dress." He bit his lip, and his chest heaved. "Where are you at right now?"

"What?"

"This matters a lot to both of us. We work together, right next to each other," he said, his voice soft now. He pushed my hair over my ear as he gazed down, and my heart fluttered. "Our chemistry is explosive, but I need to let you set the pace. We spent a weekend together, all weekend, but what next?"

"Why?" I ran my hands over his shoulders and got a thrill when he shook a little.

"Because I know how important your job is to you, and I can't risk ruining this and making work tough for both of us. I love teaching, but it's a part of who you are."

Oh my God. I closed my eyes at how much he understood me. "Christopher...what you said was perfect."

"Yeah?" He grinned now, the cocky look coming back into his eyes. "Good. I meant it." He wrapped his arms around me and lifted me up so we were face-to-face before he kissed me again, this time without the crazy heat. "Forgive me. I'm going to stick to my plans for the rest of the night, but I'm going to try to kiss you as often as you let me."

"Often. Very often," I said, earning another grin. "Now show me your book."

He laughed and set me back on my feet. "Ah, is this your choice for me?" He bent down and picked up my book. "I've always wanted to read this but never had a push. You recommend it?"

"Yes, absolutely. It's worth the read." I smoothed down my dress and watched him study the back of the book. There was something so sexy about him holding the book, deep in thought with his lips still red from kissing me. "That author has quite a few books like this, stories woven together out of true events."

"Okay, I'm in. I'll read it."

"Yes! Now what did you get for me?"

He blinked a few times before reaching onto the shelf behind me and grabbing a book. "It's a thriller."

"I love them," I gushed, yanking it out of his hand and reading the back. *I Am Pilgrim.* "Wow, this sounds insane."

"It's one of the books I read two years ago, but I still think about it." He smiled and watched me with an unreadable look in his eyes. "Did we just start a two-man book club?"

"Uh, hell yeah, I think we did," I said, my heart growing eight times in size at how much we had in common despite our differences. "This was perfect, Christopher. Seriously. Best part one of a date, ever."

He smirked and put his arm around my shoulder, guiding us out of the aisle and into the main foyer where we could check out. "Wait until you see part two."

Chapter Twenty

PART TWO WAS CHEAP BURGERS AND FRIES AT ONE OF THE OUTSIDE restaurants where you could eat in your car. It was ten dollars total, leaving another ten dollars for part three if we wanted to stay on his budget plan.

That was ice cream at a picnic table.

I was focused on part four, and the way all the casual touches built up to the point my mind could only think about touching him.

The car was filled with a comfortable silence as he drove me home, but the way he gripped my hand was a huge hint that he, too, was anticipating the next step. He wanted me to set the pace, and I wanted *more.*

Especially if I knew telling him the truth could change everything. Sleeping with him, taking my time with him…hell yes. I wanted that.

He parked on the side of the street, got out, and he grabbed my hand as I led us to my front door, all without speaking. It was only when we stood right outside it, with my keys in my hand, that he bent down and bit the part on my neck that connected with my shoulder. I groaned and dipped my head forward, letting my forehead rest against the door.

"You smell so good," he said into my skin, trailing his teeth up until he bit down on my earlobe. He brought his hands to my sides, grazing the sides of my breasts, before pulling me tight against him. "Open the door and go inside before I do something stupid out here. I haven't touched you in *days*. I'm dying."

Lust overtook my brain, and I fumbled with the keys a few times before getting it into the lock. I swung it open but barely stepped inside before he lifted me off the ground. "Oh!"

He had my legs wrapped around his waist, his hungry eyes staring into mine, and he pushed me against the door. "This *dress*." He slid his hands under the flimsy material and cupped my ass, his eyes going wide as he felt the fabric. "Lace?"

"Uh-huh," I said, so keyed up it wouldn't take much for him to get me off. One touch was all I needed. I rocked my hips into him, and he stilled, bending down and kissing me hard. This kiss had tongue and teeth. It was messy and desperate. I clung to him as he ground his erection in between my legs, the only thing separating us my thin panties and his pants. "Christopher," I said, begging for something. Anything.

His frantic movements and rigid muscles eased my mind that I wasn't alone in wanting to go straight to the bedroom.

"Are you wet for me, Gilly?" he said after removing his mouth from mine. "If I reach into your panties, will you be soaked?"

"God, yes." I arched my back and willed him to just do it. Touch me.

But he laughed softly and carried me from the door to the couch.

"No, bedroom."

"Not yet." He placed me on the sofa and spread my legs wide, the dress still covering all my parts. "I want to look at you, taste you, make you go crazy. I don't plan on rushing a damn thing with you. Can you handle that? Going nice and slow?"

"Uh-huh," I mumbled, right before he slid one strap of my dress to the side.

He wasn't kidding about taking his time. He stared at my bare shoulder before sliding the other strap off, alternating between kissing my skin and flirting with the edge of my dress. His gaze felt like a warm caress, and I shivered with need.

"Sit up for me," he said, reaching around my back as I did and unzipping the back of the dress. His chest heaved when he pulled the bottom of the material, slowly revealing my pebbled nipples to him. He groaned and traced one with the tip of his fingers, making me buck underneath him. He teased both of them with his hands, pinching and squeezing until I was going to lose my goddamn mind.

"Patience. I promise it'll be worth it." He bent low, licking the tip with his tongue and flicking one nipple before sucking it into his mouth.

My clit swelled with need as he sucked harder, gripping my hips with his hands as he tastes every inch of my chest over and over. I fisted his hair in my hand, the sensation almost hurting it felt so good, and he stopped sucking them.

"God," he said, panting like he'd run a mile. "You're gorgeous."

He spent so much time on my breasts, I was wet and needy, but if I tried to pull away, he bit down harder, taking my nipple between his teeth and pulling.

"Christopher," I moaned, loving the blurred line of pleasure and the sting.

"I want you so much. Every way," he said, kissing up the center of my breasts and looking up at me with the sexiest *loving* expression.

I cleared my throat, shifting the emotional scale.

"Are you trying to kill me?" I asked, arching my hips up so he would get the hint to go further with me. He made no moves though. He took the dress and slid it down the rest of my body, sucking in a breath when he eyed my panties. He bent down and bit the hemline of them, pulling the material down with his teeth. "Oh, wow," I moaned, honestly afraid one could die from a lack of an orgasm. "Christopher, please."

"Almost there," he said, taking my panties off and spreading my legs wide. He saw all of me, completely bare, and before I could over-think our position, he bent his head low and licked me. It was torture in the best way. Fast, then slow. He hummed against my most sensitive area and flicked his tongue right where I needed him to. Pressure built almost to the brink, and then he slowed down and flashed a dangerous grin at me. "I *love* your body, Gil. Your sounds, your taste."

I couldn't even mumble a reply when he flattened his tongue against me. My muscles tensed, and he held me down with one hand —so hot—as my orgasm started tearing through me. It was like a sucker punch. The air left my lungs as pleasure exploded to every limb. All I could hear was his content groan against me, and all I could feel was him. His hands over my stomach and thighs, his tongue and teeth between my legs, and I arched my back, losing control.

I saw stars when I caught my breath. "Holy shit."

"You okay?" He pressed another light kiss on my inner thigh, and I wanted to melt. It was so tender and kind.

"Oh yeah," I said, sitting up and grinning down at him like I was drunk. I kind of was. Drunk on Christopher Callahan. "My toes are still tingling."

"Good." He stared between my thighs with a slack jaw, his mouth wet from me. It was the sexiest thing to see him disheveled because of me. No more Mr. Rigid.

"I want you naked," I demanded, desperate to touch him, to make him feel what I was. My heart worked twice as hard, and I couldn't get close enough to him.

"Do you now?" He grinned, and I pushed him back so I could have access to his shirt. I slid the jacket off his arms and furiously undid his buttons. "You seem in a hurry, Gilly."

"I am. To see you naked."

"What if I'm not done with you yet?"

"Don't care." I fumbled with the last button and almost cheered when he was shirtless. I ran my fingers over his muscles, his chest, stomach, the line of hair that disappeared below his belt. I bit his pec and sucked the salty skin into my mouth.

He released a shaky breath and his grip on my body tightened, and I licked his nipple before saying, "Pants, gotta go."

"Not yet." He stilled my hands and gave me such a heated look, I got the familiar tingle in the base of my stomach again. "I know you need more than one orgasm. I plan on doing that before I slide inside you. Give me what I want, Gil. I haven't had you in *days*."

My head spun from how sexy that sentence was, and I gulped when he pushed me back onto the couch. He moved me so I lay on my back completely while he was still on his knees. The position put his face by mine, but his hands were *everywhere*. "I remember how much you liked it when I sucked your nipple as I stroke you. Tell me, have you thought about this since this weekend?"

"Yes," I moaned as he made his words true. He bit down while swirling his thumb around my already sensitive area. I gasped when he slid two fingers inside me, curling to the point I arched my toes. "Shit, this is…*yes*."

"Would you touch yourself thinking about me?" he asked before biting down on my other nipple. "I think about you all the damn time. Even before this weekend."

I groaned as he worked me faster, harder. Putting the right pressure and pace together to the point I was close again. "Tell me," I demanded.

"Tell you how I thought about me putting my mouth on you like this?" He sucked my sensitive breast, hard. "Or imagining my face between your thighs? Or how tight it'd feel sliding into you?"

"Yes," I moaned, feeling the second orgasm take over. He kept his eyes on mine as I fell apart, and before I could catch my breath, he picked me up.

"Bedroom?" he asked, his voice deep and tense.

"Second door on the right."

He kicked it open and set me on the bed before undoing his belt and finally sliding his pants and boxers off. He was hard. Incredibly hard. I gulped as he stared down at me with so much heat and warmth in his eyes.

"I'm really into you."

"I'm into you, too," I said, cupping his face with my hands. I ran my finger over his jaw and his bottom lip, and a moment passed between us. We were in this together, and none of the previous worries came up. We were on the *same page*, and that made the entire experience with him better. "*Really* into you, Callahan."

His body stilled when I dragged my hand down to pump his very hard shaft a few times, and then he snapped. He gripped the back of my head, kissing me hard, and his heart pounded in his chest against mine.

"Condom," I said, reaching a hand out to my nightstand. "Top drawer."

He got one and handed it to me. "Put it on me."

I don't know why him telling me to do it got me hot again. Never it all my hookups had I put it on the guy. They always did. There was something sensual about sliding it on his dick and feeling him pulse around my hand. "Okay."

"Okay," he said, repeating me and lowering me back onto the bed. His gaze remained on mine as he bent down to kiss me, slowly. He seemed to find his control again because he kissed me for what felt like hours, nipping at my lip and rolling me over so I lay on top of him. He dug his fingers into my hips and groaned my name. "Gilly, goddamn it."

"Me too," I said, knowing exactly what he meant. I ground against him, and he flipped us over again. He put his weight on his forearms and stared down at me, a question on his face. "I want this, you, all of it."

I barely finished the words before he thrust into me. He felt so damn good, and I clawed at his muscular ass as he found a rhythm. It wasn't frenzied. It was slowly building up to more, and he reached underneath me to lift me up at the right angle. He went deeper, slid in and out faster, and held on tighter. He found my mouth with his and kissed the hell out of me while he continued thrusting. Sweat pooled in between our chests, and I could smell my musk on his beard, but I didn't care. It was intoxicating to be touched and kissed by him.

"This is perfect," he said between sucking my tongue into his mouth. He fell on his side, bringing me with him so I was on top, and he helped guide my hips up and down. "God, you're sexy."

"Yeah?" I grinned, moaning as he went deeper inside me. He reached over to swirl my clit with his thumb, and I bucked at the almost too-sensitive nerve. "Pinch it," I said. He did.

It was what I needed, and his jaw tightened and his mouth went slack as he thrust up into me simultaneously, giving me a third orgasm. I grabbed his chest as I rode out the pleasure, unable to breathe as it continued. My body convulsed around him, and he barely got a word out before his legs tensed, my name leaving his lips as he yanked me down to kiss me as he came. When he stilled, neither one of us moved. I lay on his chest, my face resting next to his, and our all I could hear was my heartbeat. He waited a few minutes before getting up and disposing the condom in the trash before crawling back to bed.

He ran his hand up and down my back and chuckled. His breath tickled my skin, and he kissed my shoulder. "Hey."

I opened one eye and rolled to my side, not bothering to cover up with sheets. "Damn."

"My thoughts too."

"My body is still tingling, and I don't think I can move." I sighed, perfectly content, and stared at my bedmate. "Don't take this the wrong way, but I don't want you to leave."

His answering smile made my chest feel funny, and he snorted. "Don't take this the wrong way, but I wasn't going to leave."

"Glad that's settled then." I tried not to turn into a complete puddle of feelings when he pulled me toward him so my head rested on his arm. I wasn't a cuddler. I got too hot and itched too much to enjoy it, but with Christopher, I wanted to wrap his hard body around mine. Even in the hotel, we passed out away from each other, but this time felt different. There was so much to admire about him, physically and emotionally. I trailed my fingers over his chest and over the scar I remembered—tickling his side just enough to make him jump. "Yup, still ticklish."

"Gilly, don't even." He grabbed my hand and brought it to his chest again. "I'm trying to enjoy my post-sex vibe, so knock it off."

"You're bossy. I don't recall you being that way before," I teased, the weird feeling in my chest getting stronger.

He rolled his eyes and pulled me onto him so I lay on his chest, but this time, there wasn't a frenzy. He played with the ends of my hair and met my gaze. "I'm really falling for you. You're amazing in so many ways. I just...you inspire me at work. You care so much about your students and your friends." He swallowed and ran a hand over the back of his neck. "I'm in awe of your constant positivity, and it's selfish, but I want to be around you all the time. I know that's intense, but I want you to know where I'm at."

"Wow." I blushed tomato red at those words. That was the best compliment I had ever received. My face got hot, and my body hummed like I'd been electrocuted. I glanced down, staring at his chin instead of his expression eyes, and nodded. I should tell him about the money, the past, the false narrative he had of me, but I was selfish. This was amazing and had nothing to do with money, and I wanted more. He wasn't the only one who was falling into a dangerous, can't-come-back-from-this type of feeling, but I held my cards closer to my chest. Saying that out loud was too much, too fast. Instead, I exhaled and said, "I'm falling too."

"Thought I'd have to work harder to hear that from you."

"Don't ruin the moment by talking," I said, earning a smile from him. "It feels trivial to say that, but I don't think I've said that to someone in a long time. It's weird."

"I know what you mean. This is new for me too. We just gotta take it slow," he said, his voice deep and sweet. "Well, maybe not. I need to see you naked every other day, or I might not make it."

I laughed and rolled off him, stretching and trying not to blush as his gaze raked my body. "Want something to drink?"

"Yes."

He got off the bed with me and slipped on his boxers while I slid into an old T-shirt with *Parks and Rec* quote. I slipped into a new pair of panties and turned to find him staring at me.

"You good?"

"It's weird." He scratched his chest with his right hand as he tilted his head to the side. "I cannot get enough of you. Seeing you in just a shirt and those tiny red panties is driving me crazy."

"Christopher Callahan is a sex fiend. Noted." I winked before walking out of my room but yelped when he caught up to me and smacked my ass. "Hey now."

"Couldn't help myself." He grinned and cupped the back of my head to give me a deep, slow kiss. "Mm. Yeah. I need more."

He slid his hands up my hips and pulled me close, kissing me until I lost my breath before he let go. "Mm."

That's all he said before sitting on one of the barstools. His kiss flustered me. It was a *just because* kiss, and I had very little experience with those. With wobbly knees I considered what-ifs, and the possibility he would end this once he knew the truth unless I proved to him money wasn't everything.

"Okay, uh, drinks. Water, tea, wine, beer." I had my back to him, needing the extra space at the sudden intensity of the moment, and I inhaled slowly. *Chill out, Gil.* "I'm going for some white wine, you?" I said, turning to look at him. His brows were furrowed again, and he stared at me, hard and unflinching.

"Your posture got all straight, typically a sign something's wrong." He ran his hand over his jaw.

Did he know me that well?

"Nothing is wrong. I swear." I wiped up dust that wasn't there on the counter to keep my hands busy. "You said we'll take it slow, but some of these experiences are new for me. Post-sex drinks, kissing that doesn't lead to the bedroom, that sorta thing makes me overthink stuff."

His shoulders relaxed, and his smile held so much warmth and tenderness. "I appreciate your honesty."

"We gotta be honest for this to work," I said, shrugging before turning around to pour myself a glass. *I'm a goddamn hypocrite.* I got him a beer after he finally responded, and I chose to stay on my side of the counter.

He winked as we took a sip, and when we set them down, the uncertainty grew again. He must've sensed my turmoil because he walked to my side and tilted my chin up for another kiss. It was a kiss a girl could get lost in, and my eyes fluttered shut at the gentleness of it. "I have the best idea."

"What's that?" I mumbled, feeling drunk on him *again.*

"We spend all night and morning together. Then I can give you a ride to school if you want."

I could always use more time in my classroom and knowing he, too, dedicated so much time to it made me swoon. "That sounds perfect."

"Then tomorrow could be part two of our date." He grinned and dropped another kiss on my mouth before taking a sip.

"We're not done with date one yet, Callahan." I let my voice go low, and his eyes widened. "Let's enjoy the rest of tonight, hm?"

Chapter Twenty-One

"Hey," Christopher said, nudging me with his shoulder as we stood in the teacher's mailroom, checking our boxes and totally not flirting at work. "Nice dress."

His gaze dropped to my red polka dot outfit that I loved, but his heated stare made me blush. He had stayed the night, again, a week later, and had fun reaching under the flared skirt before we left for the school that morning.

"Behave, Mr. Callahan."

He winked before rubbing his hand against mine for a quick second. Then he exited with a large pile of papers from his slot. I had a few envelopes that I hoped were last-minute donations for the Future Teacher Scholarship that I wished Kayla would win. I had to drop all the funds off at the bank that afternoon. I shoved the letters under my arm as I carried a large stack of old magazines down the hallway. We were doing a messy creative lesson where students got to build their dream cast of a story we read, and it required glue, scissors, and a broom.

Many brooms because last year I'd found little pieces of cut paper months after the activity was done.

"Gilly, got a second?" APD said, poking his head out of his office.

His eyebrows were drawn together like normal, but there was more tightness around his eyes.

"Sure, yeah."

I went in, and he shut the door. That was the first sigh of alarm. He never shut the door unless it was a private conversation, which could be a lot of things. Maybe he'd found out about Christopher and me, and there was an HR rule or something. That was probably it. I took a deep breath and tried to decipher his mood. He didn't seem angry—if anything, he looked irritated. He spoke fast and tapped his pen against the desk.

"How are you?" he asked, sitting down in his squeaky office chair and putting his arms on the desktop. He sat still and tall, and I arched a brow at him.

"Dave, what's going on? I'm fine."

"I've dealt with a lot of crap in my time as an AP, but this is a first." He ran one hand over his face before opening the right side drawer. A yellow envelope came out. It was large and had Dave's name written in all caps. "I debated telling you about it because for one, I don't care. I need you to know that. It's your life and your business. There is nothing newsworthy of this. But I'd want to know, and I'm pretty sure you would too."

"What is it?" I asked, my voice going three octaves too high. Was it a bank statement? Proof of my money? A flash drive with evidence of me doing a kegstand in college? A photo?

Shit.

The photos Samantha took.

The magazines fell from my arm, making a loud slap on the tile, and Dave seemed to wince. "This." He pulled out some card stock and pushed them across the top of the desk.

Sure enough.

It was the photo of me on top of Christopher—who remained hidden—where it was clearly me. She had to have gotten right next to the car to get this detail, and damn. It looked raunchy. I was on top of a guy, in a car, making out with fogged windows and everything. I sucked in a breath, and all the blood rushed to my face.

How goddamn embarrassing to have this conversation with my boss.

"I-I..." I couldn't finish. Shame and anger consumed me. I stared at the ground instead of his face. If he was disappointed or disgusted or anything, I didn't want to know. "Was there a note or anything?"

"Just a sticky note saying did I really know my employees. Honestly, this doesn't even get my blood pressure raised. Someone has beef with you, they don't do this kinda bullshit at a school. Again, this isn't going to get you in trouble or fired or anything like that. I just want to warn you. Something doesn't sit right with me about it. Have you gotten any threats or messages like this?"

Just Samantha.

"No," I lied, gulping and meeting his worried gaze. "Nothing."

"Be careful. If you do, I think we should file a report that you're being watched." He took the photos of me and Christopher and shoved them back in his envelope. "I'm going to secure these in a file cabinet for a few weeks, and then we can destroy them. I don't want to get rid of evidence if we need it later."

"Right, yeah," I said, trying to relax and settle the blood from rushing to my ears. This was a whole new level of bullshit from Samantha. Telling Fritz or even Christopher was one thing, but the pictures? To my boss? At my job? This was a new low, and that meant she was getting desperate.

"You'll tell me if you feel unsafe or anything, right?" he asked, his tone reminding me of my father's for a second, and it made me smile. He did look out for his staff, and I appreciated his anger on my behalf.

"Yes. I will."

"Good. Try not to worry, and I'm sorry I had to tell you this. Just wanted to be upfront."

"Got it. Appreciate the truth," I said, wincing at my hypocrisy. I collected all my materials and stood up, making sure I had the donations still intact, and went out of his office with my mind swirling.

What was her goal here? To get me fired? To scare me into paying her more money?

I wasn't so sure because this made me all the more determined not to pay her a cent. Not one penny. How dare she do this? Yes, I made the mistake of paying her to leave all those months ago, but I was done.

This was it.

I stormed into my classroom, set the materials on my desk, and took the donation checks and put them in my top drawer with the rest of the money. I locked it with a tiny key I wore around my ID badge and paced the front of my room. I felt like I'd run two miles from the walk from Dave's office. That's how hard my pulse raced, and sweat coated my skin. I had to end it. But what would be the best way to get Samantha out of my life?

Two little knocks at my door broke my intense brainstorm session, and I forced a smile for whoever was there, but it fell off my face when Samantha stood there, her red lips curved into a wicked, terrifying grin. "Oh hello, Ms. Carter."

"Get out of my classroom."

"Oh, see, I can't do that." She waltzed in and giggled as she handed me a sheet of paper. "The volunteer coordinator placed me here. There's some kid who needs extra help or something. I don't know, don't really care. I'm thrilled I finally get to work with you all day."

My eye twitched. "I don't want you around my students."

"Too bad," she said, eyeing the top of my desk and laughing again. "You seem…tense. Tough day being an heiress?"

I wasn't a violent person, but the urge to shove her against the wall made my hands twitch. She hurt my brother, tried to get me fired, and would be around *my* kids? No. Absolutely not. "Listen, you—"

"Gilly!" Christopher came into my room, his beaming smile stopping my heart for a full two seconds. It was so beautiful and filled with warmth and joy, all directed at me, and when he walked up to me and lifted me off the ground in a spin, he planted a loud kiss right on my mouth. Right in front of Samantha. "She got it. Kayla got the scholarship!"

"Wait, really?" I put my hands on his shoulders, trying to get him to take a step back, but at this point, Samantha already knew about us. I cleared my throat and jutted my chin toward my unwanted guest, and Christopher turned his head to his left a bit and winced.

"Ah, excuse me, Samantha. Sorry about that," he said, laughing, and a hint of red tinted his cheeks. "Got a little carried about with my girl here."

Samantha tilted her head to the side. "Aw, how cute."

"My sister won a scholarship for future teachers, and Gilly here is a huge reason for it. God, I'm so happy and thankful for you," he said, pulling me into a half-hug again. "My parents are thrilled. She got the email ten minutes ago. Will you come over for dinner to celebrate?"

"Uh, yes." I nodded, tears almost stinging my eyes at how happy he was for Kayla. My bullshit and mess had no place in this moment, and with a lot of effort, I pushed all thoughts of Samantha to the back of my mind and gave the man I liked, a lot, my attention. "I'd love to celebrate with you all. She is so deserving."

"Tonight." He grinned again and ran a hand over my shoulder and squeezed. "I can't believe my sister wants to be a teacher. I know the amount isn't huge, but it's enough to show her she can do it. She can apply for scholarships and get financial help and go to school. She's been so glum about it all, and this sparked a new wave of motivation. I cannot thank you enough. Seriously."

I stared into Christopher's tender and excited gaze and knew this was more than just *liking* him. So much more. It was in my bones, wanting to see him and his family happy and thinking about him all the time. "She'll be phenomenal."

He shook his head a few times and turned to Samantha again. "Sorry to interrupt you ladies, just had to share the news."

"Interrupt anything, Christopher. I don't mind," Samantha said, her flirtatious tone obnoxious as hell.

Christopher didn't notice, or if he did, he didn't give any indication of it and stared at the magazines. "You working in here today, Samantha?" he asked, the same kind tone he always used with the students, which irritated me. He had no idea she was a literal monster.

"Yup. Got assigned to the Ms. Carter for a while. Heard all about these grants she writes for all this stuff. Isn't it amazing how her room looks like this?"

"Amazing is a word. I'd go with busy, overdone, distracting," he teased, winking at me and making my face flush hot. "But yes, Gilly is…the best."

Samantha did not like that. Her facade cracked. An ugly snarl overtook her face. Christopher was too busy staring at me to notice, and I needed to get him out of there, stat.

"Could I trouble you for help for a second?" I asked him, his eyes lighting up, and he nodded before I even finished the sentence.

"Anything, yeah."

That one word, *anything*, said in his teaching tone sent the last wall around my heart crashing down. He meant it. He would do anything for me, and the fear that this wouldn't last when he found out the truth was enough to cause my stomach to cramp.

"What you need, Gil?"

"Scissors. Lots of them."

I walked out into the hallway and toward the teacher's lounge where we stored supplies we could use and share. There were boxes of crayons, markers, glue, scissors, tape, and cleaner. I got two boxes of scissors and he got the glue, but before we headed out of the empty room, he stopped me near the door by putting one hand out and resting it on my hip. His face was serious—all hard lines and a firm mouth, and anxiety had my throat closing up.

"What is it?"

"I'm so glad I met you." He looked around the room before dropping a slow, wonderfully teasing kiss on my mouth. He tasted like coffee and perfection, and I leaned into the embrace. "I know we shouldn't do this at work, but I had to. You helped my sister. That's…" He stopped, shook his head with a little smile, and ran his thumb over my bottom lip. "Moving back to this town made me nervous. Was worried I wouldn't like it or feel stifled. But damn, teaching next to you has been worth it."

"Christopher." My damn eyes were stinging again.

He smirked, like he knew the absolute chaos raging inside my heart, and he let his finger drop when someone approached the door. We didn't say anything else when we made the way back to my room, and we dropped the materials off at my activity table. The kids were going to lose their mind with this activity. They loved it, every year, and even if Samantha was assigned to my room, it would be too chaotic for her to do anything damaging.

Or so I hoped.

DESPITE HER BEING IN MY ROOM, SAMANTHA WAS uncharacteristically quiet most of the day. She was kind to the students, which was the only redeeming quality she had in her gold-digging body, and as long as she treated the kids with respect and kindness, I wouldn't glitter glue her ass. The last student left for the day, and once he was out the door, I shut it and turned to face her. She was at least helping me clean up the mess, but there was no way there wasn't an ulterior motive.

"You're done, Samantha. I'm not paying you a dime after the shit you pulled. Tell Fritz, Christopher. I don't care. You came after *my career* when you know how much this means to me." My voice shook a bit as I stared down someone who I had thought was a good friend. A woman I thought would be my sister-in-law. Her eyes got wide, and she took a step back from me.

Good.

"You can attempt all your blackmailing and bullshit, but it is done. You are not worth a penny."

"I'll get back with Fritz," she said, lacking all her normal confidence and bravado that made me waltz around like she was in charge. That was no more.

Dave said I couldn't get fired from those pictures.

Fritz was interested in another woman.

Christopher…well, I had to tell him before she did.

"No, you won't." I laughed and crossed my arms over my chest in a power move. "What are you going to tell him? Oh, *your sister paid me money to leave.* He'll see right through it. Why would you take my money?"

"I'll make something up. I'll say you threatened me."

"Why would I do that when I was helping him pick out a goddamn engagement ring?" I said back, my adrenaline making me feel invincible. How the hell did I let this woman rule my mind the last month? She had nothing. No power but her empty threats and two lies that I could fix. Fritz might be pissed at me, but there was no excuse for her leaving.

She flinched and blinked really fast, her attention moving to the wall I shared with Christopher. "I'll tell him."

"Right, because he wouldn't understand the power of sibling love. You heard him talk about his sister. Why wouldn't he side with me?" I asked, almost believing my own words. "End this scam. You will not win."

Samantha's lip curved up into a terrifying scowl, and her hands shook. "Fuck you, princess. You don't deserve this life."

She stormed toward me, and I readied myself for a punch or a slap or something, but it didn't come. She burst through the door, and her footsteps disappeared into the hallway.

Holy shit.

In our constant back and forth, I'd won that round, and damn, it felt good. I leaned against the door and took a deep breath, confident in what I told her. Fritz and Christopher would forgive me. I knew it. But I still had to tell them before it was too late.

Chapter Twenty-Two

Dinner with the Callahans was nothing like the ones Fritz and I had growing up. We had fancy tablecloths and extra silverware. There were always guests and proper dinner conversation. We took turns speaking, and we had to ask to be dismissed from the table.

The Callahans were loud and messy, and it was beautiful. Christopher's mom would talk over their dad, and Kayla would interrupt with something absolutely off topic. They each played a different role within their familial unit and seeing them all together made me miss my parents.

They weren't neglectful or anything, but they lived abroad and traveled all around the world, often too busy to visit. That's how my upbringing was until high school. Traveling and never being in one place too long. Seeing Christopher smile at his mom or joke around with his dad—even though he was frustrated with his dad's behavior —just showed how much love the man had for his family. He wouldn't let his mom carry anything to the table from the kitchen, and his manners just made him sexier.

"My little girl...a teacher like her brother. Isn't that something?" their dad, Curt, said, patting Kayla's hand a few times before going back to their pizza. He was built like Christopher, strong and lean, and had graying dark hair that fell over his forehead. His smile was a lot like his son's, tight but lit up his face.

I also learned pizza was the go-to celebratory dish at their house. Specifically, pineapple and ham, which weirded me out because pineapple on pizza was weird. It was a fruit. Fruit did not belong on pizza, but whatever. I didn't judge. Not when our family was over the top in our celebrations. We had lobster at ours, usually with some imported wine from France too. But having cheap beer and pizza seemed so much more special.

"I don't know if I want to teach first grade though. The kids seem messy." She cringed, giving us an apologetic look, making Christopher and me laugh.

"What grade would you want? Do you have a preference? I could talk to our boss to see about you observing a few classrooms at each level to see what you like best," I said, taking a long swig of the beer. "I had no idea I wanted first until I student taught second grade and realized yeah, that wasn't the level for me."

"That would be amazing!" she gushed, her young face bursting with ideas and potential.

I loved how excited she was. The scholarship wasn't enough money to pay for a year of school or anything, but it was a starting block.

"Gilly is the reason she even got this grant," Christopher said, putting his arm around me and scooting his chair closer to mine. "She's the treasurer for the program and works with the junior high and high school on getting donations."

"Thank you, Gilly. We cannot tell you how much this means to us," his mom, Carrie, said, her gaze moving to where his hand rested on my shoulder.

He didn't introduce me as his girlfriend, but he made it obvious we were together. Her light blue eyes were so similar to Christopher's. It was quite clear he was a replica of both his parents. He had his mom's thick brown hair and eyes, but his dad's build.

"Oh please, this was all Kayla. I heard fifteen students applied for it. Your application and letter of recommendation must have been impressive."

Kayla burst into a smile again, and I felt her joy in my bones. "This is the coolest, honestly. I didn't think I'd actually get it, you know? I can't believe there is like a whole lunch for it, too this weekend."

"I know! I love how they make a big deal out of it. It's impressive, and you deserve all the food they'll provide," I said, looking forward to the luncheon the high school ran that Saturday. All the sponsors helped out to make it run smoothly, and while I enjoyed seeing students get recognized for their hard work, it would be more special knowing Kayla won.

A brief silence came over the table, and we all took a few bites to finish the food. It amazed me to see their dynamic—how Christopher doted on his sister and mom and obviously loved his dad, but there was tension.

The money. The con man.

I wondered about that night we were together and he'd suspected I stole from him. He never said if the money turned up, and I made a mental note to ask him about it. I finished the beer and looked up to see his mom staring at me with a half-smile on her face. I grinned back, hoping it didn't come across weird because his mom was totally sizing me up.

Was I good enough for her son? I hoped so. It had been years since I met a guy's family, and the butterflies made me feel like Kayla. A high school girl meeting her teenaged boyfriend's parents before a dance. Sweat dripped down my back and pooled just above the waist-line of my dress, and I shifted in my seat.

"So, Gilly, Christopher seems quite fond of you."

"Mom, stop it," he said, the tips of his ears getting red. "I told you, none of this. That was the deal. I'd invite her over, but you don't say a word."

Kayla giggled and rested her chin on her hands, watching us like a tennis match.

I winked at her before leaning into Christopher's side. "Aw, you're blushing. How adorable. You're fond of me, huh?"

His gaze sliced to me, but amusement circled around those mesmerizing eyes. "You damn well know how I feel."

"Well, would you enlighten us about it? It seems Kayla knew all about her, yet I know nothing," his mom said, making it really dramatic and elongating her words. "Sorry, dear, my son just thinks that being an adult means he doesn't have to share things with me."

"No, that's totally fine. I like it when he's off-balance. He's too in control at work, so I like when he's flustered. Makes me feel more normal."

Everyone snorted at that, and his mom's eyes warmed. "You work right next to each other? So, this has been going on since the beginning of the year?"

"Not exactly," I said, smirking as Christopher's thigh tensed against mine. "We were enemies at first."

"Wait, is *my brother* the guy you were telling me about that day?" Kayla asked, her eyes big and wide as she stared back and forth between Christopher and me. "No way!"

"Yup. Sure was."

Christopher groaned and finished his beer before running a hand over his eyes. "Okay, we're leaving. We came here to celebrate Kayla's accomplishment, not embarrass me and talk about feelings."

"Oh, but it's so fun," I said, pulling his shirt when he tried to get up. He let me pull him back down because he was obviously larger and stronger than me, and my stomach swooped like I went upside down on a roller coaster when he kissed me right there, at the table, in front of his family.

That was a message.

I blinked at him, something like love dancing along my skin at his attention and sweetness. It was exhilarating and terrifying to feel my body being attuned to it.

He sat back down with a loud sigh and kept his hand on the back of my chair. "Thirty more minutes. That's it and no grilling her, please."

They followed his wish, and the rest of the time was spent chatting about Kayla's senior year and how they liked living in the house. I told them all about their neighbors, my best friends, and their dad knew who Brock was and was a huge fan. I might've led him to believe

Brock was really friendly. I snickered to myself, already imagining him getting grumpy.

"Ready to head out?" Christopher said, hugging both his parents and sister before coming to stand next to me. "I have to finish reading my book tonight."

"Like you have homework," Kayla scoffed, rolling her eyes and leaning in to give me a side hug.

"We have a book club. You should try it sometime. Might learn something, kid," he said, high-fiving her with a grin. "Seriously, congrats again. You deserve it. Can't wait for the ceremony."

She smiled and looked at me. "I get the check next week. I appreciate not waiting until the end of the year because it could help pay for the college application fees. It's stupid that they charge just for an application. Don't they get enough money?"

I cringed at the truth to her words. This wasn't an issue I even knew about or thought about, yet it was very real for a lot of students. "So glad you got it, Kayla. Happy for you."

"Thank you, Ms. Carter." She smiled at me before pulling out her phone and walking away without a glance. It made me laugh. Kids were still kids, no matter the age. They could be talking to an adult one second and technology or something more exciting pulling their attention the next second.

Christopher put his hand at my lower back as we said good-bye to his parents and walked outside. It was just after eight, and the evening had already begun. Fall would be here soon, and that meant scarves and pumpkins and bonfires. I smiled up into the air, taking a deep breath at the fresh scents.

"That wasn't so bad, right?" he asked, giving me a weird look when I opened my eyes and smiled at him. "Are you smelling the air?"

"Yes. It almost smells like fall. It's my favorite."

He shook his head, pulling me up against his chest and hugging me. My body warmed at how close we were. I reached up to run my fingers through his hair. He trembled a bit, and I made up my mind then and there.

I was telling him this weekend. Before this got deeper.

"Any way I can convince you to come to my place tonight?" he asked, his voice deep and sweet and so tempting.

I shook my head. "I need to see my brother. We haven't caught up in weeks, and that thing I was telling you about? It's not cleared up."

He frowned and nodded in understanding. "Yeah, you better take care of that. I know it's bothering you."

"But this weekend…" I said, waiting for him to make the move. He did, and I sighed when his lips touched mine. It was a polite kiss, but it wasn't enough. It didn't matter that we were outside his parents' house and that they could be watching. He tasted like beer when his warm mouth parted, and I took advantage and *kissed* him hard.

He groaned into my mouth and clung to me harder, like he couldn't get close enough to me, and my body hummed with emotion, for him. He pulled back, breathless, and let out a strangled breath. "Okay, don't kiss me like that and leave me alone. Not fair."

"Didn't mean to go that far," I said, wiping the back of my hand over my mouth. "Damn. You tasted good, and kissing you makes me forget to think."

He hummed in response and pulled me in for a tight hug. "Go talk to your brother. I'll see you tomorrow, and I swear, you better not have plans tomorrow night."

"Not even with you?"

"That's my girl." He patted my ass and watched as I got into my car. My body felt heavy with dread, and I wished I could hold on to this joy for a few minutes longer. Putting on the radio, I made my way toward Fritz's place, chewing my lip to the point it stung.

But when I got there, I thought I might throw up that pizza and beer.

Gilly: I'm outside Fritz's place. I can't do it.

Grace: You don't have a choice. Get it over with.

Gilly: I might be halfway in love with Christopher. The truth could make them both hate me.

Gilly: I'm shaking.

My phone buzzed, and I answered it, almost on the verge of tears. "Hey."

"Fritz will be furious with you, but it won't last. You keeping this from him and he finds out another way…that is what you're avoiding. Don't back out. I know he has this new girl, but we both know it's a rebound. That man thinks love is a joke now."

"It could ruin our relationship."

"You already are by lying," she said, her voice curt and unhappy. "Call me when it's over, but Gil, this is me playing the best friend card. Suck it up. You did it—you tell him the truth."

"Right," I said, my throat throbbing from the nerves. "Okay. Okay, I can do this."

"I love you, no matter what. Now stop stalling." She hung up, and I called my brother.

"Gilbert, what's up?"

"You home?"

"Almost. Why?"

"I'm outside your place. I need to talk to you about something, in person." I cleared my throat, and I swore I heard him suck in a breath. "Everything is fine…just…how soon?"

"Ten minutes. What's going on?"

"We'll talk when you get here. It's about…Samantha."

"Not making me want to drive faster."

"Please, Fritz. This is important."

"Okay, be there soon." He hung up, leaving me with ten awful minutes to fill my time.

I scrolled through my phone and checked work emails, replying to the NHS sponsor for the high school, saying I'd deposit the money that I collected tomorrow so it could go to the winner. Thinking about Kayla and her smile made me feel a little better. Not a lot though. Headlights appeared on the street, and I gripped the wheel a few times before getting out and leaning against my car door.

Fritz parked his Beemer, got out of the car with his tie loosened, and narrowed his eyes at me. "Okay, what is it?"

"Let's talk inside?"

"You're freaking me the fuck out, but fine." He rushed to get the door open to his place, and once he shut it, he crossed his arms and stared me down with the same intensity he did to anyone who messed with us.

He just didn't know it was me who screwed up this time.

"What did that *woman* do?"

"It's...about me, actually." I twisted my fingers together as every part of my body told me to lie, to avoid this, but I couldn't. "I'm the reason she left you."

"How do you figure?"

"Because I paid her ten thousand dollars."

Chapter Twenty-Three

MY BROTHER FROZE. HIS EASY SMILE WAS NOWHERE TO BE FOUND, and he looked like a gargoyle, stuck in place with hard lines around his eyes and his lips in a flat, disappointing line. Thirty seconds, then forty, went by, him not saying anything or moving at all, and tears filled my eyes at what I had done.

"Fritz…let me explain."

"You better fucking explain because there is no *rational* reason that I can think of that makes sense as to what you said. So please, enlighten me." His jaw turned to stone, and he crossed his arms over his chest and stared at me with nothing but fire and loathing in his eyes.

"She was conning you. I saw her at a bar with another guy and went up to confront her and overheard them talking. She wanted the ring, for you to make it official, so she could steal from you. It was all part of her master plan with this other guy. She knew about the proposal, the bank accounts."

He swallowed hard and blinked. That was his only physical reaction to my words.

I dug my nails into my palms.

His nostrils flared, and he pushed off the door, pulled on the ends of his hair, and stomped into the kitchen. "And you thought what? Paying her *off* was the right move? You didn't think to tell me about this shit then?"

"You were going to propose to her, and she was a master manipulator, Fritz. She already prepared for that scenario when she saw me. She would've painted me as the bad guy."

"So you assumed I wouldn't believe my goddamn sister?"

"You were blind to her! You loved her! I couldn't take that risk! I made a call and had to live with it. Now, she's at my school, black-mailing me again and—"

"*What?*" he yelled, his face getting blotchy and red, and he slammed a fist on the counter. "She is back, blackmailing you at your school. You didn't think to tell me any of this this whole fucking time?"

"Yes."

"Gilly." He took a long breath and clenched fists at each of his sides. "You can't just throw money at all your problems. You should've told me...I would've...God. I can't even look at you right now." He closed his eyes, and I could see him physically shaking. Each tremble felt like a stake in my heart.

"She's been threatening to get back with you this whole time, to convince you she needed space, that commitment freaked her out." My voice came out scratchy and hoarse, and my stomach tightened with nausea. "She took my car for a week and is trying to get me fired. I just...I'm sorry. I'm so goddamn sorry." A sob escaped my resolve, and I hunched over, hating myself a little bit.

My brother, normally one to hate to see me cry, stood stock still, his lip curling in disgust as he stared at me, hard. "You don't get to be the victim here," he said, his words cold and icy, a tone he had never used on me.

"I know. I *know.*" I sniffed and wiped my eyes with my hands, the mascara from that morning melting off and making me look like a rabid raccoon. "But Fritz, I'd do it again if I had to. That woman, that *con artist,* is the devil."

"This entire time...the past six months...I've thought it was me. That something was wrong with me. That I wasn't allowed to fall in love. That it wasn't for me. But now I find out my sister *paid a woman* to leave me. This messes with you. God, I can't..." He huffed and went into the fridge and got a beer, twisted off the cap, and downed half of it. "Did you and Grace just laugh at my self-pity this whole time when I whined about how she left me? Did you enjoy seeing me be pathetic?"

"No, of course not. She didn't know." I moved to grip the back of one of the barstools and took a shaky breath. "She's a terrible human being, Fritz. I might've paid her, but if that meant protecting you from her, I'd do it a million times. Everything I've done, that I'm not proud of, was because I love you. So be pissed at me, I deserve it. God, I do. But there is nothing I wouldn't do for you."

His eye twitched, and he pressed his lips together until they were white. "There are so many fucking ways this could've been handled, and it's so *typical* Gilly to use your funds to fix things. I'm so pissed." He shook his head, and a vein popped up on his forehead. "I need to be alone."

"Right, yes, I'll leave." I wiped under my eyes and made a movement to head toward him but stopped. The look on his face made me second-guess myself. "I love you, Fritz. I'm sorry I kept this from you, but I'm not sorry I got that bitch out of your life."

He didn't say anything as I walked out of his condo, and the second I got outside, the door locked, and another wave of tears fell down my cheeks. We never fought. Not in junior high or high school or as adults. We worked things out and figured a solution. But this... I'd crossed a line, and I deserved the consequences. It just hurt not knowing how long it would take for me to repair the damage.

I sat in my driver's seat with a heavy heart that just felt worse when Christopher's text came through.

Christopher: hoping it goes okay with your brother—he'll forgive you, Gil. Your heart's too big.

God. I groaned into a fist, imagining what he would say when he found out the truth about me. He'd *hate* me. I cried again, already mourning the best relationship I'd had in years because there was no doubt it would end when the truth came out.

FRIDAY MORNING DIDN'T HOLD THE TYPICAL BUZZ AND EXCITEMENT. My mind and heart weighed heavier than normal, knowing I could've done irreparable damage to my relationship with Fritz. The way he looked at me, like I disappointed him behind measure, had my throat tightening and my eyes stinging as I walked into the building. I forced a smile as I walked by other staff members, but it felt tight. Fake.

I was upset about Fritz, and Samantha, but the fear bubbling up in my chest had more to do with Christopher. He admitted, multiple times, that money was a trigger for him, and telling him the truth could ruin us. *If I could just wait…*

"Hey, Ms. Carter," he said, smiling at me as concerned lurked in his beautiful eyes. "I made you your favorite tea this morning. I figured you'd need an extra pep in your step." He lifted up a navy-blue thermos and shrugged, like it wasn't absolutely adorable seeing him bring me tea.

That meant he bought my favorite kind and made it at home. It was so *him* to not just buy it at a café, and my heart swelled. "Thank you, this is so nice."

"I don't like seeing you sad." He voice dropped, and we walked shoulder to shoulder to my classroom. "You have this…energy about you that is addicting. I love how positive you are, and the way you bring joy to everyone. The least I could do is bring you tea," he said, moving his hand to brush his fingers over mine. "You want to talk about it?"

I sighed and *hated* how the guilt making my words come out choppy. "No. Maybe."

"Ah, well," he said, bringing his teeth over his bottom lip and letting out a slow breath. "I'm here when or if you want to talk, okay? You know that, right?"

"Yes, I do," I said, swallowing hard and knowing that I had to tell him everything. It would change things between us. That was for sure. But seeing him look at me with all the warmth, the concern, the patience…I was in love with him. The realization about knocked me on my butt. My head spun and the air was harder to breathe in, but it was true. He was my complete opposite in almost every way, but not where it counted. My bottom lip trembled as he looked over his shoulder for a second before getting closer to me. He cupped my face with one hand and half of his mouth quirked up in a smile.

"I know we're not supposed to show affection at work, but one kiss wouldn't hurt, right?" He grinned before dropping his mouth to mine in a slow, tender kiss that made everything better, and worse. "You'll get through this, Gilly. I know it."

I couldn't talk. Not when he looked at me like he might kind of, sort of love me too. I gripped the edge of his shirt, not wanting to let go because we had to talk. That night. He covered my hand with his and trailed his finger over my wrist before he said, "Let's each lunch in here today. Just the two of us."

I nodded. "Th-that'd be nice."

He let his hand drop and took a step back as footsteps sounded in the hall. He winked before leaving my classroom, having no idea the absolute turmoil going on in my mind. I sighed, sat in my chair, and gave myself ten seconds to mope.

This is my fault. I can fix it.

No, this is Samantha's fault.

No, it's mine. I paid her off. I lied to Fritz and Christopher.

Knowing the blame landed on me, and not Samantha, was a gut punch. It would've been easier to blame her, but Fritz's words seemed to penetrate my heart. I did throw money at my problems, not even realizing it was an issue. No longer though. Knowing I survived three weeks without any credit cards or frivolous fund brought me a sense of pride and joy. It was the same pride and joy I felt after receiving the Teacher of the Year award.

I spun in the chair to eye the glass award I got last year, to hold it and remind myself I worked hard and could get through this. But it wasn't on the desk where I kept it. *Weird.* I frowned, trying to remember if I'd moved it for any reason, or maybe someone cleaned my room last night. *But the crew never moved things on my desk.*

Huh.

I opened a few drawers and hoped to see the flash of glass with my name on it. It didn't make sense for me to misplace it. Sure, I cleaned the shelf from time to time, but for it to disappear? No. That didn't make sense. The hairs on the back of my neck stood on end as a rueful dread crept into my spine. Maybe it was all the shit with Samantha that had me thinking the absolute worst. This was a simple fix. It had to be. I probably moved it, or maybe it fell and someone cleaned it up. That made the most sense, even though my gut warned me this wasn't a coincidence.

I took a sip of the tea Christopher brought me just as Timmy walked into the room with a big yawn. "Good morning, Timmy. You're early today."

He finished his yawn, and like most days, he went from zero to eighty. "If you eat a lot at night, a lot in the morning, and a lot at lunchtime, you make a baby."

"Oh, really?" I asked, amused at this random conversation. It was just what I needed to pull myself out of the weird funk.

"Yes. My mom is growing a baby from all the food. My dad makes the food and feeds her. I eat a lot, too, but Mom says I don't grow babies. You be careful with the food, Ms. Carter. You'll grow a baby."

I snorted into my mug, enjoying the real laugh and smile. All my drama could wait until later—distracting myself with littles was the best plan of action. We went over our ELA lesson and then math, and soon enough, it was lunchtime, and after getting them into a line and taking them to the cafeteria, I was ready to hang out with Christopher and live in our bubble a little longer. When a couple minutes went by, I figured he'd gotten caught up with someone or something. It wasn't unusual for students to need help or a parent call to come through at lunch. But five, then ten minutes went by, and he wasn't in my room.

Now that I thought about it…Samantha had never shown up that day either. Was she in his room? I shoved my food to the side and stood up, needing to make sure she wasn't in his class telling him half-truths. My outburst at her could've made her retaliate. Fear and absolute worry had my chest heaving as I bolted into the hallway and strode into Christopher's classroom. It was empty, which was a relief and a curse. If he wasn't there, then where was he?

Where was Samantha?

I walked as fast as I could to the teacher's lounge and spied through the glass window that gave a peek into the room. Larissa was laughing with Marisa, Maggie, and Martha. No sign of Christopher or Samantha though. My sixth sense tingled like something was wrong. Where else would he, and Samantha, be?

This wasn't good. My stomach felt like a ten-pound rock sat in it, growing each second Christopher failed to show. Did he see the pictures Samantha took? Did he think it was someone else?

No. That didn't make sense. I gritted my teeth and searched every classroom on the way back to my room, still not seeing a sign of him anywhere. My nervous energy needed an outlet, and I couldn't sit down as more time went by, my gut absolutely a mess with worry. It wasn't until ten minutes later that the familiar thud of his footsteps sounded in the hallway, and I spun, seeing him stop just inside my classroom.

Wide eyes, fists at his sides, jaw tight, and I *knew*. Samantha had told him the truth. That was the only explanation for the hate in his eyes.

"Do you have it?"

"Have what?" I asked, taking a step back at the anger radiating off him. "Have what?"

"All that money," he said, shaking his head and curling his lip up in disgust.

Shit. "It's not what you think," I said, my voice losing its flare. All that dread, worry, and anxiety was exactly because of this moment. All these weeks leading up to it, and my brain seemed to shut down. All the explanations I had prepared in my mind turned to absolute mush seeing the hurt on his face.

"Oh, it's *exactly* what I think." He sucked in a breath, glaring even harder at me to the point I recoiled. There was no longer any tenderness or warmth on his face. It was pure fury, and my throat clogged up.

"Christopher, wait…" I said, unsure what to say, how to make this right. "I just——"

"You just what?" He stepped into my room, hands on his hips as he barked out a laugh. "I fell for it. Bravo." He clapped his hands a few times, the loud slap of his skin together making me jump. "Your act was *incredible.*"

"It wasn't an act." I swallowed hard and stood up. He was as approachable as a raging bull. His gaze shot to my feet, warning me to not take a step farther, and I stopped. "*None* of it was an act. What I feel for you has nothing to do—"

"Stop. I was right about you. God, I'm such an idiot. Just like my goddamn father." He rubbed his temples and looked up at my face, all traces of tenderness gone. "You must feel good at night, falling asleep knowing your entire life is bullshit. All of it is a lie," he said, spitting out the words and his face getting red. "The students, the staff, your friends…they have no idea who you are, who you really are, but I don't care. I'm done. I'm done with you. Don't talk to me again, Gilly. You've done enough to me and my family."

He stormed out of my classroom, and I went numb.

Devoid of feelings or emotions as all areas of my life were imploding. I knew my money was going to get in the way of my love life. My worst nightmare had come to life, and I couldn't stop the sob from escaping. I cupped my hand over my mouth and stifled the sound, feeling my heart break into a million pieces.

Chapter Twenty-Four

GRACE WAS TOO BUSY TO HANG OUT, FRITZ SAID HE *NEEDED TO GET out of town,* and Christopher didn't answer any of my texts. It didn't matter what I said. He was stubborn—something I admired and hated about him, and his mind was made up. My stomach soured thinking about his issues with his dad, with his friend's ex who had taken all the money from him, the emotion in his voice when he talked about Kayla's lack of college fund. His aversion to money made sense. I understood *why* it bothered him—it shaped his life in dark moments, and I got it.

What I didn't get was how it was an absolute deal breaker. Yes, I kept my inheritance from him, but it didn't change anything about us. Not how I felt, or how I would act.

My worst fear had come to life.

I was so worried about someone *using* me for my money, the realization that I would be discarded because of it was hard to swallow. A pang in my chest grew as I got ready for the luncheon. How exactly did one act after what had happened? I would apologize about not telling him about my family's month. I owed him that, but everything else was on him.

My blood burned with a little bit of anger as I put on a bright-red dress, lipstick that matched, black pumps, and an extra layer of mascara. If I had to face him, I was going to look good. That was just basic math. I knew money would hinder me from finding love or happiness or anything resembling what Grace and Brock had, but that wouldn't prevent me from making Christopher regret his decision. Finding love wasn't for me, but I still wanted to look good as I figured out how to piece my heart together. My phone went off, and while my stomach somersaulted from the sound, it was just an *I love you* from Grace.

I'd always have her, and that thought helped as I got into my car and drove toward the high school. Listening to Taylor Swift normally soothed whatever mood I was in, but her badass tunes didn't do their magic this time. Everything felt hard, heavy, and sad. Cars lined the parking lot, and I shoved my keys in my purse as I walked toward the entrance. A police officer stood outside the building, scowling as I approached.

"Morning," I said, forcing a smile.

"Gilly Carter, right?"

"Um, yes?" I frowned, instantly thinking about anything this could be about. I sped, sure, but I hadn't run any red lights or anything. "Is everything okay?"

He sighed and jutted his chin to Fern, the high school NHS sponsor. "My name is Detective Peter George. I need to ask you a few questions about the scholarship funds you collected for the National Honor Society scholarship for future teachers."

"Okay." I swallowed and held my bag tighter to my body. "I deposited the portion from the elementary school earlier this week. I could find the receipt for it if I ran to the elementary school if you need proof. Why are you asking me? Did something happen?" My pulse raced like I'd run up and down the stairs ten times without a breath, and I tensed, trying to read his facial expression.

"Yes, there's evidence of you depositing the three thousand dollars," Fern said, frowning and sharing a look with Detective George. "But, Gilly, you withdrew it yesterday morning."

"No, I didn't." Blood seemed to leave my head, making me dizzy.

I wobbled and tried to make sense of her words as I blinked away the confusion. I was at school yesterday morning.

"Gilly," she said, huffing a little bit. "I'm sure there's a reason for it. I'm not *blaming* you or accusing you of anything, but it was your signature on the deposit slip."

"What are you talking about? I didn't withdraw anything." I blinked and tried to settle my pulse, but it was out of control. Sweat poured down my back, and the same gross feeling of dread I got yesterday came back full force. Something had happened. I shook my head hard, reiterating the truth. "I was at work. At school. All day."

Fern's brows came together, and she shifted her weight back and forth. "You didn't withdraw the amount of three thousand dollars?"

"What? No. Why would I?" I stared at the detective.

He uncrossed his arms and narrowed his eyes. "Could you verify that you were at the school?"

"Yes," I said, so loudly a few people walking into the high school looked our way. "I use my key card to get in, which time-stamps it somewhere. I don't know who tracks it, but I can call my boss or something. I always get in early."

I blinked a few times, trying to clear my head. Friday morning now felt like a month ago, even though it was just yesterday. *Christopher.* The stab of hurt, disappointment, and anger hit me right in the gut, but I pushed that away. They thought I took money, which I absolutely didn't, and this took priority. I spoke to him that morning. He would vouch for me…right?

"I talked with a colleague. Christopher Callahan. He would tell you I was at the school. Could you explain to me what the heck is going on? I am not comfortable with what you are both insinuating."

"I got a call yesterday from one of the recipients," Fern said, cracking the knuckles on one of her hands. "They tried to deposit the check they received yesterday morning, and it wouldn't go through. There were no funds, so I checked the history."

Everything seemed to still at that moment. The air, my heart, the dread that I'd felt all morning finally made sense. Before she said the words, I already knew. I knew in my gut.

"There was a withdrawal check from you, with your signature and everything."

Samantha.

It had to be her. The checkbook sat in my top desk drawer, where it always had, and guilt clawed at me, inside out. I was naïve. Foolish. I never thought she'd steal from *students.* The bitch probably impersonated me. She could've forged it easily. After all, she had a check from me for ten thousand dollars.

"Well, it wasn't me. That checkbook must've been stolen from my classroom," I said, my face growing hot and my throat getting dry. I needed water, or a straight shot of tequila at this point. "I would never do that, but I know who would."

"Oh?" Detective George said, the skeptical look shifting to curiosity. "What makes you say that?"

"Samantha Sullivan. She's been blackmailing me for the past month, and I refused to pay her. Things escalated between us, verbally." God, the last thing I wanted to do was confess this to an officer and Fern. Word would spread fast, but at this point, I was done caring. My relationship with Fritz and Grace would always be there, Larissa would always have my back, and Christopher wouldn't care to hear it.

I straightened my posture and crossed my arms. "In fact, I never saw her at the school yesterday. That would be convenient for her to disappear after cashing the check, right? Make it look like me, then ditch. I'm telling you. Christopher Callahan can verify, along with the school cameras, that I was on the school grounds all morning. I would never take those funds, and I have zero motive."

Detective George nodded a few times before saying, "I'll be in touch, Gilly. Thanks for the information."

He walked away, leaving me and Fern in an awkward standoff. She blinked a bit and let out a long, nervous laugh. "It was your name. I had to call them."

"I understand, but if you would've called me yesterday, I could've explained, and we'd have a better chance of finding Samantha." I rubbed the back of my neck with a free hand and wished I could be at home, not dealing with this. It was tough to swallow the fact that this started because I paid her off all those months ago.

But what if Fritz had married her?

That was the tricky question that made me not feel like absolute garbage. Would I do it all again, knowing it led to this?

If it protected Fritz, then the answer would always be yes. That was something I'd have to reconcile with. "We won't find her though. She's smart. I can have a check for you next week to replace the funds she took."

"Gilly, that's a lot of money," Fern said, her lips parting just enough to tell me she was excited. "You can't do that."

"I have the money. It's no big deal," I said, content with knowing I could at least solve the situation myself. "I'll have it next week."

"You don't—wait, Gilly," she said, reaching out and putting a hand on my forearm. "I'm sorry."

She looked it. Her eyes were downcast and her shoulders slumped as she twisted her mouth into a grimace. "The check with your name —it was your signature. I've seen it before and assumed, well, the worst."

"I understand." I forced a smile. "Let's forget about it."

"Right, yes, of course." She let go of me and smoothed her black-and-white dress. "The luncheon. I could use your help if you're still up for it."

"Here for the students, so yes."

She exhaled, and like a snap of fingers, she went into action. "Okay, we have the food table on the north side of the gym and tables spread out for each family. I'd love help getting the vases to every recipient."

"Lead the way."

She bustled in and I followed, plastering on my best *teacher* smile at the various families and high school students all around. The ceremony was for any scholarship winner, not just the ones NHS sponsored, so there were athletes there too. It was nice to see school support all sorts of scholarships and not just sports. Fern pointed to a black table filled with vases and gold flowers—the school colors—and then gestured to the open area. "Each family gets one."

"Got it."

I scanned the room, and all the air left my lungs when my gaze landed on Christopher's table. He was here with Kayla and his parents, and his eyes were almost black as he stared a hole through my chest. Anger. Hurt. Betrayal. All of it showed through his once-tender gaze, and I looked down at the gym floor. It was too much. How could I see him, every day, and be okay? God, this sucked.

Busy myself.

I picked up two vases of flowers and made my way to one table. The family thanked me, and I set the other one at the family farthest away from the Callahans. I could come up with an excuse, pretend to be sick and leave, but that felt cowardly. I didn't want to see him, but I refused to let him dictate my actions. No. I finished putting the vases on all the other tables, and it was just theirs now.

I sneaked a glance and found him glaring at me, and it sent a wave of anger through me. How dare he look hurt and put off, like he didn't break my heart with those words? Money might've been an issue for him, but it was for me too. I'd always had to worry about people wanting me for my wealth, and while the opposite took place, it was still about money.

I glared right back at him and grabbed the final vase and made my way toward their table. Neither of his parents noticed me, and it wasn't until Kayla saw me that she smiled.

"Gilly! Hi!"

All four pairs of eyes stared at me, and I gave a half smile. "Hey, Kayla, congrats again on winning."

"I didn't know you'd be working," she said, taking the vase and smelling the flowers. "These are awesome."

"Glad you like them," I said, waiting for the ball to drop, for someone to say something hurtful, but it didn't come.

"Are you able to join us for a bit? Christopher didn't say a word about you being here," his mom said, shaking her head at her son, who she probably thought kept information quiet. He must not have told her we were over.

"Oh, I can't. Sorry." I jutted my thumb over my shoulder. "Gotta help out." I didn't wait for a reply before walking away, and my fingers trembled as I went back to Fern. I wasn't running away, but I needed a second. "I'm running to the restroom."

I found my way to the bathroom. No one was in there and I rested my hands on the sink, taking a few deep breaths. *I can do this.* I got my hands wet and patted my neck right when Kayla walked in. Her eyes, so similar to her brother's, looked sad as she approached me.

I cleared my throat. "Hey, congrats again."

"He's been horrible, Ms. Carter. Miserable. I asked him not to come because he's been so grumpy about it. I told him it wasn't you. There was no way!" She spoke fast, her words blurring together as she came up and grabbed my arm.

"What are you talking about?"

"The scholarship funds. I know it wasn't you who took it."

Oh my God.

It felt like someone poured ice-cold water all the way down my body. It flowed through my veins, going into my bones enough to make me shiver. The missing funds, the recipient who tried to cash the check, the police. Christopher thought I stole the money.

He doesn't know I'm an heiress. He thinks I'm a con artist.

I closed my eyes as the heartache intensified. This was worse. So much worse. But this had nothing to do with Kayla, who worked her butt off for the award, and I shoved the heartbreak down. "I didn't take it. Thank you for believing that. You'll get the funds though, Kayla. I promise."

She frowned, looking older than an innocent, doe-eyed teenager. "I'll be fine. I just hate seeing him like this. He's a mess, Ms. Carter, and I keep telling him it's a mistake, but he's stubborn as hell."

"What happened?" I asked, unable to move a single muscle until the truth spilled from her mouth.

"I skipped school to cash the check with my dad. We were excited, but it wouldn't go through." She blew out a breath, and her jaw trembled a bit. "We called the number on the congratulation letter, and a woman told us we needed to check with the treasurer of this specific scholarship."

"Which is me."

"Christopher didn't tell us much after that, just that the money was gone." She bit her lip and looked way to stressed and worried for a seventeen-year-old. "I overheard him tell my dad you had it, but I don't believe it.

I nodded, feeling like I was watching this happen in a movie. He didn't leave me because of my lie about being an heiress. He left because he made the worst possible assumptions about me without saying a goddamn word about it. "You're right, Kayla. It wasn't me, but we'll find who forged the check. I promise you. You earned this scholarship, and I'll do whatever I can to make sure you get it."

She gave me a sad smile, one filled with questions and worry. "He'll come around."

"Not sure that matters now, Kayla. Thanks for checking on me though." I patted her arm and left the bathroom. I didn't deserve a guy who refused to even talk to me about any of it. He ended it, and he could deal with his decision. I finished the shift with my heart in my throat and walked out into the parking lot without looking back.

I should focus on saving the one relationship that would be there forever. My brother.

Chapter Twenty-Five

MY ENTIRE WEEKEND FLEW BY IN A BLUR OF TEARS AND ICE CREAM, and Grace coming over and watching *Real Housewives* with me. She knew me well enough to let me mope. That's what I wanted. A full mope session.

The mopey weekend didn't help the heavy, constant weight in my chest as I got ready for work. I put on a denim dress with red flats and accessories, and matched my lipstick to my bracelets. I looked decent, and hopefully, I could use that confidence when facing Christopher today.

Not even my playlist could make my mood better, so I turned off the music entirely and focused on getting to school safe. I parked in the mostly empty lot, getting my teaching bag and laptop out of the back seat as a loud muffler rolled in. I knew that car. *Christopher.*

I ducked my head down, walked faster, and made it through the front doors, not even bothering to stop in the mailroom so I could find safety in my room. Why did I get involved with a coworker? How long would it take before I moved on? Why did he make me want to cry and punch his handsome face at the same time?

I moved so far into my class that I spilled scalding hot tea on my hand and winced. His footsteps neared my door, stopped, and for one second, a sliver of hope burst inside my chest like a sudden summer storm. It started as a sprinkle and quickly spread to more. *Was he going to come in? Talk to me? Admit he was an idiot?*

The footsteps continued, and his door opened, shut, and that was it.

The hope died, and I squeezed my eyes shut. Why did I keep doing this to myself? Thinking people could change when they proved to continue to resort back to themselves? Samantha, Christopher… ugh. I sniffed, checked emails, and got ready for the day.

I needed to pick up some copies and made my way to the teacher's room. Hushed tones and wide eyes greeted me as I walked in, and Larissa beelined for me with a crease between her brows. "What's going on?"

"Everyone is talking about it."

"About what?" My pulse pounded against my temples.

"Samantha Sullivan stealing thousands of dollars!"

My heart skipped a beat, and I glanced around the lounge, expecting her to be there and laughing like this was part of her plan. There was no way everyone knew. This had to be a setup. A game. Another way to make me suffer. "Wait, what?"

"There was a detective here this morning asking questions, and you know how social media is…someone posted about it, and we all know."

I gulped, scanned the room, and met every pair of eyes looking my way. I lowered my voice and yanked Larissa closer to me. "Does everyone know she tried to frame me?"

"What? No! Girl, what is going on?"

"Not here." I swallowed and tried to wrap my brain around the new information. Everyone knew Samantha was a thief and not the bubbly, flirty woman who volunteered here the past few weeks. Her act was over, which was a relief, but if it wasn't known that she tried to frame me, that meant Christopher hadn't heard the news yet. He surely would've told everyone what he thought of me. "I need to go."

She nodded, reached over, and squeezed my forearm. "We'll catch up."

I gave her a tight smile and kept my head low as I marched down the hallway. An officer walked out of Christopher's room and smiled when he saw me. It was Detective George.

"Oh, hello," I said, a cold sweat breaking out down my body. How much drama could I survive? I was about ready to overdose on drama.

"Ms. Carter. Good morning," he said, jutting his chin toward my classroom. "Let's talk for a minute."

"Yes, right, of course." God, I'd done nothing wrong, yet I was still a nervous wreck.

Christopher walked out of his room with a huge frown on his face. He parted his lips, like he wanted to say something, but I shut the door to my room and faced the Detective. "Is there news?"

"Well, we have an APB out on Ms. Sullivan, and we've been questioning the staff to see if we can figure out where she would go. I'm hoping we'll find her, and the money, soon." He eyed my desk and said, "We confirmed that you were with Mr. Callahan Friday morning at the same time the withdrawal happened. His statement, along with the time stamp of the key card, clear you."

"I would hope so," I said, annoyed that if Christopher had to submit a statement, that he *knew* it wasn't me who took the money. Yet I hadn't heard a single word from him. Not one. "So what's next?"

"We'll keep an eye out for her. Your school resource officer knows about it, and if she steps foot on campus, she'll be taken in. We'll ask a few more questions from people who knew her to see if we can find her, but after that, the case will remain open until we find her. In full honesty though, there isn't a high chance we'll recover the cash."

"I figured. Thank you for the update."

He nodded and left the room, and my head spun so much I had to sit down. When was the last time I ate? My stomach tightened with heartbreak and worry all weekend, and eating food tasted like dirt. My body felt hollowed out, and I quickly found a protein bar in my desk and took a few bites. I wanted to gag at the starchy taste, but I needed something in my body or I'd pass out.

Could I just be sick today? There were twenty minutes before school started, and the thought of smiling and being happy for students seemed like so much effort, I rubbed my palms over my eyes as loud voices came from the hallway.

"You're an idiot," someone said, the deep timbre of a voice sounding a lot like...no. There was no way. Why would my brother be here?

I looked up and saw him through the glass in my door, his face set in determination and facing Christopher's direction. *Oh no.*

"I don't care what you *thought.* You're a fool for breaking her heart. Our money doesn't define us, okay? Her money should have no role in your relationship. God, I promised myself I wouldn't say anything to you. I'm here for my sister."

Fritz shook his head at my buddy teacher before pulling the door to my classroom open. His face fell when he saw me, and he set a large bag on the floor before rushing over and wrapping his arms around me. "Gil."

That was the final straw in my fragile resolve. I cried against his chest.

"Hey, it's okay, Gil."

"Why are you here? How did you...why did you say that to Christopher?" I sniffed and pulled back, wiping under my eyes. My brother, who was always busy at his job, was at my school. On a Monday morning. "Are you okay?"

He flashed a smile before putting his hands on his hips and staring at the window. "I'm all right, yeah. Look, I needed a few days to think about everything, and the same thing kept coming into my mind."

I swallowed and watched his jaw tighten and his eyes turn dark. Without saying her name, just the thought of her made a dark cloud in the room.

"I would've done the same thing if it was you. I'd still do it if it meant I was protecting you. I get why you did. I hate that you didn't tell me about it or that you've been suffering in silence for weeks. There were red flags with Samantha. I just chose to ignore them."

"So you forgive me? We're okay?"

"Yes. I forgive you, and we're always okay." Half his mouth lifted up in a smile, and he let out a long breath. "I brought you a gift as an I'm sorry and congrats on surviving a month without money."

"Oh."

I forgot about that. Completely. Today was the day I could go back to spending whatever I wanted, but the thrill I thought would be there wasn't. Money would always be an issue in my life, whether someone else wanted it, or someone hated it. "The money Samantha stole...I could pay it back."

"What are you talking about?" He narrowed his eyes and his body seemed to stiffen. "She stole from you?"

"She used my checkbook and forged a withdrawal from the school account, so one of the scholarship recipients couldn't cash their winnings. It just happened to be Christopher's sister. You never answered my question. Why did you say that to Christopher? How did you know?"

He gritted his teeth and glared at the shared wall we had. "Grace called me yesterday and filled me in on some gaps. First, she wanted to make sure I was okay and then told me that he didn't know a thing about our money. I get why you kept it from him, but that doesn't make sense why he broke your heart."

"He thought I stole his sister's money."

Fritz closed his eyes and shook his head. "Idiot."

"He has...an issue with money. I don't know." My heart lodged in my throat as another wave of sadness hit me. "I'm so glad you're here and that you forgive me. Are you able to stay the whole day?"

"No. I have a meeting in an hour, but this was more important." He came to me again and hugged me. "Love you, Gilbert. You'll get through this."

I squeezed him tight and sighed when he broke the hug. "Love you too."

"Enjoy the present. I'm sure you'll like it." He grinned and walked backward out of the room. "Any chance I can see Larissa before I go? She is your hottest friend."

"Get out." I snorted, my lips curling up and feeling weird on my face. Smiling used to be so easy, and now it felt like a chore. *This will pass.*

The gift ended up being books. Tons of books for my classroom library. All different Lexile levels and themes, and I closed my eyes and pressed my lips together. This was perfect and the best gift. I loved stocking my classroom library, and the thought of seeing kids read them made a dull thrill of excitement rush through me.

I would be okay. I had him and Grace, and if Fritz could survive heartbreak, I could too. At least Christopher didn't try to steal money from me. With that last thought, I focused on the saying *it could always be worse* and put all my energy on my students.

It wasn't until the end of the day that Christopher stood at my door, and I got a good look at him. His hair was messier than normal, his eyes lacked their typical glint, and his jaw was so tense, it had to hurt his teeth. But that wasn't my issue. Not at all. He took one step into my room, looking nervous as hell, and he gulped. "Could we talk?"

Chapter Twenty-Six

Could we talk? The nerve of this man. We could've talked all weekend. He could've talked to me Friday instead of assuming I stole from his sister. I gritted my teeth together and hated how I still loved him. My feelings couldn't just disappear over a few days, but I wished they could. I would give anything to not feel my heart thump against my ribs when he was near me or how my skin tingled around him.

"What is there to say?" I crossed my arms over my chest and sat on the corner of my desk. "I tried calling you *all weekend.* You chose to ignore me."

He ran a hand through his hair and groaned, the sound making my toes curl into my flats. "I was pissed. I thought—"

"I know what you thought." I bounced off the desk, my adrenaline racing like I was on the Tower of Terror. His sister had clued me in on why he'd gone frigid. "That I was a con artist. That I stole from your *sister.* That I would take thousands of dollars away from a student, even though my entire passion and profession are to help kids. You thought that I withdrew the money, and instead of asking me about it, you jumped to your own conclusions. Con woman Gilly, right? Like how you thought I stole from you back in the spring all over again."

Oh, I was on a roll. I couldn't stop. The words I wanted to say all weekend flew out of me, my hurt and pain needing to release at the person who'd caused my tears. My breath came out in pants as I neared him, and the absolute horror on his face made me feel a tiny bit better.

"There's a lot you don't know about me, and yes, I will admit that is my fault. It is my fault I didn't tell you I'm an heiress. I have a lot of money. So much that I'm going to replenish the funds your sister missed without even batting an eyelash. Fritz and I don't talk about our inheritance much because someone *always* wants a piece of it."

Christopher sucked in a breath and took a step back like I'd hit him. "Gilly," he said in his deep, ragged voice, but I cut him off.

"My brother used to date Samantha, and she used him because of his money. She had a whole thing planned out to rob him after she got him to fall in love and propose, and yeah, I paid her to leave him once I found out. She's been blackmailing me all school year for more, threatening to tell Fritz the truth about what I did. I was ashamed and let her play me because my brother is my best friend. But I'd had enough. When I finally said no, she stole the scholarship funds and framed me. I get that it looked bad, but Christopher...you couldn't even ask me about it or even think there was a mistake?" I sniffed. My eyes stung as I looked at the ground. "You never trusted me."

"Is that why you didn't you tell me about your money from the start? Because of Samantha?" he asked, the sadness oozing out of his voice and wrapping around my body like a hug. A small part of me wanted to hug him, to comfort him, but he'd hurt me too much, and the trust was broken.

"Yes. Money is an issue for me too, Christopher. I wanted someone to love me who didn't care about my money or what I could do for them."

"Gilly, I do—"

"No." I held up my hand, stopping him. I couldn't hear anything else from him. "I don't think there's anything left to say anymore. You made sure of that when you refused to talk to me during the worst three days of my life."

His gaze shuttered, and his entire face crumpled. "I'm sorry."

"Yeah, me too. This could've been something great, but you broke my heart." I took a breath and closed my eyes, hearing his footsteps echo on the floor as he left my room. This was for the best. We were done, the truth was out in the open, and we could move on with our lives. Even though it wasn't my fault, that it was Samantha who did it, I felt guilty that Kayla would suffer because of me, and that wouldn't do.

I typed an email to my financial advisor, asking for a check to be made to the NHS fund. At least that piece of my heartbreak puzzle would be fixed.

THE NEXT DAY WAS LIKE A SCENE OUT OF A MOVIE. I WOKE UP, preparing to suffer from seeing Christopher, but it went in a totally different direction. My phone rang, and Detective George wanted me to come to the police station. They'd caught her. Now they needed me to verify that the checkbook they found in Samantha's car was mine, as well as another item found in her possession.

The best part wasn't even that they found her by searching for her —it was because she ran a red light. The irony of it all brought a real smile to my face, and my stomach exploded with butterflies as I drove toward the police station. I called APD on the way there and explained everything to him—the blackmail, the truth about my back-ground, everything, and his only response was *I'll get you a sub.*

It was at times like this, I was grateful for his unwavering business tone. I parked and smoothed down my dress before walking into the front doors of the station. I had never been there before, and the brick building was intimidating as hell. Was she there? Was Samantha somewhere in the building with handcuffs? God, the thought of it made me smile. That woman deserved what came her way.

"Where should I direct you?" a stern woman said as I approached the front desk. She had dark hair twisted into a bun that pulled her forehead back. It gave me a headache just looking at it.

"I'm here to speak with Detective George."

"Right. Hold on." She picked up a phone, said a few words to whomever was on the other end, and hung up. "He'll be here in a moment."

"Thank you, great." I stood back and took a deep breath, trying to figure out what the other item was. At this point, nothing she did would've surprised me, so it could've been any of my clothes, teaching supplies…I hoped it wasn't anything broken. A piece of technology? Something she took when she borrowed my car? A picture? It could be anything knowing her.

Office George appeared. "Gilly, please, come to my office with me." He ushered me through another set of doors and took us down a long hallway filled with offices.

The place smelled like stale coffee and dust, and I scratched my itchy nose as he went farther into the building. His was the farthest on the left side, and when he walked in, I saw the item right away. It was glass, had my name on it, and sat in the middle of his desk.

Of course.

That's what she would take. *I knew I didn't misplace it.*

"My Teacher of the Year award," I said, a rush of warmth going through my body. While it wasn't an expensive item, it was invaluable to me. One of my proudest achievements. Seeing it in the office made my anger return, ten times worse. How dare she take my award? How dare she take the one thing she knew I was proud of? She'd heard me talk about how much this meant to me back when I thought we were friends, when I thought we would be sisters-in-law someday. She used that information to hurt me, and I clenched my fist at my side. This woman was the absolute worst. "She had this in the back of her car?"

"Yes. Any reason she would've taken it?"

I made a raspberry with my lips and sat down in the chair and faced him. His large frame made his desk chair squeak, and I crossed one leg over the other. "She *hated* other people's happiness. It was her whole mission to ruin other's joy because she always wanted what she couldn't have." I stared at the glass award and shook my head. "For whatever reason, she targeted my brother and me. It was about our money at first, but I think it turned personal. She volunteered at my school to mess with me and fooled everyone into thinking she was a decent human being."

"When we brought her in, she didn't seem even remotely remorseful."

"She won't. She'll blame us, me, somehow." I cracked my neck from side to side, hoping that would relieve some of the tension in my body.

"I'm glad we found her then." He moved around and pulled out a plastic bag with a bright-green checkbook in it. He set it on the top of the desk and asked, "Is this yours?"

"Yes. It's the one I kept in my desk drawer." I chewed my bottom lip, remembering how I saw her leaving my classroom that one time. I couldn't find a single thing out of place, but did she take it then? Or plan to? It didn't matter at this point. "That's what you found in her possession? It almost seems too good to be true."

He nodded. "In her car. Great. That's all I needed."

"What happens now?" I asked, grateful it was *almost* over.

"She's been arrested, and now that we've verified it was your checkbook and award, we'll have a rock-solid case. We'll charge her for all the money, but there's no guarantee she'll pay it back. If she got it in cash, there's no way to trace it."

"I figured as much." I swallowed and held out my hand. "Thank you."

He took it, shook it with a firm grip, and nodded. "You're welcome. Glad we're able to figure this out, and fingers crossed she'll pay the missing funds."

I nodded and left the station, already knowing that she wouldn't have the money to pay Kayla back. I was glad I already reached out to my advisor to pay the missing amount so Kayla wouldn't suffer.

I called APD and took the rest of the day off. I let Grace and Fritz know I was at home and shutting off my phone, and I took a bath, read a book, and tuned out the world. Christopher knew the truth,

Samantha was going to jail, and I could give Kayla the funds back that were taken because of me. Once that was done, I could focus on getting over Christopher Callahan and finding a way to get my heart back.

Chapter Twenty-Seven

I took two more personal days and spent all Thursday making sure someone was in the room with me. Larissa before and after school, and I beelined it to the teacher's workroom for lunch—all to avoid talking to Christopher because I wasn't sure I wanted to hear from him. We'd said our pieces, and we needed to move on. He called me four times between Monday and last night, and a part of me knew he at least deserved to hear what happened with Samantha and the money. It was about his sister after all, and by having the conversation before the weekend started, I could get it out of the way and close the book on this drama.

I walked into the building like I'd done countless times and was met with whispers and looks. Fragments of *Samantha* and *money* and *arrested* carried my way, and I snorted. Gossip moved at a million miles an hour here, and I had no doubt word had spread about her arrest, how I was involved, and maybe even about my inheritance. Detective George talking to other teachers didn't help the gossip, but everyone knew her act was up. I didn't care if people knew about me anymore though. If people knew, they did. I had my circle I trusted, and that was enough for me.

My anxiety eased a bit knowing that Christopher had to feel awful that he got it all wrong. That was a shitty feeling, but it served him right. Two wrongs didn't make a right, but it helped to know we were both suffering.

I barely got into my room Friday morning before he was at the door, looking rougher than the previous day. His hair was messy and he hadn't shaved in a while, but the dark bags under his eyes made my breath catch in my throat. Rough was too kind of a word. Disheveled. Awful. Upset.

"Are you—how are things?" he asked, his voice gravelly like he hadn't had a drink of water in weeks. "Is Samantha..." He paused, took a breath, and met my gaze. "Has she been arrested? Is it true?"

"Yes. They found my checkbook and my teaching award in the back of her car after she ran a red light." I snorted, but I wasn't really amused. "They're going to do their best to make sure she pays the funds back to your sister," I said, keeping my voice robotic. "And if not, I will because even though I didn't steal a dime, she did it because of me."

"Gilly."

No. I squeezed my eyes shut at the raw emotion in his voice, and I held up a hand. "No. No. I can't do this. We already talked. I..." I trailed off, unsure what to say. It did no good to talk in circles, to repeat all the emotions I felt.

"I'm so sorry, I just—" he said, but I stopped him.

"Not here," I fired back, glaring at him as he winced. "There was *plenty* of time for us to talk before you broke my heart. If we do talk, it'll be when I want to. If I ever want to."

He hung his head and nodded before he opened his mouth again. Nothing came out, and thank God for Larissa because she marched into my room, not bothering to apologize to Christopher.

I updated her on the turn of events with my buddy teacher, and like she always, she had my back.

"Girl, *girl.* You will not believe what I just heard."

She wrapped me in a hug, and I melted into it, hating that I'd kept her out of everything until recently. We shared all our teaching ups and downs, but this entire thing felt like a private battle. However, the gossip destroyed any sense of privacy. "You good? You got blackmailed from someone's ex? Is that the truth? This is like straight out of a movie."

"Fritz's ex, yeah." I sighed, letting my attention move to Christopher's broken expression for a beat. "I'm not proud of it, but yeah, she blackmailed me all month, and when I finally put my foot down, she stole from a kid."

"I knew something was up with her." Larissa pursed her lips. "She would always change her opinion based on who she was talking to. It was weird, you know? But dang, I didn't realize she was your brother's almost fiancé. Your brother is *trouble*. Sexy, but trouble."

I snorted, needing the humor, and just the gesture of smiling made my face feel tight and awkward. Without meaning to, I sneaked a glance back at Christopher and regretted it. He looked so broken and sad, but it was his own damn fault. "Is there anything else?"

He flinched and shook his head before leaving my classroom, and Larissa raised her brows, a question already on her lips.

I shook my head. "Not yet. Too soon."

"You got it. Just tell me what you need because the rumors are insane. One of the PE teachers was saying you were part of a scam robbing teachers out of thousands and the other was going on about you being into blackmailed for porn?"

"Good lord, both are false. Also," I said, pausing before putting my hand on her wrist, "I should tell you before you hear a rumor. My brother and I come from money. We don't talk about it a lot, but we're…wealthy."

"Okay," she said, laughing. Not a single dark look crossed her eyes, and I was so grateful for that. "I mean, if you think we're not still going for half-priced margaritas, then you're wrong."

It was the right thing to say, and I finally felt at ease in my own classroom. Samantha had taken that away from me for too long, and it was about time. The kids arrived twenty minutes later, and Larissa stayed the entire time, catching me up on all the latest drama during the time I'd been sucked into the Samantha-Fritz-Christopher world, and I welcomed the escape.

One teacher was on an improvement plan and was fighting it,

even though we all knew she wasn't great. Another staff member was caught having an affair with a teacher at the high school. Major yikes.

And of course, Larissa informed me all about her new man.

It was the perfect way to get back to normalcy at my job, and soon enough, the students arrived all excited about the Fall Parade the next weekend. Today was the kickoff assembly for the event, and my stomach clenched remembering how Christopher and I partnered on it.

It would be so fun to work together! I said, weeks ago when I was a fool. But no matter. I'd get through it. That's what I did.

Thank God for kids because the second they walked into my room and starting rambling about elephants and toilets, I got sucked into their questions. One after another, all stemming around what the sub told them in my absence. I was *dealing with family stuff.*

"What kind of family stuff? Like messes?"

"Or someone cried? My sister cries a lot."

"Stuffed pizza? I want to miss school for stuff."

My smile was real again, and by the time the assembly started in the afternoon, I almost forgot about the tightness in my chest. Our classes were expected to pair up together and enter the gym at our specific time. It was madness trying to get hundreds of kids into the gym at once, and I got them all in single file, ready to march out the door. Tyler was our line leader, who was always in the front and led the way. He beamed when I announced the classroom jobs for the first quarter and stood in the front of the room as we all got lined up. I went row by row, ensuring our door holder, Jaime, was at the door with a smile.

Our light saver job went to Patty, who had to double-check we shut the lights off in the room every time we left, and she had yet to miss. Our caboose, the last student in line, was in charge of making sure everyone stayed in order and did their job. Ethan was our caboose, and after we were lined up, Tyler started our walk to the gym. Jaime stood at the door, checking that we all walked through before she found her position in front of Ethan. It took weeks to get it down, but damn, I was proud of my kiddos.

Christopher was in the hall with his students, and our eyes met for a second before I forced myself to focus on the little ones. They were excited and talked loudly as we made our way, and a deep soft voice stopped me.

"Hey, can we talk after school, *please?*"

Maybe it was the absolute desperation in his eyes or the way his voice seemed to shake a little bit, but I nodded without thinking it through. "I guess. We need to talk about the float anyway," I said, keeping my posture straight and not looking into his welcoming blue eyes. They were deep pools of emotion, and a trap.

He gave a tight smile and reached his hand out, like he wanted to touch me, but he stilled it and rested it against his thigh.

Deep breath.

We brought our kids to the gym and took our seats for our section, both of us required to sit on the end of the row so we could watch our kids. That put him behind me, his knees hitting my back a few times.

"Shoot, sorry." He fumbled, blushing and trying to reposition himself with long legs. It was so awkward, my God.

"It's fine."

It wasn't fine. His familiar scent of soap and laundry detergent floated my way and made me so sad. A week ago, I would've leaned back into him to tease him, or winked, or done something to distract him. But now, I could barely look at him without my heart hurting.

"Okay, Mountains!" Dave yelled over the microphone.

All the kids cheered as loud music played. Everyone started dancing, and I tried my absolute best to not think about *after school*. Our talk, what we had to say to each other. The more the assembly went on, the larger the knot in my gut grew.

The rest of the afternoon passed by in a blur of nervousness, anger, and exhaustion. Dealing with Samantha, and the emotions that the entire situation evoked, made my body sore all over. It was like I had the flu of the heart, just no fever and constantly on the verge of tears.

Thank God I wore a black shirt that day. I sweated up a storm until the last student got onto the bus, and I made my way to my room. Christopher stood outside my door, leaning against the wall and looking so out of place, it would've been endearing.

"Let's get this over with," I said, unlocking my door and walking in, not bothering to hold the door open for him. I sat at my desk, put one leg over the other, and crossed my arms. It felt like a battle stance, a *don't mess with me* position like I used all those weeks ago when he came in hot and determined to hate me.

He swallowed hard and took the chair opposite me, the piece of furniture squeaking in protest with his weight. "Will you look at me?"

I gritted my teeth and met his gaze, hating the absolute aching feeling where my heart was. "There. Happy?"

"Gilly, I can't…God," he said, putting his hands over his face and groaning. "I messed up. I messed up so damn bad."

"You said we'd talk about the float." I kept my voice firm and was proud that it didn't shake or give away the absolute misery I'd felt since he assumed I stole from his sister. "Honestly," I said, waving my hand in the air, "I don't care what you do for it. I'm out."

"*You're* not going to help decorate it?"

"No."

"But Gilly, this is your thing," he pleaded, his eyes going wide again. He sighed, shaking his head as he looked at the ground. "I did this. I broke the most spirited person on campus."

He hit the top of my desk with a fist, making me jump a bit, and our gazes met for one, two, three horribly long seconds. "I let my shit with my dad cloud my judgment and ruin what we had. I can't sleep imaging how much I hurt you, and God, I am so sorry, Gilly. I need you to know that."

"You never even let me explain," I snapped back. "You tossed me aside without even a conversation. If you told me your suspicions, I would've told you the truth about my inheritance." I swallowed. "Just do the float however you want. I'll show up for the parade because I have to, but…whatever we had is broken."

He frowned harder and wiped his palms over his eyes for a few seconds. "Is it true she took your Teacher of the Year award?"

"Yes." I huffed, annoyed that he was still here, talking to me, looking as sad as I felt. "Why?"

"It got me thinking. It would be crazy…but…that night we spent together," he said, looking at the ground and shuffling his feet together.

"The night you thought I conned you?" I said, enjoying at the way his shoulders tensed.

He sucked in a breath and narrowed his eyes at me. "One of my awards was missing. It was stupid—just a *Fantasy League Champion* award I had on my counter. Do you think it's possible, somehow, that it was…Samantha?"

I closed my eyes, thinking about that night. I'd thought about it a million times, trying to figure out if I did something wrong to make him hate me and all this time. I forgot that I *thought* I saw her at the bar. But before I could investigate, Christopher joined me, and I forgot about it. "She does seem to like framing me and stealing awards. It could be. No way to get proof of it though."

"Right."

"Right," I repeated, rubbing my lips together as the awkwardness set it. Samantha could've stolen from him all those months ago, somehow making it work so Christopher would think it was me. It was her MO. But even if he could prove it, it wouldn't change a thing between us. "Well, you should go."

He didn't say anything else. He looked at me for a second longer, his expression absolutely broken, but I shook my head. He walked out of my classroom, and that action had more finality to our relationship than everything else. We'd said everything we wanted to say.

Chapter Twenty-Eight

DESPITE KNOWING CHRISTOPHER AND I WERE DONE, I COULDN'T help but search for his car every morning I got to school and every afternoon when I left. He was there before I was and left after I did. Before everything happened, we would've stayed late together—worked on the float, gotten dinner, then probably would've spent the night at one of our places. A tiny part of me wondered how he was doing with the first-grade float. I had tons of items in my checkout cart online that I hoped to overnight ship once I survived my month of no spending, but the thrill of shopping died when my heart broke.

There wasn't the same amount of joy in buying stuff for the parade. It was easier to sit back and let Christopher do everything. He could figure out the costumes, the decorations, getting the kids the right roles for the float. It was different to take a back seat, but it was what my heart needed.

Getting over someone when you saw them every single day was a special kind of pain.

I smiled with my students, chatted about Larissa's dating life at lunch, and spent my evenings with Grace or Fritz. Everything would be okay, eventually. One day at a time, one sip of tea at a time, and one smile at a time.

Friday, the day of the parade, I woke with butterflies. Despite the funk of a broken heart, it was hard not to be excited for the celebrations. Our Fall Parade had two floats for each grade level, the middle school band came down and marched, and it was the perfect kickoff for the high school homecoming game that night.

Our town went *all* out when it came to homecoming, and if I cared more about football, I would've been able to talk about the game. But sports were Grace's thing, not mine, so I nodded when people talked about our big rival. So not my thing. I liked the apple cider, the sweater weather, the smell of bonfires that lingered all month, and the way the leaves started changing into vibrant colors all down the roads. I smiled as I got out of my car and walked into the building. The Fall Parade meant Halloween was right around the corner, and I could binge-watch horror movies and start prepping for my costume because broken heart or not, I would go all out for that. Being a witch or a princess could be fun. A witchy princess had a nice ring to it.

I hummed as I brainstormed different costumes as I neared the entrance. Footsteps thudded behind me, and I stilled, preparing to face him. He had kept his distance all week, so this sudden appearance had my nerves frayed.

"Gilly, hi," Christopher said, almost running from the parking lot to catch up to me.

He wore faded jeans and a school T-shirt that fit him really well, and my mouth dried up fast taking in his appearance. It was not fair to still be so attracted to him despite the hurt. My skin practically tingled around him.

"Hi," I said, *hating* the rush of emotions that overtook my body every time I saw him.

His expression was tight, nervous even, with a tense jaw and wide eyes. I adjusted the strap of my bag on my shoulder and shifted my weight from foot to foot, not attempting to make this situation easy on him. He shoved his hands in his pockets, and his brows came together the longer I kept quiet. He did this, to us, so he could figure out how to make it not as painful. This was not my job.

"Um, so, we got the float ready," he said, rocking back and forth.

"Great."

"I think you'll like it," he said, his voice hesitant and lacking all the confidence I was used to hearing. No smug tones, no flirty teases. Christopher was unsure of himself, and it brought me a little bit of joy.

"I guess we'll find out." I shrugged again, my heart hammering against my rib cage, the thuds getting louder the longer we were near each other. He smelled good, like he always did, and I wanted to wrap myself around him in a hug. It *sucked* how I trusted him with my heart. "I should—"

"Your outfit. I have it," he interrupted me and awkwardly dropped his bag onto the ground and shuffled through it. "Don't go. Hold on. You'll need it to get ready."

He got on a knee as he chewed his bottom lip, frowning hard as he removed everything from his bag. Bright colored shirts, a straw hat, seashells…they all were on the ground, and his breathing picked up. "I put it in here. I know I did."

"Well, if you think I stole it, I didn't," I said, hating the wave of regret flowing through me at my comment. It just happened.

He stilled. His entire body morphed into a statue, and when he glanced up, he looked a little broken. "Gilly," he said, his voice breaking on my name.

I blinked. What could I say? What could I possibly do to make everything between us better? My eyes stung a bit, and I sniffed, taking a deep breath and shaking my head. "I need to get my lesson prepared for today."

He wiped a hand over his face and stood, his mouth parted and his eyes filled with regret and sorrow. "I'll find your costume. The kids should have all theirs in your room too. Can I ask you a favor? I know I don't deserve it, but if you could…don't look at their costumes yet."

I took a few steps toward the first-grade hallway and stopped. I faced him. "Why?"

"It'll be better if you see everything at once."

"Again, why?"

He stood to his full height and took a long breath before he held my gaze. This time, there was determination and the usual *Christopher* confidence brewing behind his blue eyes. His lips curved up and a hint of his flirty smile returned, almost knocking the wind out of me. "Because it's part two of my plan."

"Part two?" I narrowed my eyes, trying to figure out why he was being so vague.

"There are three, possibly four parts."

"To what?" I asked, not bothering to hide my impatience. He was speaking in riddles, and I was already around him too much for the day. I'd have a break for the weekend, which would be great, but his *games* were annoying me.

"To get you back."

I sucked in a breath as he said the words, a slight glint to his eyes, and he gave me a half smile. One side of his lips quirked up, and he blushed, the reddening of his upper cheeks softening my attitude toward him.

Get me back.

He wanted to get me back.

Hope was a dangerous thing. The sliver of *what-if* worked its way into my heart, and the secret desire I thought about at night, missing him, came back fast. What if I did forgive him? Could I? Did I want to?

He let out a nervous laugh and ran one hand over the back of his neck. "Wow, I feel like an idiot saying it out loud like that. You look like you saw a ghost right now. I, uh, should go find your costume because I know I had it. You didn't take it, I know that. I never meant —well, I don't think...yeah. I'll see you later," he said, ducking his head down and speed walking right by me, leaving a rush of wind to hit my face.

Christopher Callahan was nervous, and I was so intrigued—the butterflies in my stomach, sweat dripping down my back, breathing heavier type of intrigued. I had an extra spring to my step as I made my way to my classroom, stopping at the door. Every desk had a wrapped item on it, and a message was written on the board.

Remember what we talked about. Don't tell Ms. Carter the surprise! -Mr. C

Oh my God, what was the surprise?

I cracked my knuckles and paced the room, absolutely torn about ripping open a bag and seeing what the hell he was up to, and wanting to be surprised. Did the surprise matter? Would the level of surprise make a difference if I did forgive him? He had a plan to *get me back*, and while it thrilled me, the more distance was put between what happened and now, the more I understood his reaction.

I didn't agree with it, or like it, and I'd lost some trust, but I understood it.

I grabbed my phone out of my bag and texted Grace. She would know what to do.

Gilly: C said he wants me back. Do I forgive him?

Grace: Gillyweed. This isn't something I will answer for you. This is your choice.

Gilly: But I need your guidance.

Grace: No. This is on you.

Gilly: I got drunk with you when you had a full meltdown about Brock.

Grace: We got drunk LAST WEEKEND.

Gilly: I miss him.

Grace: He was an idiot. He'll probably do something idiotic again. But G, he liked you without even knowing about your money. He pushed you. Challenged you. Made wrong assumptions but you LIED TO HIM too. If he knew the truth about your background, he never would've assumed you stole.

Gilly: Okay, you're supposed to be on my team.

Grace: I am, forever. That means standing up to your stubborn ass. Now, I gotta go. You'll know what to do.

She was right. Neither of us were innocent—he was just more guilty than I was. Sighing, I stretched my arms over my head and made the choice to not look. If he had a plan, I should respect it. And honestly, I was excited to see how it played out.

THE LAST HOUR OF THE SCHOOL DAY WAS DEDICATED TO OUR parade, but that meant no one could focus after lunch. Kids were so distracted and giggling and whispering all about the *secret* with Mr. C, and at that point, my face hurt from smiling. They didn't tell me the big reveal, but they told me he got us all matching costumes, he had a speech for me because he said something to upset me, the float was dedicated to me, I would get messy, and they all loved it.

It was all very promising, and before it was time to get ready for the parade, Christopher walked into my classroom with a card and a bright, hot-pink-and-purple Hawaiian shirt and a sheepish, goofy smile that made me curl my toes into my shiny yellow flats.

"Ms. Carter, we are ready for you to get into your costume." He handed the shirt over, and his eyes sparkled, like he had a million jokes to tell me but was waiting for the right moment.

I held up the very obnoxious, yet very *me* shirt. "Wow."

"You'll look great in it," he said, smirking as he winked at the students. They all got up at the same time, opened their bags, and put on shirts just like mine, large sunglasses, and mini beach towels. "Okay, you remember what we're going to do?"

"Yes, Mr. C!" they said, smiling with my buddy teacher, and nerves froze me to the ground. They were all in on this together. All of them.

"Find our float."

"Which one is it?

"You'll know." He grinned again, but held my gaze for an extra beat. "See you out there."

He hit the doorframe twice before leaving, and my kids lost their minds with excitement. Giggles and shouts, someone knocking over their stuff they were so amped up. I barely had time to register Christopher's excitement and totally forgot about it when APD came onto the speaker.

"It's parade time! Kinder through second, please find your way to your floats and get ready!"

Our line leader got up, and it was the quickest they ever got into formation as we headed toward the gym. Christopher wore a bright blue-and-purple shirt, along with his class, and his sunglasses were the extralarge kind clowns wore, and it softened my anger at him. He was such a goofy, good man.

"So?" he said as he got closer to me. His fingers brushed against mine, and that that small contact sent a ripple of electricity all the way from my head to my toes and I sucked in a breath.

All from our fingers touching. *Get a grip.*

"Can't wait to see the float." I shrugged, looking at the kids and back at him. "Guessing it's a barbeque or Hawaiian theme."

We got outside, but before we took a step, he held my hand and waited until I looked him in the eye. "Here it goes," he said, his usual confidence gone. "Our theme is *the beach.* You told my sister you never got to have a normal childhood with all the mission trips, and well, I know that's why you are so good at what you do. You want every kid to have memories—good memories—that last a lifetime, so we wanted to give you a good beach memory."

My heart lodged in my throat, and I blinked back my emotion. He guided me toward our float, and there was a sandcastle, fake palm trees, and a little pool with ducks. The kids jumped on the trailer, and one student pushed play on a boom box. Beach music started playing, and all the kids shouted my name.

"Ms. Carter! It's your first beach trip! You need to get on!"

"My mom says you need sunscreen."

"And you shouldn't get sand in your butt!"

Emotion overload. I froze, but a soft hand pressed on my back and moved us closer to the float. There was a large sandcastle right in the center and a little bench that went around the whole trailer so kids could sit. They were covered in beach towels, and one of the pools had water balloons filling it.

"What do you think?"

"It's a beach," I said, stating the obvious as I took in every detail. The seashells from earlier were on the ground. The kids laughed and danced, and Christopher's voice was smooth and really close to my ear.

"Part one of my plan was talking to my dad. I carried that wound for far too long and let his mistakes mess up my personal life in more ways than one. We talked it out and are finally in a better place, but I am *so sorry* that I let my issues get in the way of us, Gilly," he said, spinning me to face him. He didn't seem nervous anymore.

He looked hopeful, excited even with a small smile and soft eyes. "Part two was doing this float with every bell and whistle I could. Your story stuck with me, and I wanted to bring it to you."

"I love it," I said, taking in the scene. The other grades were released, and tons of kids and teachers were heading to their respective floats. Parent volunteers were all around, but they all faded into the background. Christopher's handsome face with long lashes and love swirling in his eyes had my own eyes stinging. "I can't believe you brought me the beach."

"It's part one of my apology."

"What's the next one?"

"This." He took a breath and moved us to sit down on the bench and took my hand. "I love you, Gilly. Your personality, your creativity, your smile. I want a life with you. Kids, you telling me I'm boring and me telling you that you use too many colors. I want it all, with you."

"What?" I said, damn well hearing him, but his words going too fast through my mind. *I love you* kept repeating over and over, somehow erasing all the tears and hurt from the past week. "You love me."

"Yes, God," he said, cupping my face and his brows coming together in a hard line. "I don't give a crap about your money. I really don't, and I'm so sorry I assumed you stole…looking back, there were so many reasons why you didn't. I just…I reacted without thinking, without talking to you. I will *never* do that again."

My fingers shook as he clasped them in between his large hands. He took another deep breath, his minty breath hitting my face, before he said, "Okay, this is from the heart here, so bear with me."

"Okay," I said, absolutely on edge about what he would say.

"Sandcastles are a lot like relationships. As we built one all week, I realized they are beautiful but vulnerable. Easy to break. One lie, misunderstanding, one small wave can wash it away, but as long as there is sand and water, love and trust and devotion, it can be built again. I'm also a lot like sand. Kinda boring, nothing too fancy, but paired with something like water—like you, a breath of fresh air and fun and full of life—it can become something pretty damn special. I want that with you. I'll wait until you're ready though. I broke us, so it's up to me to fix it, and I will. I'll do whatever it takes, okay?"

I nodded as he reached over and briefly ran his finger over my bottom lip, and my pulse doubled at what I saw in his eyes. Determination. Love. Promise for more. I breathed in his clean scent and had a million thoughts on how to respond, but I never got the chance.

"Ms. Carter! Ms. Carter! We're starting!" Tyler shouted.

Sure enough, the parade was starting, and the kids all cheered. We were required to stand on either ends of the trailer to make sure kids didn't jump off—because they would try. We moved to opposite ends, and while he didn't touch me, I could still feel the ghost of his finger on my mouth.

He made this float for me.

He told me he loved me.

He apologized to his dad and admitted that was an issue.

All of this...was for me. I sat on the corner as the parade started, the band playing the high school's fight song and the drums banging echoed down the street. It would take at least twenty minutes to go around the block at the pace we were moving, and I kept glancing at Christopher. He high-fived a student, looked up at me, and winked.

It wasn't even a decision at this point. I watched the man I loved laugh and throw water balloons with students. He was soaking wet, wearing stupid big sunglasses.

And I knew we'd be okay.

THE KIDS WERE ALL GONE, THE FLOATS PICKED UP, AND THE football game from the high school would start in an hour. People lingered in the parking lot, and a lot of teachers were going to walk to the high school to see the game, leaving their cars behind. I would've loved to have hot cider and put on a baggy sweatshirt and head to the game with Larissa. But this year was different.

I had my eyes set on one person.

Christopher.

He was chatting with Dave when I approached, and he hit him on the shoulder and beelined for me. All his intensity was on me, and God, it made me feel...giddy, excited, ready to move past the hurt. That focus he put into everything he did lit me up inside. I loved it about him.

"Hey," I said, unable to hide my grin when he chewed the side of his lip.

"You're smiling. This is good, right? You forgive me a little bit?" He furrowed his brows and spoke way too fast, like he was just as desperate as I was for us to be together again. It made me laugh.

"Yes, I do."

"Thank God," he said, putting his arms around me and enveloping me in a huge hug. He squeezed me against his chest for a full minute, his heart hammering against mine, and it felt right—the two of us, embracing like this after a long-ass week at work. "I'm so sorry, Gilly. Please, please know it won't happen again."

"I know. I know," I said, reaching up with one hand to cup his face. He leaned into me, and I couldn't wait longer. I stood on my toes and pulled him down to kiss me. His greedy lips met mine with a long sigh, and my mouth tingled. He tasted like gum and sweat, and he gripped the back of my head and slid his tongue into my mouth.

God, I'd missed him.

"I love you," he said, pausing between kisses. "So much." He kissed me again and again. He rested his forehead against mine, and all I could feel was the chill in the air, the way he held me so gently, and the way my skin hummed with happiness

"I love you too," I said, not caring that we had an audience and a few people clapped. My face heated, but he lifted my chin and looked down at me with a smile that showed too much teeth, but it was the joy in his eyes that had me tremble.

"My parents are at the game tonight. Want to go and sit with them?"

"Would that be weird, given...you know," I said, cringing a bit. He rolled his eyes, put his arm around my shoulders, and held me tight.

"No. They are aware of what I did. How this was on me. Kayla sure gave me an earful, even when I was a total mess."

"Oh." I pictured him telling his parents, them sitting around with Kayla, and it made my heart grow four more sizes. "Yeah, let's go sit with them then. I'd love to hear more about how much of a mess you were."

"I regret this already," he teased, and we made our way out of the parking lot and toward the main road that led to the high school field. We didn't have a typical love story, not in the slightest, but I couldn't imagine anyone better who I wanted to share life with.

Who would've thought my buddy teacher would end up being so much more?

Epilogue

EIGHT MONTHS LATER...

GRACE AND I SHOWED UP TO THE CALLAHANS' HOUSE BEARING gifts. They weren't really gifts though. They were envelopes that said CONGRATS and a lot of cash because let's be honest, that was what a senior wanted. Money.

"Is it weird to feel emotional over one of my favorite students graduating? Like this isn't my first year teaching, but she's just going to go off, into the world, and be an adult. This freaks me out." Grace frowned as we waited at the door, and her tight expression made me laugh.

"You're starting to frown like Brock does. Pretty soon you'll start dressing alike too. I heard that happens to old married couples."

"Shut up," she quipped back, right before the door opened and Kayla greeted us with a huge smile.

"Mrs. Anderson! Gilly! Wait. Can I call you Grace now?" She pulled Grace into a hug, my best friend grimacing, and I hugged Kayla right after. "Thanks for coming," she said, beaming and looking so proud.

"Of course, we wouldn't miss it. You only graduate high school once. Enjoy it!" I said, handing her the card and searching for the person I wanted to see.

Christopher stood at the counter holding a beer, his dad right next to him, as the two of them laughed at something someone said. My chest fluttered when his eyes met mine and he winked.

God, I loved him. I made my way through the crowd and he met me halfway, bending low and kissing me. "Hey, Gil," he said, resting his hand on my hip and squeezing. "You bring your stuff?"

"Absolutely." I grinned and wiggled my eyebrows. "I bought a very specific bikini for our mystery trip."

His gaze heated, and he dug his fingers into my waist. "Damn it, we have to stay here at least one more hour. Don't make it harder than it needs to be."

I lazily dragged my gaze from his face to below his belt, and he groaned, yanking me against his chest and kissing me, hard.

"Your family is *right there*. Settle down."

"Don't care. They know we do stuff."

"*Do stuff*, God, Christopher," I said, laughing and shoving him away. "You're ridiculous."

He shrugged and ran his fingers through my long hair. "You look beautiful. I was excited for summer break, but honestly? I miss seeing you every day, all day. Is that…needy?"

"No, I know what you mean." My face turned bright red, and we shared a look.

School had ended three weeks ago, and while we were so tired and ready for a three-month break from boogers, tears, long days, and tired nights, it also meant seeing each other took more effort. We'd hung out every other day, but I knew what he meant.

It wasn't enough.

"You're not sick of me yet, right?" he asked, narrowing his eyes and chewing on the side of his mouth, something he did when he had an idea. My interest was piqued, and I studied his movements.

Rigid posture. A line between his brows. My man was up to something.

"No. Why? Are you trying to break up with me?" I said, arching one brow and giggling when he shook his head back and forth too aggressively.

"Not even a little bit. The opposite, actually."

"Wait."

The opposite. Not breaking up would mean…staying together forever, which meant…*is he proposing?*

My stomach dropped, and a light ringing started in my ears. The thought of being married to him didn't scare me. In fact, I loved the idea. "Christopher," I said, my chest heaving as his eyes widened, and he paled.

"Shit. Wait, no. Not that. Damn it." He stumbled over the words, wiping a hand over his forehead and cursing to himself. He took my hand and dragged us from the kitchen, up the stairs and into the guest bedroom. He shut the door, leaned against his, and angled his face to stare at me with absolute wonder. "What did you think I meant by that?"

"The opposite of breaking up is marriage." I sat on the bed, and he sucked in a quick breath, his nostrils flaring as he neared me. He got on the floor, on his knees, so his face was level with mine, and he put a hand on either side of my thighs.

"I've thought about it. I think about it all the time."

"Really?"

"God, yes." He cupped my face with one hand and used the other to run it along my side, ending at my thigh. "Being married to you would be…the best thing."

"Yeah." I burst into a smile, and I wanted to throw myself at him. "It would be the best thing."

"I thought…" he said, trailing off and looking nervous again. He gulped, and I moved to cup his face with my hands this time. He blinked, and his lips parted when I brought his face to mine for a deep kiss. He tasted like beer, and he groaned into my mouth, biting my bottom lip and pulling it a bit.

He slid his tongue into my mouth, tilting my head back so he could kiss me deeper, and God, I could get lost in the way he kissed me, using his whole body to make me feel him everywhere. I groaned when he stood up and leaned over me, kissing down my neck and jawline.

"I love you, Gilly Carter. I want to be with you every damn day. I will marry you, someday, but for right now…" He paused, lifted his head from my neck and smiled at me when I met his eyes. "Will you get a place with me? I was going to ask if you wanted to move in together when we got to the beach house."

"Wait, wait, wait." I pushed up onto my elbows, my entire body humming with excitement. My legs shook with adrenaline. "We're going to a *beach house?*"

"Shit. I ruined the surprise, huh?"

"Christopher," I said, squealing and wrapping my arms and legs around him. "Holy shit. What beach? What house?"

"Well, I told you we'd be in the car for a while." He cleared his throat, grinning down at me. "We're driving to Florida."

"No. Shut up!"

His smile widened. "Yeah, I found a house to rent for four days, right on the beach, and I was going to ask—"

I kissed him. I had to. He was taking me *to the damn beach* as a surprise and holy shit. "I love you. Yes. Let's move in. Let's get married. Let's have babies."

He laughed, hard, and picked me up so I was in his arms, and he looked at me with the same emotion I felt in my soul. "Okay then."

"I do have one condition though," I said, already smiling before I teased him.

He frowned and gave me a stern look. "Name it. I'll sign a prenup. We can keep all money separate. I don't care about any of that shit, you know that."

"No, not that, you wonderful man. This place we're getting. I refuse to have plain, boring walls." I tickled his side and he yelped, trying to put me down, but I held on tighter. "I mean it. No *eggshell* white nonsense. I want colors, Callahan."

"You can paint our house however you want. It's the *classroom* that has too many distractions," he said, so serious that it made me love him all the more. "I want a home with you."

"Then that's what we'll make. A home. Together."

He rested his forehead against mine, his body almost vibrating against me, and he set me on the ground. "We leave for Florida in forty-nine minutes. Let's go mingle, do what we need to for Kayla, and get the hell out of here."

"I like your thinking," I said. He held out his hand, and I placed mine in his, absolutely content and ready to start a life with this man.

Because I knew it wasn't now, but soon, I'd become Gilly Callahan, and that name had a really nice ring to it. That was for damn sure.

THE END

Thank you for reading! Did you enjoy?

Please Add Your Review! You can sign up for the City Owl Press newsletter to receive notice of all book releases!

And don't miss more romance like PAINTING THE LINES by City Owl Author, Ashley R. King. Turn the page for a sneak peek!

Sneak Peek of Painting the Lines

BY ASHLEY R. KING

Amalie scanned the bar, looking for Romina's raven hair beneath the dim lights. For a Tuesday night, quite the crowd had gathered inside Oakley's, a trendy hangout in midtown Atlanta.

"Can I get you something else?" Bryan, the cute bartender, asked with a boyish smile.

Amalie looked at her watch again. Romina was already fifteen minutes late. Tonight of all nights, when Amalie needed her best friend most.

Amalie's father, mega-billionaire Andrew Warner, had just dropped the hammer with his latest ultimatum, and Amalie needed Romina's sage advice, help, magic—*anything* that might help her figure out what to do. Her father had been pushing her to work for the family business, something she had no interest in doing. If she didn't, she'd be disowned and disinherited from the great Warner Hotel fortune. To some that might not be a huge deal, but to Amalie, who had no back-up plan, it was everything.

She sighed and took one last sip of her daiquiri. "No, that'll be all. Thank you."

With a quick nod, Bryan moved to the other end of the bar, where a seat had been claimed by a man who, even sitting down, was still taller than most. Amalie couldn't help but give him a once-over. He had a powerful frame, even if soft around the edges, like the forgotten build of an athlete lived under his skin. But something else snagged her attention.

Amalie watched with interest as the bartender seemed to contemplate cutting the guy off for the night even though it was only eight o'clock. The man bristled, spine stiffening, fingers tightening around the empty tumbler before him. But in a half-second, his eyes flicked up to one of the flat screens suspended behind the bar and he leaned forward, completely enraptured, his face oddly serene.

As a writer, or well, washed-up writer on the hunt for her next idea, Amalie was captivated by this guy's body language. One minute it looked like he might shatter his whiskey tumbler with his bare hands, and the next his eyes were glued to the television.

Amalie glanced at the screen, surprised to find a replay of the US Open tennis finals from several years ago. She knew enough about tennis to know the names of the Grand Slam tournaments and some of the cute players (hello, Rafael Nadal), but other than that, she was clueless. Her father, who loved tennis and watched it religiously, had tried to inspire a love of the sport in her, but…it just wasn't there.

Her eyes slid back to the enigma at the end of the bar. There was a catlike tension in the way he studied the battle between Rafael Nadal and Novak Djokovic, his entire focus narrowed to the game, his muscles twitching with restrained energy. Her writer instincts screamed that there was far more going on here than a bar patron watching the rerun of an old match. Cheering and clapping erupted on the screen.

"I could've done that! *Easily!*" The man pounded his fist on the bar and exploded from his seat with such force that his barstool tumbled backward. He was just as tall as she imagined, well over six feet.

Amalie gasped and took a step back. The man downed his drink, slamming the empty glass onto the bar with a thud, wiping his mouth with the back of his hand.

"Another," he growled at the bartender.

He shifted slightly and when he turned, she caught sight of his lovely eyes in the dim light, but they were marred with heavy bags beneath them.

"Hey, man. Julian, come on. You've got to chill," Bryan pleaded.

Julian. Amalie rolled that name around in her mind, tasted it on her tongue. She supposed he looked like a Julian, though to be fair she hadn't met a single Julian in her twenty-eight years. She studied him, his calves and thighs muscular beneath his khaki shorts. Yes, shorts, despite the cold. Even his arms looked like they had once been powerful, but judging by the slight beer gut he was rocking, Julian had missed a workout or two. He was ridiculously attractive, though, even if Amalie struggled to reconcile that fact with his brutish behavior.

She studied him further, imagining his story and committing his features to memory, a memory she would later take out, dissect, and piece together into one of her fictional heroes. Romina always teased that Amalie was more voyeur than participant in life. Perhaps that's why writing was so important to her.

Julian's burnt umber hair fell in unruly waves across his tanned forehead, his nose almost too flawless. But no, when he turned, she noted a slight bump, perhaps hinting at a fight at one point in his life? Or maybe, if he was like Amalie, a pretty nasty run-in with a suspiciously transparent sliding-glass door.

Julian's profile, with his sulky lower lip, was a thing of beauty, and she found herself wondering why such loveliness had been wasted on a staggering mess of a man.

As if feeling the levity of her gaze, or rather her judgment, Julian met her stare. Now *that* was completely unfair. His eyes stood out against his dark skin, a stunning green that reminded her of lush trees in the spring, and there were tiny lightning strikes of sparkling gold darting from the pupils.

Wait...

Holy crap, she was standing directly in front of him, having gravitated towards him without even realizing it. It didn't matter how hot he was, how *big* he was, she didn't want any part of this.

As if he heard her thoughts, he raised a perfect, dark eyebrow, a quirk she was sure was meant to be sexy and had probably worked on dozens of other women, but at that moment it only came off as sloppy and awkward.

"Like what you see?" he challenged. His sultry voice would've made her panties melt if not for the slur accenting it.

Amalie recoiled, cheeks hot as she leveled the behemoth with a sneer. "Excuse me?"

Julian tilted his head, studying her with a drunken intensity that made her squirm. "I said, do you like what you see? My place isn't that far…if you think you can keep your hands off me that long."

Bryan snickered as he shook his head, pretending to be mesmerized by the cleanliness of the beer mug in his hand.

"Can you believe the balls on this guy?" Amalie hooked a thumb toward Julian as she looked to Bryan. For what, she had no idea.

"A filthy mouth, too." Julian shot her a wink and sat back down at the bar. "My *favorite*."

"You are out of control." Amalie huffed. "I can't help it that I naturally gravitated toward *this*"—she waved her arms around, motioning and flailing at Julian—"train wreck. I thought I might've had my next book idea. But yet you disappoint, something I'm sure is very common."

There. She hated to be a mean girl, but he'd totally asked for it.

Julian reared back as if she'd slapped him but quickly recovered. "Enough of the spoiled little rich girl act. It reeks."

She faltered, the sting hitting home. "You don't even know me."

"Right, and you don't know me either, princess."

Princess? Anger burned inside her as she poked her finger into his surprisingly hard chest. "You have no idea who you're messing with, mister."

He puffed up, straightened his broad shoulders, and gave her a scalding once-over. "Yeah, I'm shaking in my boots. Listen, I'll have you know that you're looking at a US Open contender." He leveled her with a hard glare, daring her to argue.

Interest piqued, Amalie remained in place, her finger falling away.

"*You're* a tennis player?" she asked through gritted teeth while mentally berating herself for continuing this conversation.

Julian paused a beat too long before answering with a shrug. "You could say that."

"Okay…" Amalie stretched the two-syllable word into three and cocked her brow as if to silently say, *I call bullshit.*

Julian blinked, but his gaze was still hazy as he responded with a surprising amount of vindication in his voice. "Actually, I'm going to qualify for the US Open." His eyes widened, as if his words were a revelation to him as well.

Interesting. Amalie's nails tapped the bar in an easy rhythm as she assessed him. "So I gather you used to play?" She almost mentioned his fading physique, but he was being oddly civil now, and she feared an observation like that would bring out the pig in him, *again.*

Julian averted his gaze, studying his hands, which now gripped the edge of the bar. He gave her a tight nod, then he seemed to slowly deflate. "I used to be the best. Before it all went to shit. Now I'm just a has-been, stuck selling pharmaceuticals day after day. I had everything I ever wanted right here"—Julian lifted a hand, palm open, his stare searing into his own flesh—"then I let it all slip away."

It was a surprisingly coherent statement, one that echoed and mirrored things Amalie felt about her own life. But before she could dwell on it, electricity hummed in her veins, the wheels in her head spinning wildly.

A tiny spark of sunlight filtered through the cracks of the prison that had slowly become her life as an idea quickly formed. Ever since New Year's Eve, she'd been mulling over goals, and writing a book was at the top of her list—this was perfect. The threat of having to work for her father receded as she pulled in a deep breath and let the realization settle over her bones. *This* could be her next hit, a novel that chronicled the rise to the top of a former tennis great. Hadn't her agent, Stella, recently hinted that sports romances were making a comeback? Besides, everyone loves a good underdog story. She could see the headline now: *Washed-Up Tennis Player Makes Run for US Open.*

What were the odds that he played the only sport she knew even a little bit about?

Right now, it didn't matter that she hated tennis. It didn't matter that her father always rubbed it in her face that her older sister, Simone, was such a great player. It didn't matter that he'd tried to force Amalie to take lessons even though her instructor was the meanest person on the planet and cut her down every time she made a mistake

Her past with tennis was exactly that *the past.* An opportunity had presented itself, and she was hellbent on taking it. Stella had been adamant that Amalie write something "real and honest," something more along the lines of her debut, *Breaking the Fall,* the story that shot her into the next-big-thing stratosphere at the ripe age of nineteen. Of course, Amalie didn't want to let her down. Stella Frenette of Frenette Literary had been a hard win after Amalie lost her first agent for being a little twit high on fame and her own wealth. She'd bailed on so many commitments and haggled over stuff so stupid it made film and book people walk away. Yeah, film—that's how close she'd been to the big time.

Somewhere along the way, Amalie also lost the gift of natural storytelling. Every time she set pen to paper or fingers to keys, it felt forced. Her words read like *See Jane run. See Jane jump. See Jane suck at writing.*

Her last two novels fell flat because the characters weren't realistic. To fix the problem, Stella suggested Amalie study real people. Her bestseller had centered around a heroine based on none other than her sister, Simone. The intimate knowledge shared by sisters had given Amalie the means to create a three-dimensional character readers adored, which was really no surprise. Who didn't love Simone?

Amalie's follow-up books hadn't had that benefit and suffered because of it. She struggled to craft characters who leapt off the page, and she had no doubt the reason was because, other than Ro, she hadn't let anyone get close. Not even her ex-fiancé, Maxwell. Not really. Amalie failed at human connection because people broke hearts, and her heart already had enough cracks. It couldn't survive another quake.

She cringed as she thought of her early writing days, trying to reconcile that person with who she was now. Sadly, though she was ready to write again, the human connection thing was still a problem. But maybe Fate had given her a workaround. Readers—and Stella as well—would love that this novel was based on a real tennis player—one who was gorgeous and, with some training, would have muscles popping by the time the tournament rolled around. It would be so easy to capitalize on his looks and to even use the momentum of his rise to the top for promotion of the book.

She couldn't let fear get in the way of her dream this time. She just needed to get this Julian fellow to the US Open.

Just as Amalie was about to open her mouth, Julian slumped over the bar, passed out cold. The bartender dipped his head and smiled. "From what I hear, he does this all the time. He's pretty popular with the ladies, so usually he's already secured one or two to go home with. Looks like he didn't get that far with you." He had the audacity to smirk.

"Hard to imagine that he's popular with the ladies when he acts like a Neanderthal."

Bryan leaned forward on the bar conspiratorially, his voice hushed. "He was different tonight. Besides, I think you got under his skin because you called his bullshit. But hey, that's just my opinion."

Amalie sized up the situation *and* Julian, her mind calculating a million possibilities at once. "Was he really a great tennis player?" she asked Bryan, needing to know for sure before she made her next decision.

Bryan nodded. "Hell yeah. You never heard of Julian Smoke? They called him 'The Smoke' in college because he was a beast. He was even pegged as the next tennis great of his generation."

Amalie studied Julian's face, willing herself to remember him from one of her father's endless tennis ramblings. "What happened?" she asked, bringing her gaze back to the bartender.

"That's his story to tell. You'll have to ask him."

Amalie drummed her fingers on the smooth surface of the bar one last time before releasing a deep breath and making a decision she was sure she'd regret. "Help me get him to my car, will ya?"

Don't stop now. Keep reading with your copy of PAINTING THE LINES by City Owl Author, Ashley R. King.

And find more from Jaqueline Snowe at www.jaquelinesnowe.com

Want even more romance? Try PAINTING THE LINES by City Owl Author, Ashley R. King, and find more from Jaqueline Snowe at www.jaquelinesnowe.com

"King debuts with a delightful, character-driven rom-com! Fans of slow-burn romance will be swept away." - Publisher's Weekly

Amalie Warner wants another shot to prove that she can be a successful writer. After hitting the bestseller's list nine years ago, she's lost her spark.

Feeling pressure from her father to leave her writing behind and to work for her family's lucrative hotel business, she's desperate to find inspiration for her next big idea, something that challenges and excites her, something *real*.
Enter Julian Smoke, a failed tennis player making a dream run for the US Open.

After a chance meeting at a bar, Amalie hates him instantly. He's cocky and arrogant, but Amalie knows his story could be her big break.

Could he be more?

Everyone knows that in tennis, love means zero, but these two are about to change that.

All reviews are **welcome** and **appreciated**. Please consider leaving one on your favorite social media and book buying sites.

Escape Your World. Get Lost in Ours! Romance and speculative fiction from City Owl Press at www.cityowlpress.com.

Acknowledgments

Some stories burst out of you. It's like magic. Others, like Teaching with the Enemy, are hard. This story was the most challenging and hard to write. Maybe it was because it was 2020 and work-home-family life had no balance anymore but the biggest and warmest hugs to Mary Cain. She is a phenomenal editor and pushed me past my comfort zone for Gilly and Christopher. I'm so proud of this story and I appreciate all the brainstorming, re-writes, and guidance.

Another huge, huge, huge thanks for my sister in law Kacie. She teaches littles in an elementary school and provided a lot of wonderful stories for me. The thought of teaching first graders makes me skin break out in hives, but you have such a gift! Thanks for being such a good support, friend, aunt, and soon to be mom! Teaching is NOT an easy job. That is for damn sure. I should also say...If there are any errors in how to run a classroom, they are completely my own. I took some fictional creativity a few times.

Writing is never a solo journey. Thanks for your insight, Heather! I'm so glad we connected this year. And Kat! I appreciate your insight and am so so so glad we are CPs!

As always, thank you to my husband. 2020 proved there is NO

ONE else I'd rather be stuck in a house with for nine months and counting.

A huge shout out to Tina, Yelena, and all the wonderful hard-working people at City Owl Press. I love working with you all!

To the teachers of the world. You are the backbone of society and put so much blood, sweat, and tears into what you do. I come from a FAMILY of teachers (you saw the dedication... those are all the teachers in my family haha) 2020 was a mess for a lot of reasons but teachers stayed positive and helped kids get through it.

About the Author

Jaqueline Snowe lives in Arizona where the "dry heat" really isn't that bad. She identifies as a full-blown Gryffindor and prefers drinking coffee all hours of the day. She is the mother to two fur-babies who don't realize they aren't humans and a new mom to the sweetest baby boy. She is an avid reader and writer of romances and tends to write about athletes. She is usually watching sports with her baseball-obsessed husband when she isn't writing.

www.jaquelinesnowe.com

f facebook.com/jaquelinesnowe

🐦 twitter.com/jaquelinesnowe

📷 instagram.com/jaquelinesnowe

BB bookbub.com/profile/jaqueline-snowe

About the Publisher

City Owl Press is a cutting edge indie publishing company, bringing the world of romance and speculative fiction to discerning readers.

Escape Your World. Get Lost in Ours!

www.cityowlpress.com

www.ingramcontent.com/pod-product-compliance
Lightning Source LLC
Chambersburg PA
CBHW031215260626
47169CB00007B/2069